GRAY MEN

by
Tomotake Ishikawa

Translated by
Jonathan Lloyd-Davies

VERTICAL.

Published by Vertical, Inc., New York

ISBN 978-1-935654-50-6

Manufactured in the United States of America

First Edition

Vertical, Inc.
451 Park Avenue South, 7th Floor
New York, NY 10016
www.vertical-inc.com

TABLE OF CONTENTS

CHAPTER ONE

1

I recalled a proverb: "The weather's bad when it rains." It's a metaphor for the obvious, the self-evident.

The strong persecute the weak.

I guess that's par for the course, too.

Enduring his usual headache, Ryotaro stared vacantly into the locker. His legs burned, stiff with fatigue, barely able to support his exhausted frame.

His office locker contained a bag stuffed with his valuables and a change of clothes. A cloudy-white liquid had been poured into the bag, giving off a stomach-churning stench.

Rancid milk. Ryotaro fished the contents out of his bag one by one, dwelling on the thought. The awful stink of the liquid made breathing a chore. He held his breath and continued to work. *Just like schoolyard bullies,* Ryotaro cursed them, but no anger welled up. There was no space for it. His heart was buried so deep in despair and exhaustion that he couldn't "afford" it.

He had just finished emptying the bag and sighed heavily when, as though on cue, somebody came into the office.

"What's that smell?" came Yoshimura's husky voice from

behind. Just hearing it was enough to make Ryotaro's stomach wince in pain.

Shinohara, his face twisted in an attempt to suppress laughter, said "What, indeed," and let out a cackle as offensive to the ear as a nail scraping down a blackboard. With his generous portions of flab, Shinohara reminded Ryotaro of a swollen rice cake.

"So you're the culprit, Sakuma?"

Ryotaro twisted his trembling body to face in the direction of Yoshimura's menacing voice.

"What the hell is it? The whole damn office stinks. Is that your B.O., Sakuma?" Yoshimura gave Ryotaro a scornful look, the corners of his mouth curled tight. He stood with his chest thrust forward to boost up his needle-thin frame—all the better to intimidate.

Ryotaro smiled vaguely. The expression was a survival technique, the only response that would be forgiven in this scenario.

"Look at that smirk. Makes me sick," Yoshimura spat. He was the only person in the store with a spare key to the locker so it was pretty easy to narrow down the suspects. But Ryotaro couldn't say a thing.

"You're useless at work, you don't speak, you got a creepy smile, and you mess up your locker. As if your stench wasn't bad enough already. I'm sick of looking at you, so hurry up and deal with this, clean up and get outta here. And don't forget to lock up. We've got an important exhibition in two days. Why don't you go get some plastic surgery, fix up that glum mug of yours while you're at it," Yoshimura barked before leaving through the back door.

"Pardon me for leaving first!" Shinohara jeered before bustling out in Yoshimura's wake.

Left alone, Ryotaro emptied the liquid from his bag into the toilet and then wiped the inside with toilet paper. He spent about an hour cleaning the empty store in silence. He couldn't let his mind wander, as missing anything would be reason enough for another tongue-lashing.

Having spent the entire day on his feet without a single break, his body didn't respond properly. By the time he finished cleaning he was so worn out he felt he might collapse at any moment.

He made sure all the doors were locked, set the alarms, and turned off the lights. Ryotaro sighed and, stinking bag in tow, left the jewelry store.

August, 2013.

Outside, it was a humid and sultry night. Dampness hung stagnant in the windless air. Ryotaro walked towards the station. He immediately began to sweat and his shirt clung to his skin. Eleven o'clock. Hardly anyone around.

He caught an image of himself reflected in the store window and inadvertently came to a stop.

He traced a hand over his sunken cheeks, combed it through his grown-out hair. Exhaustion led to him spending his days off sleeping, so he couldn't even muster the time to get a haircut. He hardly ate a decent meal, which was probably why he looked pale and sickly—the overall impression was that of ill health.

Ryotaro let out a heavy sigh and concentrated on moving his legs forward. Suddenly, everything before him went black.

"Shit…"

Anemia. Clenching his teeth, he just managed to overcome the urge to pass out and started to walk again. Working all day while hardly eating a thing had left him feeling sick.

Yoshimura, the manager of the store, always made sure to find something for Ryotaro to do when it was his time for a break, which meant Ryotaro never had the chance to eat or rest. He worked over a hundred hours of overtime a month, but of course, he was never paid for any of it.

By the end of the day, Ryotaro would be a barely breathing zombie. Even after finally getting to sleep he would frequently wake during the night. He never felt properly rested and was consumed by physical and mental exhaustion.

He boarded the Keihin-Tohoku train and found an empty seat. He mindlessly flicked open his cell phone, but no one had called. His hand that held the phone trembled from sheer fatigue.

He fought off drowsiness as the train rocked and swayed during the half-hour trip to Tsurumi Station. He peeled himself up from his sunken position in the seat, stepped down to the platform, and staggered unsteadily through the exit.

He was so tired he no longer had an appetite. He went through the compulsory motions of buying a couple of rice balls from the convenience store in front of the station, then started the walk home.

Ryotaro's apartment was in a neglected thirty-year-old building roughly fifteen minutes from the station. Entering the cramped one-room space, Ryotaro mechanically flicked the switch to turn on the TV and collapsed into bed. The dispassionate voice of a female newscaster flowed from the TV, vibrating the air in the room.

Fearing shortages of the resource, China, which controls 93 percent of the market, and other resource-rich countries including the U.S., Australia, Canada, Greenland, and South Africa have declared restrictions on the exports of rare earth minerals. Accordingly, Japan, which has no such resources of its own, must now explore potential substitutes and alternative supply routes.

His body sank heavy as lead into the long-unaired futon. The sensation of descending into darkness was luscious. *How great it would be never to have to wake up. I don't want to open my eyes again.* Ryotaro held the thought, wishing from his heart for it to be true.

Rare earths, an essential resource for national security and industry, are also used in household items such as digital cameras, digital audio players, cell phones, and laptop computers. A shortage in rare earths could cause Japan's industry to stagnate.

A life of being bullied day in, day out by your superiors, of constantly having your character belittled, with no escape. Was there any value to putting up with a life like that? Was there really any meaning in a life where you're screamed at for being a waste of space, where you have to chip away at your sleep and force a smile just to receive a meager salary?

Substitutes are being developed but have not attained viability. In an attempt to bring a solution to the issue, the government has decided to inject 500 billion yen into the Tomosun Corporation, which holds mining rights in parts of Mongolia. Enough rare earths have been discovered in these areas to break free from dependence on China. The financing decision will enable Japan to secure a significant quantity of rare earth resources. In addition, profits are expected from exporting excess levels to other countries.

The seemingly endless monologue broke off and was followed briefly by a man's voice—his throat likely a casualty to smoking—before ceding to a commercial.

The music from the ad piqued Ryotaro's attention. He glanced across to the heretofore unwatched screen.

Chopin's *Revolutionary Etude.*

Ryotaro blinked and tried to focus. The video, ill-matched to the music, was some footage for a shipping company: a truck driving down a road, followed by a superimposed company logo and a voiceover of a short message: "Creating new value in logistics!"

That was the whole of the commercial, but for some reason it left an impression.

The company had been a hot topic in the financial papers about two years ago. An obscure venture business had acquired the sixth-ranked company in the industry, then soon afterwards had bought up the third and the fourth. Through expanding and streamlining their distribution networks, the company had brought about a breakthrough low-cost "revolution" and now ranked in the top class of the industry. But it had its mysteries; it never went to an IPO, and the CEO eschewed media exposure.

The next commercial was a generic beer advertisement. An actress wearing an ear-to-ear smile held a glass of beer to her cheek, chattering away. Ryotaro remembered that he had some beer in the fridge and, grimacing, got slowly up.

He pulled out a beer and sat back on the bed, gulped down half the bottle, and crammed one of the rice balls into his mouth. The food didn't taste like anything.

He felt his body flush, not from the alcohol but from a thought: *It wasn't supposed to be like this...*

Ryotaro had lost both his parents at an early age and was raised at his aunt's along with his younger brother. Having no children of her own, she had been loving—they had never felt any particular lack—but Ryotaro had spent his days subconsciously on edge, some part of him always harboring a nagging discomfort. Perhaps because of this, he had resolved to find work in Tokyo after graduating university. But the tough job market at the time had meant a string of rejected applications, and he found himself with nowhere to go. By the time it dawned on him that he couldn't afford to be choosy, most company recruitment windows had already closed.

He ended up helplessly relying on an introduction from his aunt to get a job at a jewelry store in Tokyo. He had not been eager at first, having no particular interest in jewelry and no customer service skills to speak of, but on starting, the working conditions and pay seemed good enough. He had ended up drifting into the decision to stay with the job.

Then a single incident caused everything to go downhill.

Now his days were spent in misery; he was put to work like a packhorse, hounded incessantly. Worked to exhaustion day after day, he no longer maintained any meaningful personal relationships. He had been living this hellish existence for half a year. He had considered leaving but felt obligated to his aunt and also had to pay tuition for his brother, who enrolled at a college prep school after failing his university entrance exams. He couldn't quit. Besides, the recession meant that the chances of finding new work would be low.

Ryotaro washed the rice ball down with some beer and reflected on his day-to-day life. *How have I ended up like this?* The thought weighed heavy on his heart.

Casually glancing downwards, he caught sight of the insurance documents on the table. For the past few days he had been closely scrutinizing the contents of a life insurance policy he had taken out on his aunt's suggestion. It seemed the policy, which he had taken out immediately when he started work, would pay out a certain amount even in the event of suicide. It wasn't much, but it would probably be enough to cover his brother's tuition.

I want out of this cursed existence. I've got this ridiculous quota for the exhibition in two days. Who knows what they'll do to me if I don't meet it...

Ryotaro squeezed his eyes shut and sat rocking for some time. The depths of his body ached in silence.

The noise of the TV, the meticulous ticking of the clock, the din of traffic. The sound of a heart breaking.

Ryotaro opened his eyes and made his decision.

He had lived for twenty-six years. It felt like more than enough.

2

Ryotaro opened his heavy eyelids to a jarring electronic noise.

A white ceiling dominated his field of vision. Hanging directly overhead, it felt like it was bearing down on him.

Ryotaro brushed his damp cotton blanket to one side, got up, and walked over to the mirror above the sink. The same reflection as always, no change. He looked sick, like a green pepper.

He rinsed out his mouth and, without washing his face, crossed to the living area.

5:30 a.m.

It was bright enough outside, but he felt no desire to open the curtains. He made toast and put on some coffee in the half-light. He conveyed them to his mouth and swallowed robotically.

It was a still morning. As per his routine, Ryotaro put on a work shirt and looped a tie around his collar. He stared at his black suit on its hanger for a while, then put it on.

When he stepped outside, the air was still fairly cool.

He came to a brief stop and took a deep breath before starting to walk, keeping the same pace as always.

He took the work-bound Keihin-Tohoku Line train, but a short time later got off at Kamata station and changed to the Tokyu-Tamagawa Line.

People cycled through, boarding and leaving the train. There were many different types of faces, but they all had the same tired expression. Ryotaro wondered how long he had been on the swaying train. He heard the name of a station announced:

"Tamagawa, Tamagawa."

He decided to get off. He rushed from the station as though fleeing, pushing through the crowds of people flowing in. Before him sprawled the Tama River. Its dull-hued, gently undulating surface reflected the morning sun.

For some time, Ryotaro wandered aimlessly along the riverbank. He found a dilapidated bench and sat down.

The time was 9:25. Five minutes until he was supposed to clock in. Ryotaro switched off his phone, only feeling a slight twinge of guilt. He looked around the lonely area. People were sparse, perhaps because it was a weekday. He dragged himself up and started to walk with a purposeful stride. He tried to imagine where he would die as he made a pilgrimage out of finding the perfect place.

Soon, I will die.

Ryotaro thought about the rope in his bag. It was white and sturdy, the type used on sailboats. He'd purchased it from a houseware store. He traced the riverside for close to an hour. He was having difficulty finding somewhere suitable. He branched away from the river and began to explore further afield. A quietly disintegrating shack, a forgotten shrine, gentle, lushly forested hills. None fitted his ideal location.

He took off his jacket and loosened his tie. His calves and the soles of his feet ached since he'd been walking for a while. He kept his eyes down, avoiding eye contact with others. The scent of incense tickled his nostrils as he passed a temple—the

Dairakuin. He found himself coming to a stop as he glanced up at the gate. For some reason, it felt as though it had been opened for him. Before he realized it, Ryotaro ducked inside.

The grounds were hushed and deserted. The buildings were decrepit for a metropolitan temple, the main gate warped with rain and pockmarked from termite damage. The main hall had an imposing carving of a dragon on its roof and the stone lanterns leading up to the building were engraved with a similar motif. The temple had all the signs of importance, but no one seemed to be maintaining it. The roof was missing tiles, and the enclosing wall was discolored and crooked, its paint peeling. Strangely, the atmosphere was not one of ruin; rather, there was an air of graceful calm often lacking at more splendid and luxurious temples.

Ryotaro admired the grounds for a while. Then, as though something was urging him on, he started to walk down the narrow path lined with stepping stones that led towards the cemetery at the back. The thought hit him that visiting the dead would perhaps give him some kind of insight into death. But when he arrived, the dead had nothing to show him, remaining silent under their tombstones. Ryotaro noticed some incense burning at a grave off to one side. Suddenly wary, he started to walk towards it. Had someone just been there? There was an arrangement of irises and the incense was new. Ryotaro cast his gaze around, but there was no one to be seen.

He looked at the grave again. Sprigs of white clover bloomed along the sides. The small flowers stirred in the breeze. Ryotaro stared at the tombstone for some time and realized that he had unconsciously pressed his hands together. He pulled them apart and rushed out of the Dairakuin temple as though running from something. His face was burning red. He felt disgusted for having appealed to the dead for salvation. He went back to following the Tama River and redoubled his efforts to find a place to die.

I should just do it at home, a thought crossed his mind, but his legs refused to stop. He was ready to kill himself, but the idea of simply decomposing, of no one finding him, was too horrible.

He wanted somewhere to kill himself without interference, but only if his body could be easily discovered.

He continued on until he found himself getting close to Tamagawa Station again. He looked around and sighed. His gaze fell on a sign: *The Kamenokoyama Tomb*. Without thinking, Ryotaro turned to follow the direction it pointed toward.

At the end of a route lined with grand houses, he came to a grove of various types of trees. He stepped off the road. The ground was damp despite the lack of rain, probably due to the cover of trees. The copse was well-maintained with a walking path, the kind people would visit for some light walking during the weekend.

Not bad.

This being a weekday afternoon, the grove was empty and quiet, as if forgotten. Ryotaro followed the hiking path through the cool seclusion of the woods.

The Tama River was intermittently visible between the trees. Here and there, blue tarp tents were rigged among the shadowed thickets, shying from view.

Something about the place, far removed from the daily grind, helped harden Ryotaro's resolve. The air was cool despite it being a summer afternoon, and occasional streams of light poked through the trees to stroke his skin. Ryotaro felt a tiny seed of relief take root inside his despair-laden heart. If he could just hold onto it, life might be worth living. But to return to the real world was to return to purgatory.

Hope was the last thing he needed.

He bought a can of coffee from a solitary vending machine and found a stone bench to sit on and cracked the can open. The sound reverberated gratifyingly.

As he sipped at the coffee, vaguely considering that it could be his last, he heard a voice.

He felt his body stiffen. He turned to look, keeping his head down.

A mother and her child. The young girl was chattering excitedly, clinging to her mother as they walked by. Ryotaro stayed motionless, watching them pass.

"So pretty," the young mother said as she held her daughter's hand.

The girl nodded happily. "Red-orange!" she called out, her voice filled with joy, pointing to the sky that peeked out between the tree branches.

The mother beamed with delight. The innocence of the girl's voice carried Ryotaro's glance to the sky, but he looked straight back down and sighed deeply.

"That's right! Red-orange," the mother's voice echoed softly.

Ryotaro narrowed his eyes as he watched them. They were like the embodiment of happiness. They had bright futures before them.

The polar opposite of a wretched guy like me.

But he felt no envy. He had only himself to blame for his predicament.

He took another sip of his coffee as he watched the duo fade into the distance. The sweetness that spread inside his mouth brought on a wave of sentiment.

He looked back at the sky, but he was no longer able to discern its beauty. The crimson of the sky appeared gray.

Death was close, he knew it.

He retained almost no memories of his deceased parents. His aunt who raised him often took him and his brother on walks. His brother had loved her as he might have his real mother. Like the girl that had just passed he would cling to her, his face beaming. Ryotaro would watch them, always a step behind. It wasn't that she'd failed to treat him with love. It was just that a part of him had always felt awkward.

"Is this seat taken?" came a voice from behind. Ryotaro jumped and swung around.

There stood a man in gray.

The man was over six feet tall and dressed in a gray suit with a gray waistcoat; even his tie was gray. His shoes were black, but they might as well have been gray. The whole attire looked immaculate on him. Apart from the glint of his jet-black eyes and his wavy black hair, everything about the man was gray.

His age was impossible to pin down. He looked young yet old at the same time. The deep wrinkles carved across his face like marks of suffering contributed to the uncertainty.

The man held Ryotaro's gaze with a peculiar expression. Ryotaro couldn't tell if it was a smile or a grimace.

"…Gray."

The shock of this man appearing from nowhere caused Ryotaro to blurt out that word because he immediately thought of the Gray aliens. It wasn't that the man bore any physical resemblance to the typical image of a Gray with its oversized head and eyes and shrunken frame. Something about his presence was so unreal it seemed only natural to compare him to extraterrestrial life. Ryotaro had the inkling that if Grays did exist, they would probably look like the man before him.

The man cocked his head to one side and chuckled. "May I sit here?"

The words brought Ryotaro back from his reverie. He looked around with wide eyes. There were three other benches, all of them free.

"Sure…" he answered vaguely and nodded, aware that his face was turning red.

Still smiling, the man sat next to him. The man's gaze was fixed towards the path so that Ryotaro could only see his face in profile. Although he had a prominent nose and the length of his crossed legs suggested he was a foreigner, he seemed somehow Japanese, too. Ryotaro would have believed him to be Middle Eastern, even European if the man said so. His nationality was totally unclear.

The man's long hair hung in dark waves with bangs that reached his eyes and covered half of his small face. When the man turned towards Ryotaro in response to his staring, Ryotaro hurriedly looked away.

A vibration in the air told Ryotaro that this had made the man laugh.

"Gray?" the man inquired softly.

Ryotaro hesitantly returned the man's look. The man stared at him with large eyes filled with determination.

"Err... Sorry, it's nothing," Ryotaro replied, wanting to deflect the intense curiosity behind the man's gaze.

Perhaps feeling that he was being shunned, the man narrowed his eyes and lifted the corners of his mouth into a smile. "I must seem quite the suspicious character."

Ryotaro hesitated for a moment before nodding slightly. The man's smile was warm, enveloping.

"It's only natural that, from your perspective, I appear suspicious. But, as the word suggests, I am merely questionable—certainly not dangerous. Are you the type to punish the suspicious?"

Ryotaro shook his head, maintaining his look of apprehension. Even so, he felt vaguely amused by the man's phrasing: *the type to punish the suspicious.*

"Good, for the time being it seems I'm safe from punishment. Next, would you implement torture—such as used during witch trials—to determine the true form of someone you deemed suspicious?"

Ryotaro shook his head at the man's bizarre words.

"Good, I'm relieved. A narrow escape, but it doesn't look like I'm going to be burned at the stake. I don't mind heat, but being lit on fire would be a little too much." The man smiled brightly, then continued. "Last question—would you feel uncomfortable if we kept on talking? I do not mind your impressions of me, but it is not my wish to make you feel uncomfortable. And don't worry, I'm not here to sell you on religion." The man peered into Ryotaro's face as he spoke.

The realization that the man was trying to diffuse the tension in the air caused Ryotaro to break into a broad smile. "Sorry, I'm a little shy with strangers."

The man laughed bashfully in response. "There's nothing wrong with that. Shy people tend to be quite thoughtful. Personally, I believe that it's very important to carefully scrutinize things in life. Of course, there is the tendency to overthink things and become depressed."

Ryotaro stared fixedly at this man who had appeared from nowhere and who looked completely out of place, like he had escaped from a movie. His looks were utterly unique and his voice was deep enough to shake the earth. The more Ryotaro looked at him, the more he was convinced that the fellow wasn't human. At the same time, their conversation made him seem more approachable than when Ryotaro had first beheld him.

"Please don't take offense, but when I saw you just now the first thing I thought of was the Grays."

"Grays?" the man repeated, tilting his head to one side.

"The aliens, Grays. Err... Not to say that you actually look like a stereotypical Gray. Just that there was something a little alien about you. How should I say this…" Ryotaro stopped, becoming flustered as he tried not to insult the man.

The man listened quietly and looked up at the sky before nodding in apparent satisfaction. "So I reminded you of the Gray aliens? I wouldn't say that's rude at all. If anything, I feel honored."

"Honored?" Now it was Ryotaro's turn to ask.

"Think about it," the man's large eyes glistened. "Being a Gray means being something other than human. I wonder, is there compliment greater than being told you're not human?"

Ryotaro laughed ambiguously, unsure of how to reply.

"Well, are you happy to be thought of as human?"

"It's just ordinary, I guess… So I wouldn't be happy per se."

"Sure. So, would it feel good to be thought of as *ordinary*? Ordinary, in other words normal, commonplace."

"I guess that doesn't sound too good." Ryotaro was beginning to enjoy the man's word games.

"It follows, then, that you would rather someone you've just met to think of you as not human, but a Gray."

"No one's ever said that to me, so I wouldn't really know…"

"Nor did I, until now. I'd never known the happiness of being mistaken for a Gray," the man chuckled classily, clearing enjoying himself. Then, suddenly quiet, he looked Ryotaro from head to toe. Finally, he said, "You don't look like a Gray, by the way."

"That's a shame," Ryotaro responded with a grimace and sipped his coffee.

The man re-crossed his legs and rubbed his fingers against his sharp chin. Each movement was executed with a natural grace. Ryotaro bit his lip, suddenly wondering if he was dreaming. Surprised at the cliche, a laugh bubbled up from inside him. A deeply heartfelt, genuine laugh.

"Did I miss something?" the man asked, slightly angling his head.

The burning determination behind his eyes made Ryotaro want to cling to him. Words started to spill forth the moment he formed thoughts. "Things…have been very difficult."

As he said as much, Ryotaro felt his body grow heavy like lead. He couldn't expect whining would make this man help him. It was nothing more than self-gratification. Ryotaro felt disgusted with himself and scowled deeply.

The man's eyes, unblinking, remained focused on Ryotaro's profile. He nodded slightly, like something had been clarified.

"This is a day you should commemorate. Your first close encounter of the third kind. May we talk a little longer?"

"Yes." Ryotaro finally managed a nod.

"What was it that made you think of me as a Gray? I should tell you, no one has ever mistaken me for one before."

"Y-Your clothes. Anyone would…"

The man made a surprised face, as though he had somehow failed to notice that he was dressed completely in gray. He plucked at his suit with his long fingers. "I don't like clothes that stand out," he stated softly.

You stand out well enough, thought Ryotaro, but said nothing.

The man looked back to the path. "May I ask you a question?" he asked, his voice almost a whisper.

"Of course," Ryotaro answered, letting out some of the tension in his shoulders.

"Looking at your suit, I'd say you're employed somewhere.

It's not normal for you to be in this type of place at this time on a weekday, correct?"

Ryotaro sat in silence, having no idea how to answer the question.

"Perhaps you're paid to spend your days fighting evil and saving the world?"

"Nope," Ryotaro corrected, the man's words making him smile.

"Maybe you're a UFO researcher on the lookout for Grays?"

"Definitely not."

"Don't tell me you're from Area 51 in the U.S., here to capture Grays?"

"Just an ordinary salaryman at a jeweler's in Okachimachi," Ryotaro answered honestly. He feared that the conversation would become increasingly absurd unless he told the truth.

The man looked down, appearing to be in deep thought, then quickly looked back up. "So what is a regular salaryman doing in a place like this?"

Ryotaro was lost for an answer. He couldn't possibly tell him he had come here looking for a place to die. There was no point in saying so, and putting it into words might cause his conviction to waver. Ryotaro screwed his lips shut.

The man laughed cautiously as if picking up shards of broken glass, eyes still on Ryotaro. "Whatever your reason, you're here and the two of us met."

The words made Ryotaro look up to meet the man's stare. "And just who are you?" he asked.

The man's eyes narrowed, as though he had been waiting for the question. "Me? My name is Gray." He grinned briskly and gave a bow. "From now on, that will be how I introduce myself," he added. Gray stood up and extended a hand to Ryotaro, still on the bench. "What are you doing after this, uh…"

"Ryotaro, my name's Ryotaro Sakuma," Ryotaro said, self-consciously shaking Gray's hand as he stood up.

"Ryo-ta-ro… Ryotaro, Ryotaro." Gray put his right index finger to his temple, making a show of memorizing the name. "And what is Ryotaro doing after this?" Gray's powerful eyes focused on him.

"I'm not really sure," Ryotaro dodged as he struggled for words. *I'm going to die. I've made up my mind. So what if I've met this off man. It's too late to go back on it now.*

Gray watched as Ryotaro made to shut him out. Then he ventured cautiously, "Please forgive me, I know we have only just met. But…" the man paused for a moment. When he continued, it was in a whimsical tone: "Would you reconsider dying and help me with something instead?"

The words almost caused Ryotaro's heart to leap out of his chest.

3

Electronic noise.

Ryotaro awoke to the strangely comforting sound of his clock. He sat up and checked the time: 12 p.m.

Ryotaro walked drowsily over to the sink and gave a long yawn. He had slept well for the first time in ages and felt a little better.

He made some toast in the kitchen and ate brunch, then got into his suit. He left the apartment at 2 p.m. and began his journey to the National Diet train station. He took the Tokyo Metro Chiyoda Line and then changed to the JR Keihin-Tohoku Line before arriving at the National Diet and going into the Grand Capital Hotel just across from the station.

He found the waiting room where Shinohara and shop manager Yoshimura already stood waiting along with the rest of the staff.

"Hey! Yesterday you go AWOL and today you're the last to show up. Are you trying to fuck with me?" Yoshimura glared at Ryotaro, his cheeks twitching neurotically.

Ryotaro felt suddenly ill, as though he had plunged to the bottom of a deep valley. He had taken yesterday off, then phoned Yoshimura in the evening to tell him that he'd caught a cold.

"Good morning," Ryotaro said, trying to avoid eye contact with the man. His heart was beating erratically, and he couldn't catch his breath. Just seeing Yoshimura's face was enough to make him hyperventilate.

"Don't 'good morning' me. Taking the day off because of a cold? Setting up has been a fucking nightmare thanks to you." Yoshimura's plan had been to make Ryotaro do the set-up at the Grand Capital by himself.

"I'm really sorry," Ryotaro said in a small voice.

"Shithead. A germ like you catching a cold? That's a fucking joke. But it's not like your being here's gonna improve sales. When are you going to wake up to your uselessness and just quit? Taking the day off, indeed. You'd better be ready, if you don't meet your quota at the exhibition today I'm going to have you writing apologies until you die." Yoshimura clicked his tongue in frustration as he let loose on Ryotaro.

The exhibition, known as the *Yushokuten*, was hosted by major diamond companies and held a number of times each year. It was a venue for jewelry makers, distributors, and jewelers to offer their stock to society's elite. Guests received special invitations from the sponsors to be treated to dinner and shows in addition to a chance to purchase the latest accessories that were not yet commonly available. In preparation for this *Yushokuten,* Ryotaro's store had crafted a showpiece ring studded with over 300 million yen of rubies and diamonds in an attempt to reel in new clients on top of their regulars.

Twenty tables were laid out across the space of the Grand Capital's Vermilion Bird Lounge. Invitations had been extended to over two hundred elite guests. The entrances and exits had been fitted with detectors designed to react to the precious metal and special tags attached to the jewelry, and the place brimmed with security guards. The lounge shone brilliantly as lights installed in the numerous glass cases reflected off the jewelry. The grandeur of the space was elevated by nine-foot-tall *ikebana* flower arrangements on both sides of the central stage. Between 3:00 and 5:30, the upper-crust guests were free to walk around the displays, try items on, and make purchases. The system was designed so clients only had to sign purchase orders at the exhibition; actual payment would be made at a later date when the client visited the jeweler's store.

Ryotaro stood towards the back of the booth, taking in the bustle of the exhibition, while Yoshimura and Shinohara interacted with clients from their advantageous positions at the front.

People dressed in unbridled extravagance were all smiles as they chatted and browsed the diamonds on display. Given that the rest of the country was in the grips of a recession, this room was an *aberration*, Ryotaro mused. The elite few that had received invitations to the Vermillion Bird Lounge presided as life's winners. Money begat money and the rich got richer. That had become clear during his time at the jewelry store.

Ryotaro froze as he caught a glimpse of a familiar figure, the woman responsible for everything.

He watched as her flabby body rippled with every step—fat doubtlessly born from the choicest of meat. The room was not hot, but even from his distance Ryotaro could make out the sweat glistening on her forehead, pasting her bangs flat. She resembled a swollen anaconda, her eyes wide open in excitement as she drank in the gems on display, her thick, heavily rouged lips oddly clammy like some animal's, in contrast to the strikingly white foundation plastered on her face. Ryotaro couldn't help but frown in disgust.

All of Ryotaro's problems had stemmed from a single mistake. His job had, at first, gone well. Ryotaro's easygoing manner, together with a talent for English, had made him popular with the store's clients. He had been a valued member of the team. A number of clients came to ask for him directly and his sales were among the highest of his colleagues. Even the manager, Yoshimura, had liked him.

There was one customer who was very good for business. A middle-aged woman, her body flabby from expensive food, who lavished herself with expensive jewelry. She would visit the store a couple of times each month, and each time she would buy more than the last trip. She was virtually a tree that bore money.

Rumor had it that after the death of her husband she had inherited land that had been in the family for generations. Able to live off the unearned income it generated, her fortune apparently just kept growing. Yoshimura, desperate for her business, was fervent in his attempts to ingratiate himself. Ryotaro, for his part, was careful not to offend her.

She took a liking to Ryotaro until, eventually, he came to be her exclusive attendant. Sometime after her total purchases were over a hundred million yen, she invited him to dinner. Ryotaro already had his suspicions of what would happen after the meal. He consulted Yoshimura and was told, in no uncertain terms, that he had to accept. Despite his total lack of enthusiasm, Ryotaro felt that he had no choice.

As expected, the venue was a restaurant in a glamorous hotel. After dinner they had drinks at the hotel bar until they were slightly drunk, then checked into the hotel's most expensive room. Ryotaro had resigned himself to grin and bear it, since it was only one night. But when the time came he found himself shaking uncontrollably. Before he realized it he had fled the room, overwhelmed with disgust for the woman and disbelief in himself. As he made his way home, still flustered, he fully considered himself to have made the right choice.

The next day, the woman filed a formal complaint with the store. She singled Ryotaro out and swore she would never set foot in such a "despicable" store again. When Yoshimura got wind of the news he flew into a rage. The woman had a number of connections and knew many of the store's other regular clients. The result was that sales crashed. Yoshimura's name was added to the list of prime candidates for redundancy as he came under increasing pressure from headquarters.

From that point onwards Yoshimura's attitude, along with those of his other colleagues, completely changed. Yoshimura was the worst—he would begin shouting for no reason and hurl personal insults at Ryotaro.

Useless scum. You're a pain in the ass. Fucking quit. Asshole.

Garbage. Die.

Ryotaro's other colleagues joined in with the insults, as though following suit. Out of all of them, Shinohara seemed to enjoy it the most. In the midst of Yoshimura's relentless bullying, Ryotaro began to make mistakes on the job. Each time, the chain of insults worsened. Eventually, Ryotaro began to exhibit symptoms of depression. The abuse had continued for the last six months.

Ryotaro began to walk away from the booth, trying to avoid the woman as she approached.

"Where do you think you're going?" Yoshimura said, glaring at Ryotaro and grabbing his shoulder. Yoshimura's hold tightened, and the man's fingers dug into his flesh. "You haven't helped anyone yet, have you? Are you planning to do any work today, huh?" His voice was low, so no one would overhear, but his eyes were full of menace. Ryotaro felt completely cowed. "Don't think you can leave here before meeting your quota. If you try, I'll run you down. I won't stop until I convince you that *another option that's not living would be the lesser evil for you.*" Yoshimura pushed Ryotaro's shoulder away.

Ryotaro couldn't stop trembling. He stood rooted to the spot, completely frozen.

5:30 p.m.

The clients sat at big round tables, enjoying the lavish banquet that was served. The exhibiting stores footed the bill for the food and drinks. Each dish was an elaborately presented plate of fusion cuisine. As they devoured the food, the clients discussed the gems on display.

In terms of quantity, there were relatively few items on display in the Vermilion Bird Lounge, but each was of the highest quality—the total value of the exhibition was close to ten billion yen. Moreover, each piece on offer was newly designed and not yet available in stores, which provided an endless source of conversation for the clientele.

Shortly after the last dish was served, the doors were shut

and the show began. A female MC greeted the audience before welcoming onto the stage a well-known female jazz vocalist often seen on TV. The crowd burst into applause. The lights dimmed and the performance began. The woman's sultry voice melded with the piano's melody, weaving an atmosphere of calm through the hall. It was seven once the half-hour performance ended.

A different female MC, wearing a school uniform for some reason, her face obscured by a hunting cap, came on stage, said a few appreciative words, then called out in a lively voice, "For the next part of our show I am pleased to announce tonight's utterly amazing surprise guest!"

Sated by their dinner, the guests all turned to the stage.

"Who could it be? Let's welcome him!"

The lights dimmed, filling the room with silent darkness. A spotlight fell on the stage to reveal a tall man in a gray hat. Everything he wore was gray. A quarter of the guests cocked their heads sideways, not sure what was happening. Another quarter took a loud intake of breath—remembering *the incidents*—but, deciding it was a prank, soon broke into applause. The final half scowled, thinking it was a bad joke.

"Greetings, blessed individuals! How are you today?"

The gray man smiled. His face was hidden under the rim of his hat, and only his mouth was visible.

"It is my honor to make your acquaintances, you who use your wealth to exploit others, you who plaster your bodies with money. I ask you please to bear with me for the short duration of my show."

The gray man bowed, cuing for the lights to come back on. Radiance flooded across the room, revealing ten or so people in black ski masks positioned around the edges. They were concentrated near the exits and held guns.

"I have a few requests. First, no matter what, do not raise your voices, and please stay where you are."

The gray man swept a burning gaze over the crowd before lifting up a hand. In response, the unidentified people along the walls began to smash the glass showcases and offload the gems into bags.

All muttering ceased instantly. There were a few screams, but the majority remained silent, in accordance with the gray man's demand. Most were frozen with terror, unable to make a sound.

The people in ski masks packed the jewelry away with efficiency. The small quantity of the items on display allowed them to complete their work in the blink of an eye.

"And now for my next request. Please remove all jewelry you are wearing and place them at the center of your tables."

The guests sat still, seemingly unable to respond immediately to the demand.

The man in gray sighed. "I would prefer it if I did not have to repeat myself," he said, pointing off-stage.

All eyes followed. They saw a man, held at either side by two masked men. Ryotaro's eyes opened wide. It was Yoshimura.

"You wouldn't want to leave with a nasty aftertaste, would you?"

One of the men pulled out a gun and leveled it at Yoshimura's temple. The guests hurriedly tore off their jewelry, throwing the gems onto the tables before them.

The gray man nodded in satisfaction. The masked men circled the tables, retrieving the jewels. Ryotaro spied the woman who had tried to force him into bed. He could see the flab under her chin swaying as she quaked with terror.

Yoshimura was released when the masked men finished gathering up the jewelry. Suddenly free from their grasp, he crumpled to the ground and wet himself. For the briefest of moments the man in gray—who had been focused on overseeing the operation—turned to meet Ryotaro's gaze and narrowed his eyes. In the next moment he turned back to the crowd and tipped the rim of his hat with his fingers.

"I thank you for your cooperation. My final request is that you close your eyes. You have seen nothing. Heard nothing. You shall inquire into nothing. If, that is, you value your lives."

The gray man's words caused the audience to shudder all the more. They squeezed their eyes tightly shut.

"All that remains is for me to wish you an enjoyable evening."

The lights went out. There was a bustle of footsteps and the sound of doors opening. When the lights came back on, the gray man had vanished.

In the blink of an eye, it was all over.

Ryotaro was given a brief, perfunctory questioning after the police had rushed to the hotel. Once cleared of suspicion and free to leave, he headed straight home.

The next day, as per Gray's instructions, he headed to the entrance of the park of the Kamenokoyama Tomb. Yoshimura had been admitted to hospital for shock, so the store had been closed temporarily. A car pulled up before him at the promised time of 2 p.m. The back door swung open. Ryotaro hesitated for a moment, then steeled himself and stepped in.

"Let's go," Gray said to the bald man in the driver's seat as the door closed.

The man silently guided the car forwards.

"My thanks for yesterday," Gray said. Ryotaro bowed his head slightly.

The young girl in uniform was also in the back seat. She silently placed a duffel bag on Ryotaro's lap. It was stuffed full.

"The bag contains your reward—150 million yen. Would you also like some diamonds?" Gray asked, his voice bright. Ryotaro shook his head. "Are you certain? Thanks to you I've come by ten billion yen in diamonds for a mere 150 million yen in expenses. Don't feel shy."

Gray winked at Ryotaro through the rearview mirror from his place in the front passenger seat. Though Ryotaro averted his gaze, he found himself sneaking a look at Gray's expression. Gray, however, had turned to look out of the window.

When they had met two days ago, Gray had requested Ryotaro's assistance in a robbery. Ryotaro had accepted. He'd told Gray all he knew about the circumstances, timetable, and security of the jewelry exhibition.

Why had I accepted such a wild proposal?

Ryotaro could not be sure. In his dire mood, ready to die, Gray's presence had been too fascinating.

"Um, could I ask a question?"

"Of course," Gray answered. His carefree tone was in stark contrast to Ryotaro's timidity.

"Was it really okay to do this?"

Of course it wasn't. Ryotaro understood as much, but he had to ask nonetheless.

Gray considered Ryotaro's question in silence. The car came to a stop at a red light. They waited; the car filled with quiet. A few vehicles passed in front of them. The light turned green and their car began to move gently forwards.

"I only steal from those in advantageous positions, and I take care not to trouble individuals," Gray said. "The jewelry exhibition was fully insured. The insurance companies are, in turn, insured by other insurance companies, thus diffusing risk. As a result, no single individual will suffer any significant hardship. In yesterday's case, we stole jewelry from wealthy clients, which amounted to a tiny portion of their sprawling fortunes. They won't become destitute as a result. We have already discussed this much previously. Your participation was built on that under-standing."

"Yes."

"Then I shall continue." Gray sounded particularly jovial. He was clearly enjoying his explanation. "There are reasons why I must steal. I do not steal for personal benefit. Instead, I have a greater goal, one that requires me to amass funds. And there is my talent."

"Talent?"

"Yes. *It allows me to spot those who have decided to end their lives. I have a radar for despair.* It is a meager talent, but it is enough to assist me in getting closer to my goal."

"This goal, is it something big?"

Ryotaro thought himself absurd for becoming an accessory to robbery without being party to the motives behind it. He had offered his help from a position of total ignorance. Yet it was only now that it struck him as odd. He felt a measure of guilt, but everything seemed dream-like and inauthentic—the reality that he had committed a crime had yet to hit him.

Ryotaro watched Gray's face through the rearview mirror. The man's seemingly bottomless eyes were turned to the world outside, watching it flow by. Ryotaro was increasingly fascinated by the burning sparkle within them.

"You want to know?" Gray asked, his tone suddenly smug.

"Would that be okay?" Ryotaro replied, beginning to feel like a puppet being made to dance on someone's hand.

Gray narrowed his eyes and said in a deeper voice, "You must not speak of this to anyone."

"I suspect no one would believe me if I did."

Gray chortled quietly, nodding. "My plan is to *redistribute*."

It took Ryotaro a few seconds to wrap his head around the word. Even when he did, he was unable to glean its sense. "Redistribute?"

"Indeed. *That is all I can tell you at this stage,*" Gray emphasized the words in a lively voice. "That is why I thought to enlist your help for our latest venture. Ask me whether stealing is a good deed and I would have to answer no. Yet I must steal in order to achieve my goal of redistribution. What I need most right now is money and people." Gray homed in on Ryotaro's gaze in the rearview mirror. Ryotaro was unable to look away.

"Do you steal people, too?" Ryotaro's voice was shaky and thin when he finally spoke.

"That depends on how things go. I readily welcome those who would offer assistance."

Ryotaro's resolve was deepened by Gray's meaningful smile. He gave the duffel bag back to the girl. She responded with a welcoming smile.

"I'm not sure if I can be of assistance, but could I offer it regardless? For this redistribution."

Gray turned to face the rear of the car and smiled as his chillingly charming eyes met Rytotaro's. Ryotaro felt his cheeks warm and his body flush as if he had spontaneously burst into flames.

"It would be an honor. Welcome to my little party."

Gray extended him a long hand.

4

They drove for a while as the car followed a twisting route, as though trying to lose a tail. When they reached an area of office buildings near Tokyo Station the car pulled into an underground parking area of buildings tall enough to force one to strain to see their tops.

"As your joining us was *unplanned*, I want you to have some time to get to know us," Gray said cordially, grinning through the mirror.

They parked in the space closest to the staff entrance. The bald man pulled up the emergency brake and sat quietly, awaiting Gray's instructions.

"Where are we?"

"My company's building," Gray said, smiling, and got out of the car. Ryotaro hurriedly opened his own door.

When Gray, Ryotaro, and the uniformed girl had all gotten out of the car, the bald man drove away. Gray made sure the care left before leading the three of them to an elevator. The building had thirty floors. Gray pushed the button for the top floor.

"Nervous?" Gray asked as the elevator continued upwards. The elevator's movement was so smooth it hardly felt like they were moving.

"A little," Ryotaro answered honestly. Considering his involvement in the raid he felt strangely relaxed. He knew that it was Gray's presence that allowed him to be so calm.

The person who had saved him from hell.

The presence that had pulled him away from death's abyss.

The mysterious man who had made everything go away like a summer's wind leaving only a clear, blue sky.

It was hard to think of him as human. He was something greater.

Ryotaro had no evidence to back it up, but he could not help but think so each time he felt his gaze, his presence, each time he saw the scars of terrible pain in his features and eyes. Ryotaro's mind wandered as he kept his eyes on Gray's taut profile.

Gray saved my life. That is why I must help him.

Ryotaro nodded to himself in confirmation. The young girl to his side watched him surreptitiously.

When the elevator reached the tenth floor a man in a suit got in. He was wearing a navy blue tie and a starched shirt. His eyebrows were shaped like an inverted 'v', giving him a bothered look that suggested a timid personality. He was in his thirties and thin to the point of looking ill.

"Ah, welcome back."

"Thank you. Good to be back."

The man smiled, welcoming Gray with clear affection. Gray smiled back. On hearing Gray's response the man's smile grew until it was impossible to imagine a broader grin. He greeted the girl and then Ryotaro. He said nothing else and got off on the eighteenth floor.

Two men got on. One was large like a judo enthusiast, one short with neat, even features.

"Welcome back."

The two men greeted Gray with the same look of respect and affection as the first man. Their faces lit up like happy children's when Gray returned their greeting. Just like the first man, the two then took turns greeting Ryotaro and the girl in uniform. Then they stood in silence until getting out on the twenty-sixth floor. All three men had shown respect for Gray and extended genuine smiles to Ryotaro and the girl.

Reverence. The word did not do justice to the force of emotion they had shown towards Gray. *A religious leader and his devotees.* The analogy was closer, Ryotaro thought, but not quite right.

The elevator came to a halt at the thirtieth floor and the trio stepped out into a plushly carpeted corridor. The light gray carpet was surprisingly thick, and Ryotaro stumbled several times as he followed Gray's lead.

"Here we are," Gray said, knocking at the door.

Knocking? Ryotaro cocked his head to one side. There would be no need to knock on one's own room. The door was heavy and thick; it gave every appearance of being the door to the company's top executive suite. *Gray knocking. Does that mean the company has someone above him?* Ryotaro found it hard to believe in the existence of such a person. A muffled voice sounded from inside as Ryotaro's thoughts raced.

"Come in!"

Gray opened the door. The room was decorated exclusively in blacks and whites. The walls and floor tiles were white, but the furniture—sofas, desk, chairs—were all black; it was like stumbling into a three-dimensional rendering of Othello, the board game. The only incongruity was a set of decorative plants, inconspicuous along the window. A woman sat glaring at a stack of documents fanned out across a black desk. She was in a Prussian blue suit, wearing glasses with thin, silver rims.

"It should be quite obvious that I'm busy. If it's not of immediate personal benefit to me then shred it," the woman snapped, eyes still on the desk, looping her longish hair over her ears.

"Please accept my apologies for taking up your time."

The woman jerked her head up in response, like a dog reacting to some noise. Her face was feline. "You usually warn me of your visits. What brings you here today?" The bespectacled woman pulled a sour face, throwing a glance at Ryotaro before looking back at Gray, but her tone was ever so slightly softer.

"Yes, sorry to barge in like this, but I have a favor to ask."

"And that would be?"

"Some laundry."

The woman looked momentarily surprised but soon regained her composure. "Well now, haven't done that in a while," she sighed, crossing her arms. "I hadn't heard any talk of that recently, so I was beginning to think you'd moved on. I assume yesterday's raid was your doing, then?"

"Indeed, a whole year since the last one. It did take a while to get into the stride of things after such an interim." Gray stared off to the distance, looking lost in reflection.

"Nothing since August last year."

The words kindled a sleeping memory inside Ryotaro's head. A series of robberies, dubbed the "August Raids." How had he forgotten such a sensational event? He looked at Gray's back.

He was *the gray man.*

"Well, those vulgar weekly tabloids continue to run articles on you, even though you've kept a low profile. And yesterday's robbery is all over the papers," the woman said in a tone of exaggerated politeness. She indicated the table in front of the sofa with her chin.

"Ah. One would imagine the media would have better things to do than continue writing about those incidents. Quite the honor." Gray flashed a wry grin as he picked up one of the tabloids. "Now this headline I like. 'Japan: Incompetent Police State.'" He gave a brief sigh before putting the paper down.

"So, what's the precise job this time?" The woman circled around to the front of the paper-strewn desk and leaned against it. Ryotaro willed himself to look away from her tight-fitting suit that accentuated the natural curves of her body and the short hemline of her skirt.

"A few gemstones."

"How many?" The woman sounded surprised.

"About ten billion worth."

"That's all?"

"That's all."

"Ah," she noted suggestively, then sighed heavily. "Gems are a pain to clean, you know. Well, I guess it's worth a try. What I'd really like to know is why you'd steal gemstones for the paltry sum of ten billion? I can't imagine that much would make the slightest difference to you."

"How long will it take?" Gray asked, ignoring the question.

"At the quickest, about ten days." The woman maintained the calm in her voice, but the corners of her eyes twitched at the slight.

"That will be fine. Takano has deposited the stones in the usual place."

"You want Japanese yen, like always?"

"Please."

"Fine. For this much I should be able to get it through Hong Kong. Expect about seven billion in cash," she said before looking at Ryotaro. "And this one? An abandoned cat brought in from the rain?"

"He accompanied us on yesterday's job. He's one of us from now on."

"Hmm." The woman looked Ryotaro over as though assessing his worth. She let out a sigh of dismay. "Too banal for someone you scouted out. Tell me, do you have any particular talents?" she asked Ryotaro with a scornful look.

Ryotaro made to say something, but the woman's overbearing directness had overwhelmed him.

"Cat got your tongue? Talents, skills."

"I can manage a little English," Ryotaro finally managed.

The woman snorted. "Come on, you're not some graduate at a job interview. Anything else?"

"Other than that?" Ryotaro was sweating. His chest was tight, constricted like when Yoshimura was beating him down. "Nothing, really."

The woman responded by giving Gray a puzzled look. "Why did you bring him in?"

"As you know, I don't bring in help based on an assessment of talent," Gray answered cheerfully.

The woman scowled as though the answer had been insufficient. "Fine, whatever. Either way he's one of your Forty-seven Ronin now, right?"

"Forty-seven Ronin?" Ryotaro blurted.

The woman twisted her mouth in displeasure. "Meaning you're one of a bunch who have pledged loyalty unto death," the woman snarled, revealing white teeth and a sadistic streak.

"Let's leave it at that, shall we?" Gray cut in, his tone warm but warning he'd brook no backtalk. He turned to the girl in uniform. "I'd like you to take Ryotaro on a tour of the building."

"Of course."

"And provide him with a brief overview of what we do here."

The girl nodded, turned on her heels, and left the room. Ryotaro rushed after her. She walked briskly into the elevator and, after checking that Ryotaro was behind her, pressed the button for the fourth floor.

The elevator quietly carried the two of them down. Ryotaro made a few abortive attempts at conversation but, at a loss for anything to say, ended up staring at the girl's back. She was in school uniform and seemed to be about high school age. The girl's attire seemed completely out of place. Her hair was luminous and lovely, large eyes graced her smallish face, and the corners of her lips were curved into a permanent smile. She was cute, but "attractive" seemed a better fit. Her slender legs were covered in finely patterned black socks up to her knees.

"The difficult type, isn't she?" the girl asked without turning around.

He was not expecting the girl to address him at all. Ryotaro's face reddened, and he rubbed it as he tried to banish his head of *lewd thoughts* before he spoke. "Well, she didn't seem very nice," he ended up speaking his mind, unsure of how best to respond. The woman had seemed different from the other people he'd met in the building so far. That sharpness to her personality, that flashy fashion sense, her attitude towards Gray. Everything about her had been wildly different.

"She left the worst first impression on me, too." The girl's eyes traced the ceiling as if recalling a memory as she crossed her pale legs under her skirt. "But really, she's not that bad. She's one of us, of course, but she's 'special grade.' It can't be helped that she's a little different from the rest of us."

"Special grade?" Ryotaro wanted to take his head in his hands. He was about ready to explode as question marks filled his mind.

The girl turned to face him and shrugged, chuckling, perhaps empathizing with his reaction. "It's like falling into Wonderland, right?"

"That's exactly how it feels." He raised both hands weakly in defeat.

"We've got plenty of time to talk, so don't get flustered." She laughed again, her face rounding, making her look closer to her age.

The elevator doors slid open and the girl walked out to a white-tiled corridor. Ryotaro followed behind as he took in the surroundings. The fourth-floor corridor was lined with glass-walled booths, each designed like a meeting room, and though the glass exposed the spaces to the corridor, no sound leaked out. Some of the rooms had people sitting at the tables, facing each other. There were people in expensive suits, college kids in casual getups, women decked out in designer accessories, wealthy-looking elderly couples. Men and women dressed in immaculate suits tended to the people, all of whom appeared to be clients. The staff were a variety of ages but all looked sharply intelligent.

"What exactly does this company do?" Ryotaro asked as he looked into the booths.

"Have you ever heard of Tomosun Securities?"

"Tomosun… No, I don't think so."

"It's not that well-known. You need at least 200 million yen to open an account here, so I guess your average person would never know of it."

"Two hundred million." Close to the lifetime earnings of a typical salaryman.

"Of course, no one who barely clears the threshold comes here. Most have assets around 500 million."

"Five hundred million?" Ryotaro felt a twinge of sadness, as he could not begin to wrap his head around such an amount.

"Tomosun is a word-of-mouth business for the upper classes." As she spoke, the girl opened the door to the last room of the corridor and motioned for Ryotaro to enter.

The room was designed to offer total privacy, although it looked the same as the other booths they had passed—a rectangular desk, comfy-looking chairs, and decorative plants in the corner. Nondescript. The one feature to distinguish this room from the others was a single painting on one wall. It was of a woman with long hair, rendered in exquisite detail. But there was something mysterious about the painting; the woman was attractive, but instantly forgettable the moment you looked away.

"This is my office space. Not that I'm ever here to use it."

Ryotaro looked around the room. Everything was brand-new, seemingly hardly used.

"Shall I start with a simple description of the building itself?" the girl asked from her seat to the right behind the four-person table.

"Please," Ryotaro answered from his place on the other side; they were seated facing each other across the table.

She cleared her throat, then began to go through the details. "From the tenth floor down is offices for Tomosun Securities, where we work to increase the fortunes of the rich. The wealthy—especially the nouveau riche—want more money, so they invest large amounts with us. Business booms," she informed, her voice tinted with self-deprecation. "The eleventh to thirtieth floors belong to Tomosun Trading."

"Tomosun Trading." Ryotaro was momentarily confused by the similarity of the name. He had heard it somewhere before. Maybe the news or somewhere like that. The girl continued, interrupting his train of thought.

"Tomosun Trading was formed just three years ago with strong ties to the United Arab Emirates. It has land rights mostly concentrated in Mexico and Mongolia and turns a profit from materials exportation and extraction of natural resources. There are some affiliated companies, like Pharaon Logistics which was incorporated two years ago, but that's probably not relevant now. That's the gist of it. Any questions?"

She tilted her head slightly, waiting for Ryotaro to ask something. The gesture seemed at odds with her age. Ryotaro felt his heart race unexpectedly.

"The thirtieth floor, is that the CEO's office?"

"Oops, I'd forgotten to mention that." The girl poked her tongue out slightly. "That's the cleaners."

"The cleaners?" Ryotaro furrowed his brows. However you

looked at it, the place didn't look like a laundromat. But Gray too had referred to "laundry" earlier.

"I'm not lying. I don't know the details either, but it's where they take stolen money or things and clean it, make it new. The woman we met, Shindo, she's a pro cleaner. It's called money laundering."

"Money laundering," Ryotaro mumbled. Transforming criminal money into clean money. Ryotaro remembered reading about it somewhere: the process of routing illegitimate funds through various countries until the source was no longer determinable.

"I don't know the details, but she's a wizard at it." The girl gave him a look of pride.

Small wonder. Perhaps it had been easier once upon a time to take ten billion worth of diamonds and convert them into legitimate yen over a ten-day period, but now, with a recent spate of anti-money-laundering regulations on the books, it was more like sorcery. Ryotaro recalled Shindo's figure. A beautiful yet stern career woman was a perfect description of her.

"It's impressive she hasn't been caught," Ryotaro muttered in admiration.

"She came close, once. Before she came here, that is." The girl lowered her voice, leaning slightly forwards. "Back when she was a banker, she had a side business cleaning yakuza money. But the police got wind of it. The gangsters were exposed and she got fired from the bank."

"Just fired? Not arrested?"

"He helped her." The girl's face lit up with genuine, heartfelt happiness.

"Ah, you mean Gray." Ryotaro knew instantly who it was from her expression.

"Gray?" The girl's eyes opened wide in confusion.

"The man who stole the jewels," he explained, before remembering that he had been the first person to call the man Gray.

"Is that his name? Gray?"

"Uh... I think I was the first to call him that."

"How did he react?

"React?"

"Was he angry? Happy?" The girl's spirited gaze practically begged for an answer.

Feeling overwhelmed, Ryotaro leaned back. "If I had to say, I guess he seemed to like it."

"Huh." The girl bit her lower lip with a look of vexation, perhaps even envy.

"What do other people call, uh, Gray?" Ryotaro said quickly, as if to make amends.

"Just 'him' or 'that person.' Shindo's pretty direct with him, but she doesn't know his name. Some people refer to him as 'the unfathomable one.' Not to his face, of course."

"That's it?"

"That's it."

"So no one knows his name?"

"Basically. Anyway, 'Gray'… Does that mean 'unidentified' or something?" Her eyes bore into him.

"Or something. By the way, what did you mean when you said Gray helped Shindo?" Ryotaro changed the subject. He sensed she would be angry if he told her the name came from his first impression of the man as an alien.

The girl pursed her lips, unsatisfied, but she sighed and answered his question. "I don't know too much about it, but when the yakuza were exposed the cops also worked out that Shindo was involved. They held an investigation into her complicity, but she was pronounced innocent just as they gathered enough evidence to arrest her—and just like that, she received a full acquittal. He's the one who made that happen."

"How?" Ryotaro asked.

The girl laughed. "Anyone can do anything with his help."

"Even intervening with the—"

"Police are human too. He is greater than human," the girl said, interrupting Ryotaro in mid-sentence. She laughed with a look too seductive for her age.

Indeed, it was hard to think of Gray as just a man, so Ryotaro had no wish to argue with what she'd said. So then what was he? Ryotaro was frustrated that he couldn't think of a description that fit. He continued to ask questions, but the question marks in his head refused to clear up, and he felt increasingly confused.

What he did learn was that Tomosun Trading had rights to various parcels of land across the world and specialized in selling special rare earth metals from Mongolia and other places at prices that aggressively undercut the market. That project was funded by Tomosun Securities. China's overwhelming output of rare earths had led to the Japanese government injecting vast amounts of capital into Tomosun Trading, hoping to lessen dependence on the People's Republic. While countries other than China had deposits of rare earths, geological conditions resulted in higher excavation costs than in China. Many of those countries, fearing shortages of their resources, had restricted exports of the commodity. As a result Japan was currently finding it difficult to secure a supply route. Tomosun Trading had obtained exclusive rights to import rare earths from Mongolia and was securing huge profits through various means. Finally, he learned that Shindo, the expert at money laundering, was thirty-six and single and had never been married. That was the sum total of what the girl had to tell him.

"I'm thirsty, hang on a second." The girl had been talking rapidly. She got up, rubbed her throat, and left the room.

Ryotaro watched her as she went, then turned to look at the painting on the wall. It was definitely strange. The woman's face had been painted so that the instant you looked away it was impossible to recall. She looked to be smiling, yet also expressionless, perhaps sad, even angry. Was it some kind of illusion? With each passing moment she seemed to morph into a different person, and it was impossible to recall any of them. Her eyes had an inorganic darkness that in a way suggested madness.

"Thanks for waiting. Cola okay?" The girl bustled back into the room, holding out a can. She was slightly out of breath.

"Thanks." The can was cold enough to numb his hand.

The girl pulled open the tab on her can and gulped down a

mouthful. "Does the painting bother you?" The girl indicated the wall with her chin.

"I think it's mysterious. It's hard to pin down. She's pretty, but lacks features," Ryotaro offered honestly.

"That's who I used to be."

"You?" Ryotaro looked at her, then back to the painting. There was nothing even remotely similar between them. The woman in the painting was older and Caucasian.

"I mean, she's better-looking; comparing our features is like comparing the moon to a turtle. But the woman in the painting and the old me were *stripped of our selves and faceless*. So we're the same in that sense. The painter destroyed that model's sense of self. My old self was the same. That's why I keep it here, as punishment for my stupidity. Not that I come here much, of course." She fell silent.

Ryotaro wanted to know more but intuited that the subject was taboo. He looked at her without a word. Her cheeks had reddened, perhaps from a fit of embarrassment.

"Ah, I get so tired talking about things I don't understand," she said, sounding exhausted. "To be honest, I don't really understand enough to be able to tell you what they do here. Things I don't know about, things I don't understand. Everything I've told you so far is stuff I was told over and over until I finally got it memorized."

"Over and over?"

"Yeah. Shindo made fun of me the whole time. She gets angry as soon as you ask a question." She shrugged.

Ryotaro imagined Shindo sternly lecturing this innocent girl and started to laugh.

"What's so funny?" The girl looked indignant. Ryotaro bobbed his head in apology. He had allowed himself to relax when he felt like he'd caught a glimpse of the still-young girl behind the mask.

"Sorry, that sounded pretty funny," he said, stifling more laughter.

"How rude," she objected and puffed out her cheeks.

"Anyway, is it okay for you to be telling me all these secrets?" Still laughing, Ryotaro's voice came out high-pitched. The girl looked surprised.

"What do you mean?"

"I mean…" Ryotaro stopped, realizing that he was *one of them* now.

"Exactly. You're an accomplice now." The girl nodded, as though she had read his thoughts. "You're part of our club. But not because you helped us at the exhibition. You're in because *he accepted you*. You know what his talent is, right?"

"He can tell if someone wants to die."

"That's right. But do you really think that's a special skill?"

Ryotaro considered the question. To be able to spot someone on the verge of suicide was not something just anyone could do. "I think it's special. You can't tell someone's thinking of suicide before they actually do it."

"Not so." The girl stared penetratingly into his eyes. "It's not about predicting death. It's a sensitivity to people sliding towards death. Can you tell the difference between someone who's happy and someone who's depressed?"

"That's not so difficult."

"It's the same. If you pay careful attention to what someone might be thinking or feeling, it's easy enough to tell when they're being pushed to the brink. When people are considering suicide, they are signaling as much. It's just that hardly anyone sees it."

Logically, the girl's argument made sense. But there was a limit to the amount of information that could be gleaned from an expression or a person's outward behavior. No, the ability to read someone's thoughts just through observation was exceptional, practically a superpower.

"Can you do it?"

"Of course not," the girl answered flatly. "But he can. And as you were racing towards death he found you. He chose you to be one of us and brought you here."

Ryotaro felt his stomach tighten. *She's right. I was trying to die. I was looking for a place to die, and he found me and saved me.*

He noticed that he no longer had any desire to end his life—the belated realization surprised him. His mental exhaustion, his endless worries… It felt like a lie that he had sought a release in death. It was all thanks to Gray.

"Everyone here…" he started uncertainly. The girl nodded.

"That's right. We were all determined to kill ourselves, and we were all saved."

"And Gray is assembling people like us as part of this redistribution plan," Ryotaro mumbled, recalling Gray's words from earlier.

"He rescued us from a society in decay, one that almost killed us. We have to repay that debt. Right?"

The power behind the girl's stare demanded an answer, and Ryotaro nodded slowly in agreement. The girl's face lit up in a broad smile.

"That's why Shindo calls us the Forty-seven Ronin."

"But she's different."

"Exactly. I said she was 'special grade,' right? Sometimes he recruits people with a particular skill set."

It made perfect sense. Shindo had clearly been different from the other people he had met so far. "So it's okay to include someone like that?"

"Okay? In what way?"

"There's no guarantee that one of them's not an informer."

"Ah, that's all covered. He makes sure he knows their Achilles heels. Besides, they're all as guilty as us now."

"An atheist in the same foxhole."

"Not the best comparison, but yeah, something like that."

The girl took another swig of soda. Watching her, he wondered: *This girl wanted to die?*

"Are you 'special grade' too?" he asked. The girl shook her head.

"No way. I'm the same as everyone else. The same as you. I wanted to die from the bottom of my heart. I tried to end my life, and he rescued me." She met his eyes with a warm familiarity, a recognition of their status as equals.

Was he seeing things? The young girl faded away and a woman sat in her place. He saw eyes that had known deep suffering. The crying smile unique to those who had known betrayal. The sense of having been torn apart by bitterness, a heart cast deep into darkness and decimated.

"How long have you been here for?" Ryotaro's mouth had gone dry but he forced the words out.

The girl who was not a girl smiled softly. "About a year, I think."

She cast her eyes to the painting on the wall before slowly turning back to look at Ryotaro. Something in her eyes mirrored the expression of the woman in the painting.

"Oh, and by the way, my name's not 'you.' It's Sayuri. Good name, right?"

Sayuri smiled as if to put a lid on brimming emotions.

CHAPTER TWO

1

It was just after I started my freshman year in high school that I realized the bright city lights were cesspools and the people that flocked towards them were flies.

I was between my fourteenth and fifteenth birthdays.

It was the year that everything was corrupt. It was the year I became sullied, defiled. It was also the year I became numb to pain.

Sayuri Mizuno chewed at the straw sticking out of her plastic cup as she stared, awestruck, at the figure of beauty that sat across from her. It was September 2012. The new semester had already begun at her high school, but Sayuri was skipping class.

"After that it just seemed ridiculous to work at any normal kind of job." Ako Kurosaki laughed mischievously, narrowing her eyes like a cat. Her dress accentuated her taut figure, drawing an uncomfortable number of stares. She was 5'7" and looked even taller wearing high-heeled sandals.

Sayuri sat in the unexceptional family diner, carrying wilted fries to her mouth as she half-listened to what Ako had to say.

"I mean, you can earn crazy amounts."

"How much?" Sayuri asked.

"Five hundred thousand per person."

"Five hundred thousand?" Her eyes widened upon hearing such an unimaginably high number.

"Sometimes more, of course."

"Wow," Sayuri nodded, stunned. The sum was far greater than she had thought.

"It's five hours per person, not too much of a strain. Over in the blink of an eye."

As she took in Ako's infomercial-like pitch, Sayuri let her thoughts dwell on the idea of 500,000 yen.

"It sounds too good to be true. It's fishy." No such thing as a free lunch.

"Not at all, it's easy money. Just sleep with the guy. That's all you need to do to land enough money to have people rolling their eyes," Ako said, laughing away Sayuri's concern.

"I dunno." Sayuri narrowed her eyes, trying to discern whether Ako was being straight with her.

"It's fine, it's fine. I'm still alive and kicking, right? Look, you're lucky enough to have been born with good looks. Use your strengths, girl. Besides, you said you need someplace to live."

"I guess so," Sayuri mumbled. Finding somewhere to live was the most pressing issue she faced.

"That'll be fixed, you get a room in the building. With no charge, of course. Money and an apartment. Can't ask for more."

Ako got up and ran a hand through her shiny, straight hair. Everything she owned was designer, from her clothes to her handbag. Sayuri's uniform seemed so shabby in comparison.

"Wanna give it a go?" Ako asked, taking the bill between her slender fingers.

There was always a caveat to a good deal. But maybe once in a while a truly good offer was to be had. And there was Ako beaming right before her, the very picture of happiness.

I'll give it a go.

Sayuri nodded as she got up. Ako responded by scrunching her eyes into a smile.

Sayuri had been raised by her single mother. She had no memories of her father. Her mother was always busy with work so Sayuri spent much of her time alone but never considered herself lonely. She had certainly never been happy, but things had been such that she could keep on living. Her mother had raised Sayuri as if it was her duty but was never particularly loving. Sayuri, for her part, had never asked her mother to be more affectionate. It was enough that her mother took on her care. Selfishness had always seemed inappropriate. In her heart, Sayuri had always accepted that she was one of *the weak*.

Sometime during Sayuri's first year in middle school, her mother started to bring a man home. She lavished money on this man who was ten years her junior, bringing him into the house for sex regardless of whether Sayuri was there. Finding herself with nowhere to go, Sayuri began to avoid going home. But it was a chore to pass the time without any money.

One day, when she was in freshman year of high school, Sayuri had been hanging around Shibuya when someone called out to her. A man in his forties. Instead of the usual pick-up lines, he had offered her cash to be his "companion." Sayuri wanted money so she took him up on the offer. She accompanied him to a hotel meaning to steal his cash and make a run for it. She waited for him to take a shower before rifling through his wallet and running away.

It had been surprisingly easy.

From that day on Sayuri made a habit of cleaning out people who approached her for sex. It was highway robbery. If she stood idle among the brightly lit downtown streets, it was never too long before a mark approached her of his own free will. There were occasional bouts of self-hatred, but she rationalized them away by telling herself that the men were all bastards using money to get their way. Sometimes she would be caught red-handed, but the men's position as johns meant she had them by the balls. They would scream profanities, but she was never subjected to violence and no one ever went to the police.

Her mother's boyfriend had come to live with them after

Sayuri started high school. After a while she was bothered by the way he looked at her. It was the same look all those men had when they wanted to hire her.

As time passed, his looks became fondles. Sayuri began to fear for her safety. One day he forced himself on her. She was desperately fighting him off when her mother, fortunately, came home. But as soon as she saw what was going on, her mother exploded with anger at Sayuri as if she were her enemy. She screamed and grabbed at Sayuri in tears as though she had stolen something from her. Sayuri was devastated. Yet, as one of *the weak*, she made no attempt to stand up to her mother. She kept her emotions in check and endured the blows.

Sayuri left home without saying a word and never went back. To stay would have been too much. She knew she would suffer a breakdown.

She had crashed at her various friends' houses, but their generosity had a limit. She needed to find work and rent her own place. She had continued work as a pretend escort, thieving from her clients, but the income was unstable. It proved impossible to find a decent part-time job without the guarantee of a guardian. As a minor, she couldn't rent an apartment.

That was when Sayuri turned to Ako.

Ako had attended Sayuri's high school but dropped out within the first two months when their school discovered her involvement in an extortion racket targeting married men. But during that brief two-month period, Sayuri had come to feel a bond with Ako. They were in the same game—her tricking johns, Ako's extortion. They were two of a kind.

Ako, radiating a maturity that the other students lacked, first approached Sayuri not long after they had started school.

"I admire beautiful girls. Being smart is fine, but beauty's a talent, too. A limited talent, of course, one you lose as you get older. Anyways, you've got it."

Ako had beamed at her as she spoke the words. They were in the same grade, but it was the first time Sayuri had gotten a good look at her. She remembered feeling both envy and bewilderment.

Sayuri was fairly confident in herself, but her self-regard had been smashed to pieces by Ako's bewitching glamor. The girl's beauty and frank nature made Sayuri happy to play the sidekick.

2

Three days after their discussion, Sayuri and Ako headed to Ikebukuro together. Sayuri had visited Ikebukuro a number of times before, but in Ako's company it felt like a completely different place. People would stumble out of their way, bowled over by Ako's looks. Where the place had been a jumble of bodies before, it now felt spacious—all because Ako, with her unapproachable beauty, was walking alongside her. A path slid open before them, like the Red Sea parting for Moses.

"It's so hot!" Ako said, using her hands to fan herself.

"Yeah." Sayuri was about to pull at the collar of her t-shirt but instead copied Ako, fanning herself with her hand.

The time was 7 p.m.

They left Ikebukuro Station at the Sunshine Street exit and had a quick dinner at a fast food cafe nearby before heading towards their destination. They navigated through a street jammed with stalls to each side before taking a right at a drug store. The heat was relentless. The sun had already set but there was no breeze to cool the air. Each passerby brought an uncomfortable wave of humid air, and there were no signs of the flock of pedestrians thinning.

"We're almost there, stick with it," Ako said, flashing a smile. Sayuri was not jealous that everyone's stares fell on Ako. It was refreshing that she could simply accept this as being natural and fair.

Ikebukuro looked completely different once they moved past the blocks of office buildings. Something inappropriate that could never reveal itself to scrutiny filled the air with gloom. Just walking through quickened Sayuri's pulse, her instincts incessantly kicking up a sense of unease.

They walked for a while before reaching a street lined with

high-rise apartments. The area was quiet, a vacuum where pedestrians were sparse and the roar of the city receded into the background, with no more establishments trying to lure customers in with garish displays. To Sayuri, it seemed like a counterfeit version of Ikebukuro.

"Where are we going?" Sayuri asked, coaxed by her unease but trying not to let her agitation show.

"Just a cafe where we're gonna meet this guy. There's a little interview."

"Interview?" It was news to Sayuri. Her face went pale.

"Nothing to worry about. Just be yourself. He'll hire you for sure. Feeling nervous?"

"Not really…" Sayuri muttered, attempting to quell the anxiety in her chest.

"We're almost there," Ako said gently, smiling as though she could read Sayuri's thoughts. She came to a stop outside a shop called Floating Play. It was solid, encased in concrete, as though built to keep out prying eyes. Only a small plaque on the heavy wooden door bearing the establishment's name announced the shop's presence.

"This is it," Ako said, opening the dark brown door without a moment's hesitation.

It opened in silence, swallowed the two girls, and closed noiselessly behind them. The windowless interior was lit by the dim glow of a few bulbs. Sayuri inspected the area, keeping her hands over her chest in an attempt to shield her shrinking heart. The place was more a bar than a tearoom.

"Welcome!"

Sayuri literally jumped with surprise at the saccharine voice behind them.

"Did I surprise you? So sorry," the owner of the voice made a perfunctory apology, obviously having enjoyed Sayuri's reaction.

"Mr. Chu always likes to sneak up from behind," Ako said, squirming slightly and sounding stunned herself. Sayuri intuited that their relationship was more than just platonic.

"Come on, this way, this way," the man Ako had called Chu ushered the girls to a four-seater table and sat across from them.

He looked to be in his thirties but could have passed as a student thanks to his long hair, dyed brown. His nose was sharp and his eyes were bold and narrowed in a permanent smile. He wore a dark suit with a black sheen even though it was still September, but it didn't make him seem overly serious or sultry. He was charming, like a subtle perfume.

"This is our go-between, Mr. Chu. That's not his real name. People just call him Mr. Chu"—the word meant *middle*—"because he's the go-between. He won't tell us his real name," Ako said with a hint of reproach. The question was written on her face: *Why won't you tell me your name?*

"My name? I forgot it." Chu gave Ako an affable smile and turned to Sayuri with the same expression. "Sorry I made you jump just now." As he said the words he rapped his knuckles twice against the table.

Tap tap.

"It's...fine." Sayuri looked away, trying to escape from the smile that threatened to suck her in. Chu pulled her attention back by rapping at the table again.

Tap tap.

"Look at me properly." Chu's face was as gentle as before, but now there was a force behind the sweetness in his voice. Like a puppet, Sayuri turned back to face him.

"Name?"

"Mizuno..."

"First name?"

"Sayuri."

"Sayuri, eh. Nice name."

"Yeah," Sayuri murmured pathetically, at a loss for how to respond.

"Favorite food?"

Sayuri's mouth dropped open dumbly at the question. She had no idea what he was getting at.

"Food. Come on. Food."

"Um… Apples, I guess."

Chu chuckled at her response. "Okay, good," he said after a long period of silent observation. He nodded.

"So she's a hire?" Ako asked, looking at Chu and Sayuri in turn.

"Yup, she passed." Chu gave her the thumbs up.

"Ah! Hired on the spot. Great, Sayuri!" Ako smiled, looking elated. The smile seemed special, like it was reserved for her inner circle, different from all her smiles to this point.

Sayuri knotted her brows in a frown, confused. "Um, can I ask why?" she asked Chu tentatively, straightening her back a little.

His narrowed eyes widened slightly. The question had clearly caught him by surprise. "What do you mean, why?" he asked, tilting his head to the side.

"I just meant…why did I pass? It's not because I like apples?"

"Oh, that!" Chu laughed so hard his shoulders shook. He rapped the table.

Tap tap.

"To be blunt, for looks, on a scale from one to ten, you're a seven, maybe an eight. So you're good-looking enough but not so much that I can hire you on looks alone. Looks are just one factor. So I watch for other things, too."

So what were you watching for? Sayuri's eyes asked.

"It basically comes down to ambiance. Okay, let's take you straight to your new home."

Chu cleared the way to the exit and bowed, ushering them on.

They arrived at a high-rise apartment building about a five-minute walk from Floating Play. The main entrance was carpeted and lit up like a five-star hotel. The surrounding walls had been polished to a mirror-like sheen and the lobby was designed with a central black motif that gave the space an angular feel. It was intimidating.

"Everyone calls this place the Tower," Ako said as she looked around the space.

"Some people call it Babel, although that's like asking for bad luck," Chu said sarcastically, a lopsided grin on his face. "Sayuri, you're on the eighth floor."

He pulled a card from his jacket pocket and passed it through the reader at the call box in the lobby. There was a flat electronic sound as the thick, reflective glass doors slid open.

Their footsteps echoed smartly off the marble flooring as they stepped inside, accentuating the silence around them. A few people, probably service workers, quietly cleaned the few windows set in the sturdy walls to let natural light in.

"Ah, so today's cleaning day. Sorry to give you such an ungainly first impression."

Chu sighed as he apologized, and Sayuri shook her head to indicate it didn't matter.

"Well? It's huge, isn't it?" Ako said, sounding lively. The lobby was overwhelmingly spacious, like a palace. "The Tower is *exclusively ours.*"

"Ours?" Sayuri asked, drawing back a little. She was unsettled by the number of security cameras. They made her feel uncomfortable, like she was being watched.

"You're not the only Flower, Sayuri," Chu said, turning his head back as he walked in front of them.

"Flower?" Sayuri was confused by the onslaught of information.

"You know what you're going to be doing here, right?" Chu asked slowly, suddenly looking concerned for her.

"Mostly…"

"Everyone that works here becomes a Flower. It's a bit cheesy, maybe, but it's part of the rules. As a Flower, you live in an apartment here, and it's your job to interact with our Benefactors."

"That's what he calls clients. Tiresome, I know. We should just call them clients," Ako explained, muttering curses.

"Part of the rules. Just a codeword to help standardize the system. You're free to call them whatever you want in private—customers, bastards, whatever."

Chu pulled a sardonic grin as he pushed the button for the elevator. The door slid open as if it had been waiting for them. They walked into a space that seemed too big to be an elevator. The door closed noiselessly and the elevator ascended, almost gliding upwards.

Sayuri examined its interior. The buttons went up to thirteen, meaning the building was thirteen floors tall, but it had looked much taller from outside. The black carpet under her feet seemed thick enough to absorb her full weight, robbing her of her center of gravity.

The indicator stopped at the eighth floor and the door opened. They stepped out to a wide corridor that stretched far into the distance. Uniform, warmly tinted lamps flooded every last corner with light, but the abnormal quiet made it seem darker.

Sayuri gazed at the decorative objects on display. It was like being in a high-end hotel.

"Everything looks expensive, no?" Ako flicked a nail against one of the tall, thin vases that lined the corridor.

"Yeah…" Sayuri muttered honestly, looking at the blue vase as it rang pleasantly.

"I hear they're shockingly expensive, every last one. I plan to pinch a few when I leave here."

"Don't talk about leaving, you'll have your Benefactors in tears," Chu said, shaking his head.

"A job this good? I'll be here for a while yet."

Chu came to a stop outside one of the doors. "Room 803. This is yours, Sayuri."

The sturdy-looking door had a silver plate with the number 803 emblazoned in gothic lettering. Chu swiped a black card through the reader, opening the lock with a click that echoed down the corridor. The splendor of the room nearly took Sayuri's breath away.

"Wow. It's like the movies," Sayuri whispered, eyes gaping. The room stank of money. It looked like where a nobleman from the Middle Ages might have lived. Ako chuckled when she saw Sayuri's reaction.

"That's what I thought when I saw mine. Talk about a drag, having to live in such an uncomfortable-looking place."

It was true that the overall effect was garish, as if everything was lit from within. The curtains were open on the windows that were twice Sayuri's height. Ikebukuro was visible through the glass.

"I think you'll like it once you get used to it. Yeah, like you've become a princess."

There was something funny about hearing Chu use such a word. Sayuri burst into laughter.

"We are definitely treated like princesses. Check this out," Ako said as she stepped up to the window, gesturing for Sayuri to follow.

Sayuri approached cautiously and looked down. It was high enough to make her knees buckle, and the whole world seemed to be beneath her. She felt that the city, in all its neon glory, lay in supplication before her.

"We're so high up, but this is only the eighth floor," Sayuri mumbled distractedly.

"The ceilings are higher than usual."

Sayuri looked up at the shudderingly distant ceiling, then back down at the outside world.

"Living here, you spend your time looking down on everyone else. And when you go back down and head outside, anything you wish for comes true because you have the beauty and money to make it happen," Ako intoned suggestively and smiled at Sayuri.

Sayuri's cheeks reddened in a sudden wave of exultation.

"Hey, hey, forgotten I'm here?" Chu grumbled, coming to stand between the two of them. He peered into Sayuri's eyes. "This is all new to you. Must be pretty exhausting."

Sayuri shook her head. She didn't feel tired at all. If anything, she was surprised at the vigor she felt flowing from reserves she never knew she had.

"You're just excited. It'll hit you suddenly, later."

Chu looked towards Ako for agreement. She pulled a sulky face but didn't talk back.

"I'm sure there's more you'll want to ask, but for now you should get some rest. I'll come again tomorrow."

Chu gave her a quick overview of the room's facilities and showed her the wardrobe, then took his leave, practically dragging Ako along with him.

Suddenly alone, Sayuri felt the excitement fade away and her anxiety return. The room was too big for just her, and nothing in it was hers. She felt nervous, like a lost child.

She flopped onto the king-size bed and stared up at the ceiling, feeling completely out of place. It felt bizarre for someone like her to be in a place like this. Despite all Ako had said, she hadn't gotten her hopes up. Just getting a roof over her head would have been enough; she hadn't imagined anything like this.

This job was certainly sketchy. The avalanche of weirdness, however, had numbed her sensibility. She was emboldened by the comforting knowledge that Ako was in it with her.

Sayuri smiled at the bizarre direction her life had taken as she rolled back and forth across the bed.

About what might happen to her now, she worried not.

It would be wrong to try and find fault in the good fortune that had fallen into her lap. *I've been chosen.* Sayuri's heart pounded at the thought.

She felt too lazy to take off her makeup. She took a quick shower before wrapping herself in a bathrobe and lay back on the bed. She started to roll across it again.

She felt her head go numb from this astonishing lucky turn. But the soft ache felt pleasant, so she closed her eyes and gave herself to it.

Around the time the bed took on enough of her own familiar scent, Sayuri fell quietly asleep. She slept without dreaming.

Sayuri woke to the sun streaming in through the window. She glanced across to the large clock on the wall, still half-asleep. It was 7:10 in the morning.

She had received no directions in particular, so she took her time getting up, then went to open the closet. She found close to a hundred different items of clothing inside, all neatly arranged on hangers. They were of various sizes, but some were a good fit.

Chu had told her the day before that she was free to wear any of them. But there were so many that Sayuri's eyes kept wandering to the next, hesitating at each pick. She finally chose one.

A dress, dark red like wine. The cool, soft fabric brushed pleasantly against her skin. Looking closer, she saw that it was more like a formal dress than a summer outfit, with a slim cut designed to accentuate the waistline. Sayuri was unsure whether it would suit her, but the dress was beautiful regardless—a work of art.

She draped it carefully over a chair and continued to browse the rest. They were all made to the highest quality and beautiful enough to make her sigh, but none surpassed the dress she had put aside first.

Sayuri shut the closet and studied the dress arranged over the chair. Its measured, elegant sheen reflected the sun's rays, sparkling like diamond dust. She took the dress in her hand and the smooth, silken fabric wrapped around her palm. It was so soft it felt like it might disappear if she gripped it too tightly.

She went to pull her t-shirt off, grabbing the hem, but hesitated, suddenly feeling like someone was watching. She looked around.

The room was silent.

There was no one there, of course, and no one outside the eighth-floor window. She checked that the door was locked, then went into the bathroom. It was oversized like everything else, with a transparent partition between the sink and the rest of the area.

Sayuri inspected every corner of the room until she was happy that everything was normal, then stripped off her clothes. Her slender figure, naked apart from her underwear, reflected in the large mirror. Her body maintained traces of immaturity, and the translucent whiteness of her slight frame was lovely yet transient, like snow resting on twigs.

Sayuri regarded herself in the mirror for a while, then picked up the dress and started to put it on. After wriggling into it, she checked herself in the mirror again. It was a perfect fit. She tidied her hair with her hands and took a deep breath before turning back to the mirror.

Her makeup was a little on the plain side, but it suited her. She twirled on the spot and struck a pose. *Not bad.* She smiled. She looked a little more grown-up. Sayuri regarded herself from various viewpoints without tiring of it. She played different roles, pulling faces as she looked at herself.

"Looking good."

A chime rang out as soon as she spoke, causing her to jump. It sounded again. Sayuri flushed with embarrassment, suddenly self-conscious of being ill-suited for the dress.

Ding dong.

The chime sounded again, pressing her to hurry. She began to get undressed but the chiming turned incessant, telling her she had no time to change.

Ding dong.

Sayuri ran to her discarded clothes.

Ding dong. Ding dong.

She rushed to get the dress off, her hands clumsy.

Ding dong ding dong ding dong ding dong ding dong ding dong.

The constant chiming prevented her hands from functioning properly. She cursed to herself and scowled. She gave up trying to change and rushed to the door and swung it open, too annoyed to even check the peephole.

Chu stood in the corridor, his mouth stretched into a thin smile. "I thought you had perhaps run away." He bowed slightly, his expression certain that such an outcome was impossible. "Good morning. A little too early to visit?" He made a perfunctory show of checking his watch.

"No, I was up," Sayuri said, unconsciously trying to hide the dress under her hands.

Chu whistled in response, teasing her. "Beautiful."

"R-Really?" Sayuri scrutinized Chu's expression, not quite believing him. Her confidence was completely gone.

"Sure, beautiful. But something's missing."

Chu walked over to one of the phones in the corridor, muttered a few words into it, then came back.

"I'm coming in," he said, his tone a command. He stepped across the threshold without waiting for an answer.

"P-Please do." Sayuri shuffled out of his way.

He paced into the room as though he was out for a walk, then stopped in the middle of the room, looking around before settling on the charcoal loveseat in the middle of the room. Sayuri sat on the bed.

"Sleep okay?" He was in his same black suit. He sat with his legs and arms casually sprawled.

"I did."

"Good. Are you hungry?"

"A little," Sayuri answered, keeping her eyes around the waist of her dress.

"No doubt. You can call for food whenever you want."

"Call for food? You mean delivery?" Sayuri asked.

Chu laughed. "Nothing like that. We have proper chefs in the building. Leagues better than most places around here. If you want, you can get them to buy groceries so you can cook for yourself. Your wish is their command, even if you just want instant ramen or hamburgers. Junk food's quite the thing among you kids, right?" Chu's eyebrows arched high as if that was beyond his understanding. "I guess some people tire of too much gourmet cuisine. But that's more a fault of the person than the food. Human senses are easily numbed, and the majority of people get into a mindset where they accept something as commonplace when it's clearly not. They're just ignorant, insensitive— they don't deserve decent food in the first place. The palate needs training to appreciate good food. There's no excuse for negligence to muddle such stimuli."

Chu spoke as though he was casting a spell. His eyes were

empty, which caused Sayuri to feel an instinctual sense of fear. But he smiled once again, perhaps picking up on Sayuri's expression.

"To each her own. No one's going to force anything on you. Just pick up the phone and press '1' to connect to the person in charge and you can order anything to eat. You can call and ask for things other than food, too. You can even call them up and vent your frustrations at them, if you want."

Chu glanced at his watch. The doorbell rang as if on signal.

"Here we are." Chu got up and disappeared out the door.

Sayuri expected him to come back with Ako, but it was a man who entered.

A man?

Sayuri tilted her head to one side. The other person was clearly male, but everything about him was feminine—his clothes, makeup, the way he carried himself. He had short-cropped pink hair and high cheekbones. He wore a blue, see-through t-shirt with yellow trousers so close-fitting they could have been tights. He looked bizarre.

"Ooh. Now this girl's quality ore." The effeminate man placed a hand to his cheek and smiled with glossy lips. "This one will shine," he said, his voice rising girlishly at the end of each sentence. He sat next to Sayuri, close enough for her to note he was wearing perfume. "It's lovely to meet you, dear. Call me Kay. Short for *maquillage*. You can call me Katie, if you like."

"Maquillage?" Sayuri frowned.

"Makeup, honey. Like a stylist." Kay winked at her.

"Maquillage… Doesn't that shorten to 'Mack' or 'Maki' rather than 'Kay'?" Sayuri blurted out, eased by Kay's unpretentious attitude.

The stylist fell silent for a moment before smiling again and poking a finger onto Sayuri's forehead. "My, my. 'Mack.' How unattractive. 'Maki.' How drab. Doesn't roll off the tongue, does it?" Kay laughed riotously.

"I guess not." Sayuri nodded, suddenly serious. On seeing her reaction, Kay laughed his shrill laugh again.

"I like you. What's your name?"

"We haven't decided on one yet," Chu cut in.

"How unlike you!" Kay glanced at him. "That's usually the first thing you do."

"No reason," Chu brushed him off and looked away.

"Whatever. Now, you called me because you want me to do her makeup, right?"

Chu remained silent. Kay ignored him and pulled some cosmetics implements from the huge toolbox-like container he had brought with him.

"First we need to get rid of this childish makeup." Kay began to gently daub at Sayuri's face, removing the makeup she had on. He diligently applied a layer of foundation before starting on her eyeliner and other points. "Makeup isn't just to make people prettier. It helps you create a second identity," Kay told her as he applied mascara. "Do you know why people want to do this?"

"No," Sayuri answered monosyllabically.

"Isn't it exhausting to be yourself all the time? Plus, there's so much of the world, just one of 'you' can't access all of it. Using makeup to create a new you is necessary to get the most out of life."

"The most out of life…" Sayuri mumbled. She had never thought of life as something to enjoy. It was a barren wasteland that she'd merely clung to with all her might.

"If you're gonna live anyways, might as well have some fun, yes?"

Sayuri wanted to nod but Kay was holding her chin tight so she muttered yes.

"To live gorgeously, you need to make yourself up gorgeously. Do that, and your natural character will come through." Kay's eyes met Sayuri's as he applied her lipstick. "Such pretty eyes… You'll make me jealous," Kay muttered as though to himself, thereafter continuing her makeup in silence.

Sayuri stole a look at Chu, making sure to keep her head still. She saw only his profile; it looked like he was staring at something listlessly.

Sayuri followed his gaze. There was a painting on the wall of a woman with long hair, dressed stunningly. Sayuri tried to imagine how expensive it might be when she noticed something odd about it.

The woman had no face.

It was not that her face had not been painted in. She had eyes, a nose, a mouth. But they were utterly lifeless. Her features were like ice, deadly quiet. It was the kind of face you forgot the moment you looked away. *Faceless*. It made a strong impression on Sayuri as she felt something cold run down her back.

"Goosebumps! Did you see something scary?" Kay asked as he tidied Sayuri's hair and inspected her face. He brushed a finger over one of her earlobes when he had finished. "I'd like to perm your hair a little but this'll do for now. Go take a look." Kay pointed to the large mirror in the room.

Sayuri still felt spooked but did as she was told, getting up and standing in front of the mirror. She did not see herself. The reflection was of someone else.

"Well? Wouldn't recognize yourself, huh?" Kay said. Sayuri was breathless.

"I look like a different person…" she agreed, her eyes wide with wonder.

"Exactly, a different person. You've been reborn."

Just as Kay spoke, Sayuri heard a sound behind her.

Tap tap.

She turned to see Chu standing there, smiling.

"I've decided what we'll call you—Yuri."

"Yuri? But that's…" Sayuri wanted to point out that it was almost the same as her real name, but she held her tongue because Chu just looked so happy.

"It's fine. You just needed to lose the character for 'Sa'—it means 'small' after all," Chu continued, as though he had read her mind. He stepped in closer. "From now on your name's Yuri. The name will be your symbol while you live in the Tower as a Flower."

Sayuri nodded obediently. In that moment, Sayuri became

Yuri.

"I can't believe I could become so pretty."

Yuri turned back to the mirror, drawing her chin back slightly. The baggage called "Sayuri" was cast away. Even her words sounded more graceful.

"You haven't just become prettier. You've been reborn," Chu whispered into her ear. His breath softly brushed against her skin.

Ding dong.

The chime rang, drowning out the noise of Yuri's quickening pulse. She brushed down the front of her dress, thankful for the interruption.

"Coming!"

Kay strode quickly to the entrance. He returned with Ako.

"Wow, you look great!" Ako said, giving her a nod of admiration.

But Yuri knew that no one could be more beautiful or elegant than Ako standing there in her blue dress. Yuri wasn't being self-deprecating. She was confident in her own beauty now. Hers was just of a different type than Ako's.

"Time for re-introductions. In the Tower everyone calls me Suiren—the lotus flower." Ako plucked up her skirt and bent her knees in a curtsey, clearly having fun. "It's so embarrassing, just use it when we're here, okay? Outside, call me Ako."

"Suiren."

"Yep, Suiren. I guess you've noticed already, but everyone is literally named after flowers. What's yours, Sayuri?"

"Yuri." *Lily.*

"Huh, simple. Still, it's a good name," Suiren said, smiling.

Yuri returned the smile. She was happy to have someone compliment the name Chu had given her.

"I'd like to start explaining the job," Chu cut in, clearing his throat. "Suiren, could you leave us?"

"But I just got here," she complained.

"Yes." Chu gave Suiren and Kay a look that made it clear they had no choice in the matter.

"Fine," Suiren said and puffed up her cheeks. She let slip a look of fear.

The two of them left, leaving Yuri alone with Chu. Chu sighed softly, sounding tired.

"Sit there," Chu pointed to the loveseat he'd sat on earlier.

Yuri went, feeling a bit like an obedient puppy.

"So, what do you think of the place?" he asked, and without warning came to sit next to her. He had moved so fast that Yuri felt unsettled. Ignoring her reaction, Chu asked again. "Give me your first impressions."

"First impressions…" Yuri lifted her eyes, trying to gauge his mood. His eyes were narrowed in a warm smile.

"Yes, your thoughts."

Yuri was at a loss for words. Everything had been dreamlike since coming to the Tower. Her body felt fuzzy, and she was mostly absent-minded. If someone told her she was dreaming, she would believe it. That's how unreal this new world felt to her.

"You don't hate it?" Chu changed the question.

Yuri nodded immediately. "No way," she said, slow but clear.

"Do you want to leave?" Chu peered into her eyes.

"Definitely not!" she answered, louder than she had meant to.

Why would she want to leave? She had nowhere to go. From now on she would support herself. She had already decided as much. Chu gave her a shallow nod, like he knew what she meant, and rapped his hand against the arm of the sofa.

Tap tap.

There was no sound, as the arm of the sofa was covered in fabric, but Yuri heard it clearly.

"Your job won't be as easy as you think," Chu said, his tone a fraction harder. "You're going to be pleasing Benefactors with your body."

"I know."

"Do you think you can do that?"

Chu covered her lips with his before she had a chance to reply. She responded to the kiss to tell him that she could.

He scooped her up and lay her on the bed. She gasped for

air and writhed about. She raked her hands through her hair, squirming in response to Chu. Her blood boiled, making her feel like she might die that instant. Waves of ecstasy washed over her as her field of vision went hazy and her thoughts went quiet. She clung desperately to the pleasure that closed in on her.

Sunlight streamed through the window as her moans filled the room. Yuri felt surprise at the scope of her abandon as her body trembled in pleasure. Chu's intermittent motions pulsed through her body, and she happily accepted them.

Snap.

The bed stilled as something broke. Yuri's labored breathing was the only thing that disrupted the room's silence.

"You've got potential, Yuri." Chu's voice was soft. He was already up and putting on his clothes.

Yuri lay on her stomach, in a daze and unable to speak. Faint tremors ran through her body and she felt totally drained of strength.

"The first thing is to give it a go," Chu continued, looking into Yuri's vacant eyes. He took out a yellow pill and put it to her lips. "Now that you're a Flower, there's something you must always do. You have to take one of these before a Benefactor visits."

What is it? Yuri asked with her eyes.

"It's an antibacterial nutrition supplement. You take it to stop you from catching colds, getting ill. Take one for now, but from now on it's two each time."

Chu pushed the pill into her mouth with his index finger and gave her a bottle of water. Yuri took it from him, finally able to sit up. She washed down the pill and collapsed back onto the bed. Her body was still sensitive enough that she could feel the cold of the water spread through her body.

"Tastes weird." Yuri stuck out her tongue, looking up at the ceiling.

"You'll get used to it. I've gotta go," Chu said, turning away.

"Already?"

Yuri felt suddenly unhappy. She wanted to spend more time

together. To talk more. She wanted…more.

But the words never left her mouth. Chu looked like he was already pushing her away. His attitude had changed completely, causing her lips to freeze shut.

"I'll visit again," Chu said, leaving the room.

Slam.

As the sound of the door echoed through the room, Yuri started.

Something was wrong.

She felt something ache from deep within, and her blood began to rush. She began to sweat as her eyes shone. She could only manage shallow breaths, which became a constant moaning, and she started to tear at the bed. She tried to stand, but her body wouldn't listen. In succession she stretched and curled up, soaked in sweat and burning up. She had to bring it under control.

She used her hands to bring herself to orgasm over and over, until she was released from the fire.

Then, finally sated, she fell asleep.

3

Yuri woke to an empty stomach. She checked the clock— twelve. She jumped up like a spring.

She had been asleep for three hours. Despite having worn herself out completely, she was overflowing with energy.

She picked up the phone from the bedside table and pushed "1" and ordered some food. Twenty minutes later, a man with dark eyes brought her some pasta, salad, and corn soup, and ice cream for dessert. It all tasted fantastic. Impressed by the possibility that they actually did employ chefs in the building, Yuri stuffed herself with the pasta.

When she had eaten her fill, she lay back on the bed and cast her thoughts back to what had just happened with Chu.

Hmm?

Yuri frowned. She could hardly remember it, though it had happened only three or four hours ago. It wasn't memory loss.

Rather, it was as though the memory had been shrouded in fog, ephemeral; it was like trying to grasp air. She knew Chu had come to her, that they had made love. But she could not be sure of anything else.

She traced her memories. She had gotten up in the morning and tried on the dress, then Chu arrived, and Kay put on her makeup. Suiren complimented her… She slept with Chu… And now she was in bed. She had no problem recalling the order of events, but she was having trouble summoning the details.

No big deal, Yuri decided and laughed out loud. The one detail that remained vivid was the pleasure she had felt. To remember that was to remember Chu. Yuri felt happiness well up within her.

Ding dong.

She sensed someone enter the room at almost exactly the same moment that the chime rang. The room was filled with the sound of feet brushing against the carpet.

"You're awake?" Chu stood leaning against the wall. He looked tired. His eyes were sunken and dark.

Yuri turned to look at him. "Is something wrong?"

"It's nothing," Chu dismissed her with a wave of his hand before walking slowly to the loveseat and half-collapsing into it.

"Nothing? You're soaked with sweat!"

Chu was out of breath and large drops of perspiration collected on his forehead. Yuri wanted to wipe it off, but the man before her now seemed completely different from the one she had slept with so recently.

"Just some heavy work."

"Heavy work?"

"Taking apart a machine we don't need anymore." Chu pulled back his long hair and changed the subject. "Let's continue our discussion."

"Discussion?" Yuri cocked her head to the side.

"About your job."

"Ah, right," she nodded. She'd completely forgotten about her job. She was just barely able to keep up with everything happening to her. It was too much to wrap her head around. "Exactly what am I supposed to do?" It was the first time Yuri had volunteered a question.

"Just what you did with me, that's it."

Yuri felt herself blush.

"Really simple, right?"

Yuri met Chu's smile and nodded, still looking down.

"Okay, that's the job description. Done…" Chu said, glancing at his wristwatch. He looked like a salaryman at work. Yuri felt a sudden unpleasantness as she got the feeling that their *intercourse* had just been another part of his job.

"When can you start?"

"Whenever," Yuri replied curtly.

"What, are you angry?"

"…"

"Whatever," Chu said and got slowly to his feet. His color had improved slightly. "It's five hours per person. It's the Benefactor's job to manage his own time, so you don't really have to worry about that. It's five hours, but that includes a block of time just for tea and chatting, so you shouldn't have any problems, physically. Just think of your Benefactors as people who hold a high status in society, people possessing both luck and power. We don't get shady people, so you can rest easy on that regard. Any other questions?" Chu said without pausing for breath. He took a couple of deep breaths.

"Nothing in particular," Yuri answered sulkily.

"Your job as a Flower starts from 8 p.m. tonight. The chime will ring at 8 p.m. exactly, so make sure to answer it. If there's anything you don't understand, just press '9' on the phone and I'll answer. If you leave the building, make sure to let us know. Finally, this," Chu said, slapping a black medicine case on the desk. "The antibacterial. You start at 8 p.m., so take it shortly beforehand. Make sure to take two. You mustn't forget to take them," Chu ordered, made a peace sign, pointed again at the medicine case, and left the room.

There were over six hours until eight o'clock. Yuri had forgotten to ask if she could leave the building before then. She showered, making sure not to rinse off the makeup, then spent some time trying on clothes.

Each had a luxury brand label on the inside of the collar, and many were names Yuri had never heard of. She would try something on, take it off, try something else, and repeat the cycle. Each time she stood before the mirror she felt as though she had become even more beautiful, although her looks were still no match for Suiren.

Suiren.

It didn't sound like a person's name at all, but it suited her perfectly. Here in the Tower, Ako would sound cheap in comparison. It was the same with "Sayuri"—old-fashioned, passive to the ear. Besides, the name was nothing but bad memories. Yuri, on the other hand, was wonderful. Gorgeous, beautiful, and above all it was the name Chu had given her.

She had been reborn. The girl she saw in the mirror was overflowing with confidence. Sayuri was dead, and the girl in the mirror now was Yuri—a completely new person. She felt liberated, free from the chains that had held her down.

Once she got tired of trying on her new clothes, Yuri got back into her original red dress and looked around the room once again. It was flamboyant, designed to look like something from feudal Europe. It was wrapped in an almost unnatural quiet. The silence was deafening.

Yuri thought to pass the time with the TV as a distraction, but she couldn't find one. Nor could she find any signs of a computer or even a radio. She took out her cell phone to call Suiren, wondering if the room might have a projector or something. She looked up the name "Ako" in her address book and made the call, but the line was silent. She frowned and looked at the phone's screen—no signal.

No signal. In the middle of the city? Suddenly uneasy, Yuri picked up the room's landline. She was about to press "9" and call Chu, but hesitated. She eventually pressed "1" instead, just as when she had ordered food. The phone rang three times before someone picked up.

"Yes, how can I help you?" came a woman's voice.

"Um, I can't make any calls."

"Sorry?" the woman's tone was mocking. "If you can't make any calls, then who are you talking to now, I wonder?" Her tone grated on Yuri's nerves.

"With my *cell* phone!" Yuri raised her voice.

The woman replied with a hatefully calm voice. "Ah yes, that. The use of mobile phones is restricted inside the Tower."

"Restricted?"

"Indeed. The building has been installed with devices that block signals."

"Why would they want to do that?"

"To prevent anyone outside from bugging the room or secretly taking photos. We do it because a small minority of Benefactors persist in trying to break these rules."

"They would do that?" Yuri felt anxious.

"Please rest assured. We employ vigorous bodychecks to avoid any trouble of that kind. We hope you understand our need to exercise caution in these matters."

Yuri agreed, reluctantly. "So that's why there's no TV? Because of those signal-blocking devices?"

"Correct," the woman said, as though enjoying herself. "But that's not all. There's another reason we don't have TVs. Can you guess what it is?"

She's making fun of me, Yuri thought. Muscle twitched under her eye. "Of course I can't!" She began pulling the receiver away from her ear to hang up, but the woman responded before she could.

"The second reason is that it's unnecessary." The statement caught Yuri off guard. She held the phone still. "TV is dead. TV, as it exists, is an inadequate tool for supplying information, values, and even entertainment."

"Why?"

"Information passed through the filter of people's vested interests is damaging and of no benefit whatsoever. Isn't it just better to say no? It's more peaceful, and you stay closer to reality," the woman lectured, laughing. "In addition to not being able to use mobile phones, there are no TVs or computers in the Tower. Instead, we have something much greater. What do you think that is? Question number two."

The woman seemed to be enjoying asking things that she thought Yuri couldn't answer. Annoyed, Yuri blurted out the first thing that came to mind. "Money and power."

The woman was momentarily silent. Then she continued, sounding impressed. "A little crudely put, but yes, that is correct. Exactly. The Tower has both."

"But why are money and power better than TVs or phones?"

"Because they control information, values, and all forms of entertainment. If you have money and power, you have no need for superficial information, values, or entertainment. You can *just create it all yourself.*" The woman cleared her throat. "But I go on too much. Your query concerned your inability to use your mobile phone, yes?"

"That's right."

"And it has been addressed to your satisfaction," the woman snorted.

"Just who do you think you are, talking like this?" Yuri muttered, trying to keep her emotions in check. Her eyelids were twitching from anger.

"Your personal concierge."

"Concierge?"

"Think of me as someone to help with any questions you might have. Every one of you is assigned a concierge during your stay in the Tower. It's my job to do what I can to meet your needs. Of course, that doesn't extend to humoring a child's impossible demands," she stated as though she were trying to placate a kid.

"Right. Well, first, fix that attitude," Yuri said as she slammed the phone back in place.

17:00. Kay sashayed into the room and reapplied Yuri's makeup. This time the makeup was more glitzy, as it was for her first job.

18:00. Yuri felt hungry and ordered some dinner. Since the attitude of the woman on the phone was exactly the same as before, Yuri resolved to give her a hard time when she came up, but it was the man from before—the one with the dark eyes—that brought her her food. Yuri ate the Italian dishes quietly in the silent room, then had the plates cleared away.

The clock indicated 7:45 p.m. Even so, there was nothing particular to do in preparation. Yuri sat on the sofa drinking iced tea waiting for the chime to ring.

It's not like I have to do anything hard, Yuri persuaded herself, trying to brush away mounting worry. Just then she realized she'd forgotten to take the pills Chu had given her. She jumped up from the sofa.

Ding dong, rang the chime.

Yuri pulled the pills from the medicine box on the table and gulped a couple down with the iced tea, then ran to the door.

She opened it to find a man in his late forties wearing a dark blue suit that was clearly from a high-end designer. One hand was in his trouser pocket and the other held a leather bag. His gentle smile matched his smart clothing, and he seemed utterly relaxed.

"Good evening."

"P-Please…" Yuri stammered, flustered by his calm air.

The man nodded and let himself in, walking with slow steps. He looked around the room and took off his jacket. "Do you mind if I sit here?" He kept his eyes on her as he pointed towards the loveseat.

"No, of course." Yuri ran across to the table, scooping up the medicine case and half-empty iced tea.

"You needn't be so nervous," the man said, his voice deep. He sat on the loveseat. Yuri stood in a daze, not knowing what to do. "Why don't you sit?"

Yuri looked around, following his prompt. She saw a chair next to the window with a round table about a foot across next to it that featured a white vase containing flowers. Yuri decided to sit there.

"Sorry you have to deal with an old man like me," the man said, not looking particularly sorry at all. He took an envelope out from his bag and placed it on the table. "Today's amount. Would you check it?" He leaned back into the loveseat.

Yuri picked the envelope up from the table. It was thick and heavy. "How much is it?" she asked, overwhelmed by the envelope's heft.

The man smiled thinly. "As per the rules, five hundred thousand yen."

Yuri gulped, pulled the notes from the envelope, and began to count. She was uneasy, having never handled such a sum before. By the time she had finished counting, she was covered in sweat.

"All there?"

"Yes." Yuri wiped the sweat from her palms and put the notes back on the table.

"And here's your tip," the man added, pulling an elongated brown wallet from his discarded jacket and removing a wad of ten-thousand-yen notes. He got to his feet and handed it to Yuri. "Three hundred thousand. This is your first time in the Tower, am I right?"

Yuri nodded, eyes gaping. The man looked pleased.

"Think of it as a gratuity, for allowing me to be your first Benefactor." He walked towards Yuri and held out his hand. She felt her body tense slightly. Though she had prepared herself, letting someone she didn't know touch her was arousing some resistance.

But the man simply touched the top of her head before disappearing into the kitchen.

"Something to drink?"

Yuri felt strangely thirsty despite having just had an iced tea. She asked him for something cool.

"Of course. You sit and wait."

Yuri did as she was told. Listening to the sounds in the kitchen, she decided that the man must have visited the room before.

He came back and put one hot and one iced coffee plus a small creamer full of milk on the table in front of the loveseat.

"I hope ice coffee was okay? I haven't put in any milk or syrup, so just add what you want."

The man picked up the chair next to the window and brought it to the front of the table. They sat facing each other.

"So, how many days has it been since you got here?" the man asked as he sipped his coffee and crossed his legs.

"I just got here yesterday," Yuri answered.

"Hah, guess you're probably not used to everything yet, then."

"Well…" Yuri answered weakly.

"This place is nice to visit, but I can't say it looks comfortable to live in," he continued, looking around. It was true. The room was large but the furniture was too assertive, and finding one's place was a challenge of sorts.

"I only feel relaxed in the bed," Yuri confessed awkwardly.

The man laughed with forced mirth. He sat forward as though he had suddenly remembered something. "I forgot to introduce myself. Here, people call me 'Togo.' It's a pseudonym, but it's my real name here," he said. "I'm a big fan of Heihachiro Togo, the Russo-Japanese War admiral. That's why I chose it. And your name is?"

"It's…Yuri." This being the first time she had used her new name to introduce herself, it felt somewhat off.

"Yuri. Well, nice to meet you." Togo smiled.

Yuri got the feeling she had seen his face before. "Um, have we met?"

"No prying." Togo held up a hand to stop her and pulled smokes from his bag. "It's better for both of us that way."

He lit a cigarette and exhaled. She had definitely seen him somewhere. Yuri blinked, trying to kickstart her memory. She saw a vague image of Togo being interviewed in an expensive-looking suit, bulbs flashing everywhere. On TV, she was sure. A politician or something. His name was…

"Are you okay?" Togo asked, his tone stern.

"Huh? Yes." Caught off guard, Yuri straightened her hunched back.

"Seems a bit like your mind is somewhere else. It makes me lonely to think you're neglecting me."

Yuri struggled to keep herself from grimacing at the creepy sentiment. Her throat was parched. She poured a large portion of milk into the iced coffee before sucking back half of it at once through a straw. She could feel the liquid spreading through every corner of her body.

"Now. It was pretty hot today, I think I'll take a shower. Pardon me while I go in first."

With that, Togo got up and disappeared into the bathroom. Left alone, Yuri cast her eyes towards the wad of notes on the table. Eight hundred thousand yen in total. She looked at the time—almost 21:00.

She felt like she was burning up. All she had to do was endure another four hours, and the huge sum of money would be hers. How could she not feel excited? She wondered how much Togo was paying the Tower. She had no idea. Besides, there were more pressing matters.

What to buy? What to do?

Yuri began to lay out plans in her mind but found it hard to settle on a particular path.

"Hey, Yuri, why don't you join me?"

Togo's voice was amplified by the bathroom walls.

Yuri slowly got up and walked towards the bathroom where he waited. She wanted to hurry and cleanse her sweaty body...

4

Yuri woke to the sound of rustling clothes. She vacantly noticed Togo was dressed. He was in his dark blue suit and smiling thinly, just like when he arrived.

"Perhaps we'll see each other again."

Yuri registered the voice just as he was leaving. It was vague, shrouded in fog. She checked the time: one in the morning.

Exactly five hours had passed.

So that's all.

Thinking so, she tried to get up, but couldn't summon the strength.

She gave up and tried instead to cast her clouded mind over the last five hours, but she couldn't remember the details.

Togo had arrived, they had made small talk, he had taken a shower and called her in, they'd showered together before going to bed, they'd kissed... After that, she wasn't sure. She hadn't forgotten, but she couldn't remember.

Yuri wondered vaguely that it might be better for her not to dwell on it. She didn't feel particularly bad. She should sleep. Yuri began to doze, lying face down, and fell asleep.

The room was dark and silent as always.

Shallow breathing. Sleep breathing. Moonlight reflecting off her naked, unconscious body made it as if she were floating. And *watching her, countless pairs of eyes.*

The clock showed five.

Sunlight poured through the window, lighting the room, clearing away the darkness. Yuri's eyes twitched as she grimaced before the bright sun. She was parched, and her eyelids felt heavy as she blinked again and again. She tried to get up, tensing her upper body. She moaned as she felt jolts of sharp pain and sank back into the bed.

"What?"

Yuri clicked her tongue and bit her lip as she bore the pain, turning onto her back. The morning sun fell on her naked body.

"What the hell..."

She narrowed her eyes and stretched both arms towards the ceiling. Her wrists were covered in bruises that suggested blood congestion—slender wounds, as though she had been tied up.

She had no memory of such a thing. She took in the black and blue marks with a lax brain, then opened her eyes wide and rolled off the bed. Her whole body ached, but she ground her teeth against the pain and walked to stand in front of the large mirror. She saw the reflection of her snow-white body. Turning to look from every possible angle, she inspected herself all over. She couldn't see any marks apart from those around her wrists.

Yuri breathed a sigh of relief. She had been worried that her whole body might have been covered in bruises. She crumpled to the floor and curled into the fetal position. "Thank god," she whispered, closing her eyes as she lay on the resilient, cocoon-like carpet.

Her head felt heavy. So much was happening at once. The room was silent. She opened her eyes slowly and looked again at the bruises on her wrists. Wounds she didn't recall receiving. Her body aches might have been from sleeping in a bad position, but the marks on her wrists were clearly from having been tied up. They hadn't been there before she met Togo, so it was safe to assume that they were made during the five hours.

Five hours. Most of it was lost to her. At most she could recall the first hour or so. The latter four were a blank. There was a hole in her memory. But she could still remember the *sensation* of those four hours in the back of her mind. She just couldn't remember what they had talked about, the kind of sex they'd had.

"It's…better this way," she uttered, her voice hoarse.

Bad memories were best forgotten. She only needed the good ones.

Yuri thought of the time with Chu, but that was vague, too. Not quite as far gone as her time with Togo, but the memory was fragile and clouded.

Am I losing my mind?

At that moment the phone rang, breaking the silence of the room. Still curled into a ball, Yuri dragged herself like an inchworm towards the bed. She pulled herself onto the bed and picked up the phone's receiver.

"Ah, you're up?" came Suiren's crystalline voice. It made Yuri feel nostalgic.

"Yeah."

"So you've finished your first job? Good work."

"Yeah."

"How much did you get?"

"Eight hundred thousand," Yuri answered, looking at the cash on the table.

"Not bad, not bad!" Suiren cheered.

It felt great to be complimented. "What's up? It's early," Yuri asked.

Suiren chuckled. "I just finished a job. I wanted to invite you to go shopping at lunchtime."

"Shopping?"

"Yep."

"Sure."

"Settled, then. What time's good?"

"I'm in a little pain… I'd like to rest a bit first if that's okay." Though Yuri felt an urge to get going, the sooner the better, the pain made that impossible.

"In pain? Did you sleep funny?"

"I don't know. My whole body was aching badly when I woke up."

"Hang on, I'll bring you some pills," Suiren said and hung up.

She arrived ten minutes later in a simple purple tunic and padded lightly over to Yuri.

"For your hard work," she praised as she handed her a small, unlabeled bottle. It was packed full of pure white capsules.

"What are they?" Yuri asked, still lying on her bed.

"Painkillers. You can take up to two a day. Good for cramps and stuff like that. Take some and rest up. I'll call again later."

Suiren left. Alone, Yuri took one of the white capsules from the bottle and swallowed it with just the saliva in her mouth. She sank back into bed and fell asleep.

11:30.

Yuri opened her eyes to the ringing of the phone echoing through the room. Feeling much lighter, she sat up and picked up the receiver.

"Hello?"

"How do you feel?" Suiren's voice was comfort to her ears.

"Better," Yuri said, stretching this way and that. "Looks like the painkillers worked." Her aches had gone completely, like they had been an illusion, never existing in the first place. She felt thoroughly rested.

"Yeah? Great. Can you be ready by one?"

"Sure."

"Just wear whatever. I'll come get you," Suiren said and hung up.

Yuri got up and showered, washing off sweat and makeup, then found some underwear in the wardrobe and picked out some clothes from the closet. They were all designer items not suitable for simply walking around Ikebukuro. She looked at the plainer clothes she had arrived in, now discarded on the bathroom floor. They were the best option for walking through the city, but she couldn't wear them since they hadn't been washed. She settled on the blandest thing she could find—a blue dress— and went with a pair of blue heels to match.

She went to the sink to put on some makeup. At first she tried to mimic the gorgeous style Kay had applied but found it hard to replicate and ended up doing her usual light covering. She left the bathroom and checked the time—12:50. She hurried to the phone and dialed "1." The call connected after a few rings.

"How may I help?" It was the same woman, the one that always sounded mocking.

"I don't seem to have a washing machine. I need someone to do my laundry," Yuri said curtly.

"Wash your clothes?"

"That's right. My clothes. The clothes I wore when I came here and the ones I've worn since." Yuri looked over to the red dress balled up on the corner of the bed.

"Of course. But you have access to lots of clothes now. Why bother washing your personal clothing? I don't mean to be rude, but I don't imagine they're particularly fashionable. Not that I've seen them, of course."

Yuri felt her blood rushing to her head. "Whatever! Just get them cleaned!" she shouted and slammed the phone down.

She breathed loudly through her nose and stamped the floor in frustration. *That woman, always going out of her way to get on my nerves.*

Just as Yuri spat "What's her problem?" out loud, she heard the doorbell. Suiren had arrived.

"Looks like you're ready!" Suiren walked in, heels tapping on the floor. She peered at the still angry Yuri.

Suiren looked radiant, dressed in a short dress that was dazzlingly white. For a moment Yuri felt a compulsion to compare Suiren to herself, but the thought only lasted a second.

She straightened up, hoping that one day she would be as gorgeous as Suiren.

"What should I do with the money?" Yuri asked, looking at the pile of cash on the table. She didn't have a wallet large enough to carry it all.

"There's no need to take it with you. We've got these," Suiren said, producing two black cards from her purse and handing one to Yuri.

Yuri frowned.

"Buy-anything cards. It's a pain to carry cash with you, no?" Suiren approached the bed and picked up the phone, made a brief call, and hung up. "You just have to ask your concierge and they'll keep the money for you. You'll get a receipt to confirm your balance each time they collect your cash, so there's nothing to worry about. I've just asked them to collect your eight hundred thousand." Suiren skipped across to the doorway. "Whenever you use your card to buy something it's debited from the cash you've deposited. Pretty convenient, yes?"

"Wow." Yuri nodded, looking appreciatively at the black card in her hand.

"Okay, let's go."

Yuri followed, leaving the room with only her handbag.

As they walked down the corridor, the silence was as heavy as before. They rode the elevator, still so smooth that it was hard to tell if it was going up or down. They crossed the intimidating, black-themed entryway and exited into the humidity of the outside world.

It felt difficult to breathe in the late summer heat. As she stepped out onto the dirty asphalt, Yuri immediately pulled a face. Her ears rang slightly in response to the violent cacophony of the streets. Suiren's beautiful lips curled into a smile as she saw Yuri's expression.

"Always happens the first time. It's too quiet in the Tower, so the contrast can make your ears ring when you come outside. I was the same. Nothing to worry about."

"Sure." Yuri nodded, tensing her eardrums to equalize the pressure. The noise was so loud it was almost painful. The air felt polluted. Hard to breathe.

"You'll get used to it in no time," Suiren said as she set off.

Nothing about Ikebukuro had changed since Yuri had entered the Tower. It was all the same; the pedestrians' smiles, the general feel of the place. Suiren drew the attention of most of the men as before. The one difference was that some of them were also looking at Yuri. It was nothing compared to the number who stared at Suiren, but they existed. Yuri felt proud. They came out to a main road and Suiren hailed a taxi.

"Aren't we staying in Ikebukuro?" Yuri asked. Suiren's eyes opened wide with surprise.

"You'd never make a dent in your money if you shop in a place like this," she answered, getting into the taxi. Yuri hurried in after her.

"Where to?" the driver asked Suiren via the rearview mirror, eyes wide.

"Ginza."

"Ginza it is." The thin, balding man fiddled with the meter and shifted the car into drive. The low thrumming of the engine rumbled through Yuri's body.

"So, what do you want?" Suiren asked, looking out at the smoggy city outside.

"Uh…" Yuri wracked her brains. There were a number of things she wanted, but she had never been out to a place like Ginza before so she couldn't think of anything specific.

"What's wrong? Things you want to buy. You must have a long list." Suiren looked suspiciously at Yuri, as though she was odd for not knowing off-hand what she wanted.

Yuri avoided the gaze, looking down. Her eyes fell on her bag. "A handbag, maybe?" she ventured.

Suiren looked at Yuri's bag. She nodded, appearing satisfied. "In that case, I know the perfect place."

She gave the driver new directions, leaned back in the seat, closed her eyes, and pursed her lips. The interior of the car fell silent. There was only the constant hum of the engine, the repetitive ticking of the turn signals, the sensation of the driver's lusty gaze through the rearview mirror.

Yuri took out her cell phone as the car repeated the cycle of stopping and starting. After having been unable to use it in the Tower, it felt like seeing an old friend. She had four emails, all spam. Nothing else, no missed calls. She paged through the address book out of habit, then shut the phone.

"Boyfriend or something?" Suiren asked, still leaned back in the seat, eyes closed.

"No way," Yuri laughed. She had been approached, of course, but she had never really felt like she wanted one.

"Right," Suiren replied flatly before falling into corpse-like silence again.

Yuri watched the people outside, considering the idea. It might be worth dating Chu.

The taxi stopped and the two of them got out. Yuri had never come here before. There had never been any reason to. But more than that—she wouldn't have fitted in.

Getting out of the taxi, she felt it keenly. The buildings and people of Ginza were her polar opposite. *Haves* filled the streets, glamorously dressed. They walked like they owned the place, their rights granted by money. Ginza was generous to the *haves*. It didn't reject others outright, but it left them feeling alienated. The *have-nots*. A feeling only understood by the outcasts.

"What's wrong?" Yuri felt Suiren's hand on her back. She realized she'd been standing in a daze. "Come on."

As Yuri felt Suiren's hand push her to get her to walk, she made a decision.

From now on, I'll be one of the haves. *I'll never suffer again.*

"Okay," Yuri answered, and followed Suiren's lead.

The surging pedestrians seemed to be walking however they pleased. It was difficult to walk, each person a roving obstacle to negotiate. Despite Yuri having to make so much effort, Suiren moved easily, like she was swimming. The distance between them grew. Yuri's head began to spin from the heat and the crowds. She kept bumping into people, desperately trying to keep Suiren in sight. Just as she was close enough to be able to touch her back they arrived at their destination.

"Here we are." Suiren looked towards a spiral staircase leading downwards.

"Here?" Yuri's mouth fell open. She had expected a glassy boutique.

"Yup," Suiren said, pointing towards a black tile stuck in the wall. The name of the store was written in English. Yuri didn't know how to read it.

Suiren walked lightly down the spiral stairs, and Yuri followed. They descended one and a half turns. When they approached a frosted glass door at the bottom, it slid open with a quiet motorized hum. In a space dimly lit like an aquarium, only the bags, arranged equidistant to each other, sat dazzlingly illuminated.

"Welcome," a woman wearing skinny black pants and a tight t-shirt to match bowed her head. Her limbs were long and insect-like.

"Which do you want?" Suiren asked after giving the shop assistant a quick glance.

"Um…" Yuri inspected the brightly lit bags. The store, at over 300 square feet, wasn't that tiny, but she could easily count the number of bags on display. Each bag appeared to be giving her the cold shoulder, as if they were the ones to decide who could touch them.

The shop assistant had retreated to a corner and stood still as a mannequin. She seemed to be the only member of staff. There were no other customers.

Yuri carefully inspected each item, eyeing them as though they were part of an exhibit at an art museum. Her eyes stopped on a black leather handbag. The design was simple, but it looked expensive and elegant.

"That one?" Suiren asked. Yuri answered by nodding vaguely and craned her neck to check the price tag. There didn't seem to be one.

"Feel free to try it," the shop assistant suggested quietly. Yuri hadn't realized that she was now standing beside her.

Yuri obeyed, taking the bag in her hands. It was lighter than she had expected, and the leather was very smooth. "How much is it?" she asked hesitantly.

The shop assistant's smile looked like it had been cut out of a woman's magazine. "One million two hundred thousand yen."

Yuri's mind went into momentary shutdown. She felt her hands begin to tremble as she held the bag. She put it back, careful not to drop it.

"You don't like it?" Suiren walked up to them and picked it up.

"It's just…" *I don't have that kind of money.* She tried to whisper as much to Suiren, who suddenly gave the bag to the shop assistant.

"It looked good on you. My treat," Suiren said, pulling her black card from her purse.

"Huh?" Yuri stared at her, eyes wide open.

"To celebrate your joining the business," Suiren explained, smiling. She looked very much like one of the *haves*.

Yuri tried to turn her down multiple times; once the bag was in her possession, the mixture of gratitude and unease was enough to impede her from properly saying thanks. At the same time, she shivered at her luck.

So it's possible to earn so much. It wasn't decent, but it wasn't particularly dangerous, either. It was easy, if anything. She'd be able to treat people to bags that cost one million two hundred thousand yen just by doing *that*.

Yuri walked in a daze, amazed at how her luck had exceeded her expectations. Suiren told her she was thirsty and they decided to go to a cafe.

The establishment was part of a well-known chain, but the interior was grander than the others she had seen; the atmosphere was relaxed, with jazz playing in the background and indirect lighting.

"It was so hot out there," Yuri placed an iced tea and a latte on the round table. The air-conditioning had finally stopped her sweating.

"Thanks," Suiren said, putting her mouth to the straw, having held seats for them. Her lips moved seductively as she drank the iced tea.

"I'm the one who needs to thank you," Yuri replied, her eyes lingering on the bag Suiren had bought for her.

"Enough of that." Suiren held up her palm.

"But..."

"It's fine, it's fine. The truth is," Suiren leaned forward, lowering her voice, "I get a little money from Chu every time a someone I introduce is hired," she laughed.

"Oh, really?"

"Yup. So it's my pleasure, really."

Yuri fell silent. *How much did she get?*

"Now you're wondering how much of a kickback."

"Huh?" Yuri blushed at having her thoughts read so unexpectedly.

"Only natural. But you can't become a scout yet."

"Why not?"

"You need to gain a little trust first. Chu might say it's okay at some point. I'll let you know if the opportunity arises. If we're reckless in scouting and the Tower gets exposed, we won't just get thrown out," Suiren divulged ominously.

"That sounds scary."

"You don't need to worry, as long as you don't let anything slip," she added, smiling. But her eyes had narrowed, as though warning Yuri not to pry any further.

The cafe was busy, but since there was plenty of space between the seats and the other customers were chatting quietly, it wasn't noisy.

"How many of us are in the Tower?"

"You mean Flowers?"

"Yes."

Suiren put a finger to her lips and thought for a moment. "I can't say for certain, but I think there's less than twenty of us at the moment."

"Huh, that's all?" Yuri asked, surprised. From the Tower's size she had imagined many more. And something felt odd about the way Suiren had said *at the moment*.

"I think so. I'm not sure, we never see each other. I don't really care anyway," Suiren said flatly before changing the subject. "So tell me, how was the first go-round?" Suiren's eyes narrowed with curiosity. She was beautiful enough to make another woman blush.

"How do you mean?"

"I dunno, impressions, that sort of thing."

"Impressions," Yuri mumbled, thinking. She didn't know what to say since she didn't remember most of it. "Actually, I don't remember that much," she replied honestly.

Suiren cocked her head to one side and gave Yuri a questioning look. "You don't?"

"Um… I mean, I remember most of it, just not the details. It's not like I've forgotten, everything's just a little foggy," Yuri answered, shrugging.

"Okay, so what do you remember?" Suiren probed.

"Normal stuff, I guess."

"Normal?"

"Yeah, *we just did it normally*."

Suiren burst out laughing. "I guess everything's good then."

"Oh?"

"You'd grow to hate the job pretty soon if you remembered all the little details."

Yuri agreed. She simply did not remember them. That said,

the sensation that her memory had been erased—manipulated, even—was far from pleasant. It felt like someone had been cavorting rudely around the inside of her skull.

"Best not to worry," Suiren nodded, satisfied, and put the straw to her mouth.

Suiren's reaction helped reassure Yuri that she was making too much of things, and she put the matter out of her mind.

It was after 4:00 p.m. There were fewer customers now, and some of their conversations could be overheard quite clearly.

"So, how's the investment going?" a woman smartly dressed and in her early thirties seated ahead of Yuri inquired excitedly. It was obvious she had both time and money to burn; her gaudy accessories and heavy makeup seemed an attempt to fight back against inevitable aging with money.

"It's amazing. I put in ten million and tripled it in half a year." She was talking with a woman that looked a little younger, maybe twenty-seven or -eight who, with her hair coiled high, stank of money.

"Tripled?" The heavily made-up woman was left breathless.

"My husband manages it so I don't know the details, but he's talking about increasing our investment," the woman with the high hair noted, her tone dripping superiority.

"That's great. But—I forget the name… The company's only been going three years, right? Is that safe?" Heavy Makeup asked, envy in her eyes.

"I'm sure it's fine. I hear executives at my husband's affiliated company are pouring money into it, too. Even the government's injecting public funds, so it's a good bet. Look, what was it now… Rare earths or something? The company has a ton of rights to the stuff."

"Hmm, maybe I should mention it to my husband, too."

"You must! I'll make the introduction."

"Y-You would?" Heavy Makeup's eyes sparkled with greed.

The two of them looked like drooling animals.

"Hey, you okay?" Suiren's voice brought Yuri back to herself.

"Huh?"

"You were spaced out. Come on, let's go."

Suiren took the bill and got up. Yuri glanced at the two women as she walked to the register. *Money-grubbers.* The phrase fitted them perfectly.

The sky was dyed faintly crimson as the city lights glowed brighter. The display windows lining the streets were dramatically lit, designed to kindle people's desire.

"Shall we go back?" Suiren asked, her casual steps suggesting that she was just out for a stroll.

"What? You don't want to buy anything?"

"Me?" Suiren pointed at herself, and Yuri nodded. Suiren appeared to think for a while, then looked around until her gaze fell on a particular store. "I guess so, we've come all the way," she said and walked into a jeweler's.

The store's interior was all brown and the lamps were dimmed, but the showcases were a riot of light that glittered like a sprinkling of stars.

"This one please." Suiren pointed to a necklace studded with large diamonds almost immediately upon entering the store.

The clerk's eyes seemed to bulge for a moment, but she switched to a customer-friendly smile as soon as she recognized Suiren. "Always a pleasure," he said and opened the showcase, taking out the necklace and handing it to Suiren.

Suiren took off the necklace she was wearing and replaced it with the diamond one. She handed her black card to the clerk.

"What do you think?" Suiren asked Yuri after glancing at the shop mirror.

"It looks amazing on you," Yuri answered, completely entranced. Suiren looked surreal, such was the combination of her features and the string of diamonds.

"Great." Suiren laughed, taking her card back from the clerk. "Right, let's go."

Suiren started to walk slowly towards the exit. Yuri stole a glance at the space where Suiren's new necklace had been. The price tag read 1,500,000 yen.

They discussed whether to have dinner out but ended up deciding to go back to the Tower. All the restaurants were overflowing with people, and it was unlikely they would find anything better than the food at the Tower.

Yuri stood back and watched the passersby as Suiren looked around for a taxi to hail. She saw the smiles of the haves, the contentment of the haves, the greed of the haves. They looked genuinely happy, as though they didn't even know of the existence of have-nots.

The air outside was humid and clingy, carrying an echo of the midday heat. Yuri fanned the area around her neck with her hands. As she looked around, something arrested her gaze and seemed to anchor it, and not as an act of her will. It was as though her gaze had been *forced to settle*.

A man was walking directly towards her through the bustling crowd of pedestrians. He showed no signs of having to navigate the crowd. It navigated around him. Oddly, the crowd seemed to pay him no notice, as though he was invisible.

His clothes were a little eccentric. He was dressed in an all-gray suit with shoes that were almost gray. Even his skin was pallid. In contrast, his eyes burned darkly. He seemed to be walking in slow motion, but something about him conveyed urgency. Everything around him faded into mist.

He wasn't human. He was something more, Yuri felt straight away.

His eyes appeared to be focused on blank space as he drew closer. He came within reach.

He gently caught her gaze.

The man's cheeks tensed slightly. By the time Yuri had recognized the expression as a *smile*, he had passed right by her like a breeze and disappeared into the crowd.

Yuri was rooted to the spot, as if she'd turned to stone and her heart had frozen. She tried to turn her head to look back, but she couldn't even manage that. The fear of having faced the unknown. The awe of something overwhelming standing in one's way. She felt cold, as though all the blood in her body had sunk to the ground.

"Yuri, come on."

Suiren's voice broke the spell, allowing Yuri to breathe again. She turned to look at Suiren. She didn't seem to have noticed the man.

Yuri got into the taxi in silence, her breathing shallow as she leaned back against the seat. Only then did she notice that she was drenched with sweat like she had been doused with water.

5

After her outing with Suiren, Yuri had spent two weeks at the Tower. Granted leave to go outside alone, she had gone shopping on four or so occasions but had passed most of her time working as a Flower.

Around half of Yuri's Benefactors were people she thought she had seen somewhere before. A number of celebrities and politicians she clearly recognized from TV. In each case they used pseudonyms and avoided any discussion of their private affairs. There were many Benefactors whom Yuri had never seen before, but even they stank of money. One and all, they were *haves*.

Every day Yuri would be visited by one, at most two, Benefactors. Each time, she collected around a hundred thousand yen in tips on top of her fee. In just two weeks she had amassed savings of over five million yen.

In light of the compensation, she didn't consider her role as a Flower to be too demanding. Kay put on her makeup, she took her medicine, greeted her Benefactor and spent an hour or so on idle pleasantries, then slept with them. All she had to do was repeat the cycle.

There was only the one strange fact that she could never remember anything about the sex, but she had decided it was not worth dwelling on. After all, it was easier not to have those kind of memories.

One thing did make her uneasy. She often woke after her encounters with marks on her body. None stood out too much, but

she had cuts, worm-like marks from being tied up, blood congestion under the skin, or impact wounds. She used painkillers to
manage the pain, but even then it was difficult to fully dismiss the
marks. They were more than a mere annoyance, bad enough to
merit investigation under normal circumstances. But Yuri's head
was clouded, as though her ability to think had been diminished,
and she never feared that her wounds represented real danger.

She had no memory of how or where she obtained the
marks. Nothing came to her even when she tried to remember—
it was like someone had put on a tight lid.

I slept badly. Before she knew it, Yuri had started to rationalize
away the injuries. The fear, in fact, was there, smoldering deep in
her heart. She just failed to notice it.

Yuri lay in bed again, half-listening to the sound of a Benefactor leaving. She had begun taking painkillers at the same time
as the antibacterial medicine, so she no longer had to put up with
any pain after work.

The time was after 7:00 p.m. Her mind was still wandering,
confused. She decided to sleep and sighed out heavily, hoping it
would help. Just as she was about to nod off, the doorbell rang,
unpleasantly, as if to rub her heart the wrong way.

Ding dong. Ding dong.

Brief silence.

Ding dong. Ding dong.

The chime sounded in a regular rhythm like a pulse beating.
Yuri thought it might be Chu. She stretched her eyes wide open,
then jumped out of bed and scampered to the door. He stood
there with a hand in his pocket, one side of his mouth curved
into a crescent moon of a smile.

"Sorry to disturb you so soon after work."

"Not at all, it's fine," Yuri said sweetly, peering up at him.

"I'm coming in," Chu said, ambling into the room and setting himself down on the loveseat. That was where he always
sat. "Getting used to your job as a Flower?" he asked, lighting a
cigarette. His eyes flashed briefly to Yuri.

Yuri sat facing him. She wanted to sit next to him but somehow felt too intimidated. "Yeah, pretty much."

"Good," Chu uttered flatly. He watched the smoke unfurl from his cigarette, saying nothing else.

Yuri stole a glance, trying to gauge his mood. She had really wanted to talk to him about the marks on her body, about her memories becoming vague. Yet, perhaps because he sensed this, Chu had built a wall to hide behind, often sitting in silence thus. Kay, the makeup artist, was easygoing enough, but that in itself made it impossible to broach the subject. Yuri had also mentioned it to Suiren, who just laughed it off, telling her that she was thinking too much.

"Um…" Yuri forced her resolve and opened her mouth to speak. That alone was enough to make her heart beat painfully fast.

"What?" Chu turned his languid eyes from the clouds of smoke to look at her.

Yuri sucked in a breath, but all that came out was air. She couldn't voice her thoughts. "It's nothing," she finally managed. Chu smiled at her.

Tap tap.

His usual habit. He tapped his index finger against the arm of the loveseat. Yuri shivered. He got to his feet and pulled her in by the hips and gave her a violent kiss. Yuri went with it, her thoughts dissolving away. She was pushed onto the bed, manhandled as she gave in to both pain and pleasure. He hurt her badly, but the pleasure was even greater. It felt as though countless snakes were crawling over her, constricting, biting, and caressing with their slippery bodies. Yuri moaned from pain, groaned with pleasure.

When it was over, Chu chain-smoked two cigarettes and got ready to leave. She watched from the bed as he left in silence. As she started to doze off, she felt a blankness wash over her as though everything had been reset. She fell into a deep sleep.

Yuri did not realize that she had not dreamt once since coming to the Tower.

She checked the time when she came to. The clock read 22:00. Three hours had passed since Chu's visit.

It was dark outside, and the city lights seemed far away. Though tempted to go back to sleep, hungry to the point of nausea she reached out for the phone and pushed "1."

"How may I be of service?" It was the same impudent woman. She spoke the same line in the same tone of voice. Yuri had never met her in person, but she liked to imagine the woman as being somehow disfigured.

"Chow," she ordered bluntly. She hated the woman so much, she wouldn't have minded throwing in a few gratuitous insults.

"Chow? You will need to be more specific, otherwise you'll end up with plain white rice."

"Anything, something light." As always the woman's tone grated on her, and Yuri didn't bother to hide her frustration. "A light pasta dish. Seafood, or Japanese-style. No cream sauce or anything like that."

"You really do keep an unhealthy diet."

"Whatever, just bring it here."

"Fine, Japanese-style pasta and soup. A salad for nutrition. And a light dessert for after your meal. I'll have tea sent as well."

"Sounds good."

"Someone will be along shortly."

"Um, I…" Just as Yuri sensed the woman was about to hang up, she opened her mouth to stay her. She wasn't really sure why.

"Another request?" the woman complained.

Yuri faltered, unsure whether she should broach the subject, but her mouth was moving before she knew it. "There's something that's been bothering me."

"Something? If you are going to ask me to fix my temperament I'm afraid that won't be possible."

"Marks, on my body." As she spoke, Yuri cursed herself for talking to this woman who did nothing but put her down, but she was unable to stem the flow. "I get these…injuries…on my body."

"Oh. You want to talk. Okay, I've got a little time now, so go ahead. When you say injuries…"

"When I wake up after a job, I have bruises that I don't remember getting."

"You must sleep pretty badly. Kids are so—"

"Stop making fun of me!" Yuri cried, not loudly, but her tone revealed the extent of her distress.

Cough.

The woman cleared her throat apologetically. The gesture allowed Yuri to lower her guard.

"How bad are they?" the woman asked, also as though the wall between them had come down.

Yuri began to give her the details, all the while looking at the marks over her body. When she finished, the woman let out a barely audible sigh over the line.

"The marks are certainly a worry, but there's a bigger problem you're not noticing."

"I don't…"

"That you've waited until now to see this as a problem."

Yuri struggled to absorb the meaning of what the woman was saying.

"You've abandoned your ability to think. You've renounced your memory. How about you try not taking those 'antibacterials'?"

"But…" She could get ill if she didn't take them.

"I'm not forcing you, it's just a suggestion."

The woman hung up. Fifteen minutes later, the unsociable man with the dark eyes brought Yuri's food.

The next day, Yuri left the Tower alone. She wandered the streets of Ikebukuro, buying things she didn't need from department stores. Nothing she bought was anything she really wanted, she just couldn't think of other ways to use her money. Every time she bought something, the shop attendants bowed to her. Everyone bowed to the power of money. They revered her. They were jealous of her. It certainly wasn't a bad feeling.

It was six when she returned to the Tower with all the shopping bags she could carry. There were no hints of other people in the elevator or along the corridors. She didn't see any other Flowers, didn't chance upon any other Benefactors. *Does anyone else really live here?* she wondered, finding it hard to believe how quiet the place was.

She went back to her room, put her shopping bags down in a corner, and began to get ready for work. She had a client coming at 20:00. She showered and put on the newly washed red dress, then waited for the time to come around. Kay turned up one hour before her Benefactor was due to arrive. As always, he sat Yuri before the bathroom mirror and laid out the tools he used for her makeup.

"You've really blossomed over these last two weeks. You're like a completely different person. The power of youth is scary," Kay remarked, looking entranced as he put on her makeup. The swift movements of his hands contrasted with the relaxed tone of his voice. "You get any prettier and I'll be jealous."

"You shouldn't be. Doesn't matter how pretty I am since I'll just end up with more wounds," Yuri daringly countered.

Kay made an odd face in response, an awkward, sad expression. "The key is to not let it bother you," he said, chasing the look from his face with a smile directed at Yuri.

It took twenty minutes for Kay to finish applying the makeup. He stroked his index and middle fingers over Yuri's cheek when he finished.

"Perfect," he nodded, satisfied. After he cleared away his tools he let out a small sigh and looked at his diamond-studded wristwatch. "Thirty minutes until showtime."

"Yeah," Yuri nodded, trying to gauge Kay's mood.

He usually left as soon as the makeup was done, but he was still in his seat, seemingly in thought. After a while he got up and started to pace towards one of the room's walls. "Let me tell you why I do this job," he said, leaning against the wall. He stood so that Yuri could see him in the lit-up mirror. "I was a makeup artist even before I came here. I was fulfilled, happy enough to want

97

to spend the rest of my days that way. Then, one day, it wasn't enough anymore."

Kay laughed self-deprecatingly. "It was because I met Chu. We met at a party hosted by some big cheese. It was a little too glamorous for me, but I was hired to do the makeup for a certain actress. Of course, I had nothing to do after I was done with her makeup, so I sat drinking in the corner of this huge hall. I sat watching all these people in their expensive clothes like they were from another dimension. They were like a breed apart, confidence and arrogance oozing from their expressions, the way they handled themselves. They belonged to a race diametrically opposite to mine.

"Don't get me wrong, I wasn't pitying myself. I had my own arena and I was satisfied to live within it. After watching them for a while I noticed a dark figure in the corner of my eye. It was Chu. It was hard to believe I hadn't noticed him until then, he stood out like a sore thumb. I knew instinctively he didn't belong to my kind, but I was also certain that his was a world that differed from the rest of the partygoers'. His was a world that was hard to put into any category."

Kay hugged his arms across his chest. "Chu noticed me after a while and walked over. I'd already fallen for him. Nothing as simple as love, mind. It was more fervent, more like devotion, what you might feel in a cult, maybe. Anyway, I was ready to deny everything I was and offer my life to him. It was crazy to think all that just from looking at someone. But women can be like that sometimes." Kay smiled, and the expression looked more feminine than that of any biological woman.

"I don't remember what we talked about there. I mean, I was totally in shock. But I managed to get hold of his contact details and hounded him ferociously until he gave me a job here at the Tower. Been here ever since. I'm going to spend my life with Chu. When he's around, everything is perfect, and nothing's right when he's not. I'm satisfied as long as I'm with him. I don't let anything get in the way of that. *Even if I have to slaughter people, even if I become an accomplice to crime,* I will be with him, always."

Kay's voice lost its softness towards the end of his speech as he emphasized the words like he was carving them into his heart. He ran his hand up through his short hair and held Yuri's gaze in the mirror.

"We've only just met, but I like you. So I'm going to give you some advice." Kay walked away from the wall, came to stand behind Yuri, and placed his hands over her shoulders. "Keep taking the medicine. For your own happiness." His fingers tensed on her shoulders, lightly pinching into Yuri's flesh.

By the time he left there were only fifteen minutes left until the Benefactor was due to arrive. Benefactors always arrived on time. Yuri spent the time in turmoil.

Should she do as the woman on the phone had said and not take the medicine? Or should she follow Kay's advice and take it? She had the inkling that Kay's advice would turn out better for her. Yuri wasn't sure why, but she had sensed a kind of compassion in Kay's eyes and felt that he had spoken the truth.

But was that good enough? Yuri wanted her head clear of the fog that had built up like exhaust fumes in her head. For that, it was probably better not to take the medicine.

The doorbell rang before she finished making up her mind, telling her the Benefactor had arrived, 20:00 on the dot. Yuri scooped up two of the pills and headed to the door. She opened it to see Togo standing there wearing an affable smile. He was in an expensive black jacket and white trousers.

"Hey there," he said, raising a hand in greeting as he came into the room. He ambled into the kitchen as though he was at home. "What do you want to drink?" came his disembodied voice.

"The same as usual," Yuri replied, sitting at her place on the bed.

Togo had visited her four times since she began working as a Flower. Her other Benefactors had only visited once, twice at most, but Togo kept coming back. Yuri didn't dislike him. She didn't particularly like him, either. She could relax more around him than the others, but that was all. There were no other emotions.

After clattering about the kitchen, Togo emerged with a coffee in one hand and an iced tea for Yuri in the other. He passed the drink to her then sat on the loveseat.

"How've you been?" Togo asked, a thin smile on his lips. It had no doubt charmed a number of women, but Yuri thought it looked dated.

"Not too bad, I guess."

"Such a cold reply," Togo lamented, taking off his jacket so that he wore only a white dress shirt on top. As per routine, he pulled out an envelope stuffed with cash and placed it on the table. Taking a sip of coffee, he asked, "How's work?"

"Fine."

"Good to hear."

Yuri added syrup to her iced tea and glanced at the envelope. "What is it that you do, exactly?"

"And what brought this on?" Togo fixed his eyes on her, as though to assess the intention behind her words.

"Nothing, really. It's just wild to see someone casually spend so much money. I was just wondering what kind of jobs could make people so rich." Yuri wasn't trying to flatter him, she genuinely wanted to know. Before coming to the Tower she had never known anyone who could throw around money like it was so many scraps of paper.

"I'm not super-wealthy. I'm just one of the moderately rich."

"But what kind of work do you do to earn so much?"

"Why the interest? I told you at the start, nosing around won't do either of us any good." Togo's voice was soft, but his eyes had a sharp glint.

Yuri cringed, intimidated. "Sorry…"

"It's okay, just make sure you understand." Togo's expression softened, returning to his usual confident look. He started to chat about harmless, commonplace things.

Exactly an hour passed. It was as if he was keeping time.

Yuri had come to the realization that her Benefactors made sure to always make conversation for just the first hour. Now

Togo suddenly fell quiet, got to his feet, and slowly made his way over to Yuri. Then, wordlessly, he pushed her so that she fell back onto the bed. Yuri cried out quietly, realizing he wasn't going to shower this time. In the moment before Togo had pushed her onto her back, her eyes had flashed over the yellow pills now scattered on the carpet—*the medicine she was supposed to have taken.*

"About ready?" Togo whispered, his nose almost touching hers. The coffee stink of his breath was repellent.

Yuri nodded vaguely, unsure of what he meant. Togo's eyes glimmered abnormally as he opened a large, red mouth.

His eyes, usually narrowed into a smile, were wide open, round like saucers. A dull sound echoed across the silent room. Fireworks scattered before Yuri's eyes and she couldn't catch her breath. Togo had buried his fist in her abdomen.

"So you flunked yesterday's test?" His tone was caressing but his face was fiendish, almost demonic.

Yuri tried to break free, but Togo used his body to pin her to the bed. She wanted to cry out but she could hardly breathe from the pain.

"That won't do. That's what happens if you don't listen to Daddy," Togo said as he closed his right hand around her neck and stroked her cheek with his left.

The pain was too much. Yuri used her freed hands to claw at his right hand.

"Ow!" Togo shouted, drawing his hand away from her neck. He slapped her hard on the cheek, jumped up, and kicked her in the side of her gut. "Again? Don't you ever treat Daddy like a nuisance!"

Togo's face had gone red, his eyebrows arched high. He kicked her once more and brushed disheveled hair from his face. The intensity of the pain caused Yuri to cry out. Her body was trembling from fright.

"Hah! Looks like I'm going to have to punish you as usual." Togo lowered himself over her, letting his long tongue snake over her neck. "Right. You always make fun of me, telling me to keep away, telling me I stink. But at the end of the day I can do whatever I fucking want with you."

Yuri was shivering. She had no idea what Togo was talking about. He began to tweak her small, hardened nipples. From there his hands—hands that knew not heavy labor—traced downwards, touching her privates before digging in with nails.

Yuri couldn't speak, couldn't scream. Her eyes went wide as her entire body stiffened with panic. Her mouth went dry, she couldn't breathe. She was soaked in cold sweat and faint tremors ran through her body.

"Huh? What is it, are you scared?" Togo said, looking overjoyed. "Today's going to be the same as always. I tie you up, you serve me. Now and then I hurt you. A good deal, right? I let you live in such a great place and pay the expensive tuition for high school and cram school. You can't complain about the pocket money you get. I always buy you what you want, don't I? 'Those who work not shall eat not.' I better start seeing more appreciation outta you." He sneered as he took off his belt and removed his trousers.

Yuri watched him as her field of vision became distorted through tears. Her expression went blank, as though all feeling had suddenly vanished. Her body stopped shaking, her senses began to shut down, and her sight clouded over. She could barely see Togo. Her instincts were screaming at her to disassociate; if she didn't, her life would be in danger. She felt her consciousness float away from her body as she lay there unnaturally like a puppet with its strings cut.

Scary. But don't think. Filthy. But don't think.

When *this* was over, she would go shopping. She would buy every little thing that caught her fancy, revel in the shop clerks' attentions, and bask in the looks of envy.

I'm a have now. This is the price. No choice. Gotta bear it.

She had to stay as calm as possible. The image of that strange man from Ginza popped suddenly into her mind. The gray man. His pitch-black burning gaze filled her head, rattling her brain. She began to blink furiously. Her vision cleared a little. She saw before her a man-eating demon.

"…No."

"Huh?" Togo, his trousers off, halted.

Yuri felt a wave of nausea as her voice tore out. "No! Get off me!" she shrieked and began to wail as she mustered all her strength to push Togo away from her.

"What the hell…" Togo's mouth gaped open in shock. He seemed to be struggling to understand what was happening.

"Stay away from me!" Yuri screamed, fighting back the pain shooting through her body.

Togo's lips trembled. "Oh, no… Don't tell me you didn't take the medicine."

"Stay back!"

"Fuck!"

Yuri heard the door to the room swing violently open, almost on cue with Togo's outcry. She heard running footsteps as Chu came into view. His hair was a mess, his eyes bloodshot and huge. *I'm saved.*

Yuri looked at him, pleading for help, but he ignored her.

"I'm very sorry!" Chu bowed his head. Togo stood there without his shirt and trousers, looking ridiculous in just his socks.

"Ugh. This won't do," Togo admonished with a sigh, assuming a sickeningly self-important attitude in order to calm himself. "I was hoping to have a little more fun."

"I'm terribly sorry!" Chu repeated, keeping his head bowed low.

"Well, it's done now. I'll overlook it. Bidders?"

"We have three bids, including yourself."

"The highest amount?"

"One Benefactor has bid ten million yen."

"The auction price was fifteen, right?" Togo asked, putting on his trousers.

"Yes."

"Okay, I'll buy her."

"Thank you so much. Do you have a preferred date?"

"Today. Let's see… In six hours. I have some work to cancel and I want to take a quick nap."

"Of course."

Togo pulled a card out of his wallet and handed it to Chu. He accepted it politely, then walked out of the room. Yuri watched him as he left, shocked to have been treated as though she didn't even exist.

"What…is…" Yuri mumbled semi-consciously.

Togo finally turned back to her. "Why didn't you take your pills?"

"Why? I don't…"

"No matter, it's done. But you made a bad choice." Togo had already donned the skin of an adult.

"What are you saying?" Yuri asked, but she was afraid to hear anything more.

"I guess this way isn't too bad. I'd wanted to play a little more, but there you go." A look of ecstasy flashed across his face as he tried to keep his anger in check.

"I'm asking you what the fuck is going on!" Yuri screamed, her voice shot through with fear and anger. Togo stared at her in silence, showing no reaction. His mouth opened, splitting into a crescent, pulling strands of spit.

"You're going to get *killed*, by me."

He roared with laughter.

"Tell me, how does it feel, to hear you're going to die?"

Yuri didn't understand. Togo continued regardless.

"I'm going to rape you, beat you, burn you, and hack you to pieces. No matter how much you cry and scream, no one will come to your rescue." Togo pulled a self-satisfied smile, looking completely insane.

Run.

Yuri's head thudded with the dull ringing of warning bells. She tried to move her hands and legs, but they were too feeble from shaking. But she had to escape. As the thought came to her, Chu came back to the room.

"The transaction is complete. Here is your card." Chu bowed his head, returned the card to Togo, and took a couple of steps backwards, glancing briefly towards Yuri. "We have prepared a room for you to rest in. Was there anything else you required?"

"Make sure you tie *that* up properly. The shrew scratched up my hand. She needs to be taught a lesson," Togo said, rubbing the lacerations.

"Of course." Chu bowed.

Togo smiled at Yuri, then walked out of the room.

As soon as he heard Togo close the door, Chu walked straight up to Yuri and, without hesitation, clamped her in handcuffs and shoved her back onto the bed. His movements were so sudden Yuri had allowed herself to be restrained with no time to resist.

"Why didn't you take the pills?" Chu asked, straddling her.

The rude woman flashed across Yuri's mind, the one she'd only ever spoken to over the phone, but she said nothing about her and instead demanded, "Tell me what's going on." Her voice reflected anger, despair, and fear, but was surprisingly calm.

Chu snorted. "Tell you? It's easy. You've been sold."

"Sold?"

"Yes. The Tower's different from your average bordello or the mainstream sex industry. We're an auction house. Haven't you ever felt uncomfortable in this room?" Yuri was silent. Chu took that as affirmation. "It's because of the surveillance cameras. Countless cameras are planted all over so your life can be observed."

A shiver ran down Yuri's spine. The room had felt uncomfortable, it was true. She had felt like she was being watched. But she had thought it was due to the garish furniture and the size of the place.

"Our Benefactors use the camera feeds to observe your everyday life, then they pay money to make contact and decide whether or not to buy you. It goes without saying that we switch the cameras off during their visits in order to maintain their privacy. I watch regardless, of course, just in case of an emergency. Then the Benefactors bid against one another. They bid, then pay extra to visit you to help them decide whether or not you're someone they really want to buy. Then they bid some more. That's the system."

Yuri was unable to absorb the meaning of the words.

"And you've been bought. Admirable. Congratulations. It was a little irregular, but Togo met our auction price outright. And in just two weeks at that—a new record. You should be proud."

Proud of what? You lied to me. I trusted you. I looked up to you. Yuri glared and spat at Chu. *You smashed it all to pieces.*

"No need to look so scary." Chu left the spit on his face. He pulled out another pair of handcuffs and clamped Yuri to the bedposts. "Still, it's a shame."

"What is?" Yuri wriggled her legs to kick him but couldn't move them well as Chu had her pinned down.

"I'm going to feel a little sad to see you die, Yuri. It's something I've never felt for any of the other girls. I felt close to you from our very first interview. You see, you look a lot like the first girl I raped and killed. For a while, I didn't want to let you die by anyone else's hands. But your life has been sold for fifteen million. There's nothing more I can do."

Chu pulled away from her.

"I'll bury you myself. Call it my tribute to you."

So saying, he knocked his shoes together.

Tap tap.

6

Left alone in the room, Yuri's anger began to slowly dissipate. As it did, it was replaced by a burgeoning sadness and fear that seemed to crush her heart.

She pulled at the handcuffs with all her strength, but they showed no signs of loosening. All she achieved was to tear her skin until it bled, but she didn't let that stop her. She continued to pull against the cuffs.

The thought that it was all some kind of bad joke persisted in the back of her mind. *That's it, a sick, black joke. It has to be.* It was too surreal. People's lives didn't get sold. Certainly not in Japan. It was absurd.

But the greater part of Yuri's mind had already accepted the situation as fact. She was beyond simple fear. She was losing control, as though every emotion inside her had spontaneously blown a fuse.

Alone in the spacious room, she cried at the top of her voice. She cried and raged. She made a few more desperate attempts to break free from the handcuffs. Her wrists were red from her own blood, but the pain lost out to her increasing panic. The handcuffs rattled but still showed no signs of coming loose. Yuri wailed and cursed. Nothing reacted to her.

An hour had passed since Chu had left the room. It was strange, but Yuri didn't feel vindictive towards him personally. She would have been lying if she said she didn't hate him, but her fury was directed at those who used money to always get their way, the Benefactors.

Yuri looked around, suddenly feeling watched. Just the thought that those bastards might be watching her was enough to make her retch with horror.

Click.

Hearing the door open, she went rigid and concentrated her ears and eyes, straining her senses. Footsteps, scuffing over the carpet. A dark shadow revealed itself before her.

"Are you okay?"

It was Suiren, wrapped in a crimson red dress.

"I... I..."

Yuri couldn't get the words out. One look at Suiren was almost enough to cause her to burst into tears. She moaned for a while before finally speaking in a hoarse voice.

"Help! This... This place is dangerous. We've gotta get outta here."

"Get out? Why?" Suiren tilted her head to one side and smiled slightly.

Suddenly Yuri understood everything. "Y-You lied to me?"

"Lie? How scandalous. You took the job and came here of your own will, no?"

"You never told me about this!" Yuri bellowed.

Suiren just stood there smiling, apparently enjoying herself. "If you'd done better you might've been able to stay on, like me. Not now, though. At the end of the day, you're just one of the exploited. And I'm one of the exploiters."

"But you're a Flower, too."

"That was true at first. Maybe I might have ended up like you. But I won, got to the next round. The powers that be saw my talent at *planting* Flowers and chose not to sell me off. Head-hunting. I pick up personnel and put them to work here. Then I let the Benefactors pluck you off at the root," Suiren said as she took a step towards Yuri to the exact spot where Chu had stood. "If you'd been good and taken your pills you might have lasted longer. Oh well." She narrowed her eyes as she peered down at Yuri.

"This is just a bad joke, right?"

Yuri's voice trembled as she begged for help. Suiren said nothing in reply.

"Hurry up, tell me this is just a game!" Yuri cried and thrashed, her emotions exploding.

"It's no use. Give it up," Suiren's words came like a slap on water. "The world is divided into people who pluck and people who're plucked. The powerful few govern over the powerless many. You've worked that out by now, yes?" She sounded like a teacher chiding a wayward student. "It's pitiful. There are so many people out there who spend their lives blind to the fact that their only value is in being exploited, in being directed. They lack self-awareness, any realization that they're being consumed. Makes it all the easier to take advantage of them, of course."

"But killing people!"

"Listen to you. Even murder's just entertainment for the powerful."

"They'd get caught!"

Suiren laughed until she had expelled all the air in her lungs. "Who do you think makes law? The people in power. You think people with more money and power than the ones who enforce the law have anything to fear from it? Take the police. You think people with more influence than the police are going to be arrested? The answer is no. They talk about the rule of law, but I wonder. Only the weak get caught. We live in a bizarre country where murderers are treated with more respect than victims of crime. Or rather, it's a wonderful country, where powerful people can snuff out anyone who gets in their way."

Suiren shook her head. "I never disliked you. That's why it's a shame. I wanted you to live a little longer. The remainder of your life is going to be spent entertaining that old pervert. Seems he gets off on killing girls his daughter's age. He's always spouting serious-sounding crap on TV, looking superior, yet he kills for kicks. I hear he actually gets off from watching girls crying and screaming. But he won't be caught because he's got money and influence. The Tower is designed to bury it all in darkness. Hang in there. I guess this is farewell, forever."

Suiren gave Yuri a look like she was nothing more than an object, then waved her hand and left.

The room fell silent.

Left alone, Yuri vacantly stared at a single point on the ceiling, like she'd become an empty shell. Time ticked away.

I don't care anymore.

Though she'd suspected that the deal was too good to be true, she'd never imagined being so terribly deceived.

Even so, to end like this…

Yuri snorted, disgusted with herself.

I'm so tired. I wanted to enjoy life a little more. If I'd been raised in a decent home, if I'd led a decent life, I'd never have come to this place. A decent… I wasn't even granted that basic right.

Tears poured from her eyes.

Sad. Too sad to breathe. I want to live. Live normal. I hate the world for not even letting me do that.

But now it's time to end it.

Yuri stuck out her tongue, ready to bite it off.

She'd rather take her own life if the alternative was to die as the plaything of that bastard pervert. She focused on her quaking tongue. Then, just as she sucked in a deep breath, she heard the door open and the sound of footsteps.

She checked the clock. It was still too early.

Just get it over with.

She bit down on her tongue with all her might. She let out a short shriek, like an inrush of air, then everything went black. In her fading consciousness she only heard voices. They came from somewhere far away.

"What are you doing? Hurry up and do something!"

Huh?

It sounded like the rude woman from the phone. Yuri had never heard her sound so agitated so she couldn't be sure, but...

"I know."

A man's voice, subdued but stiff from nervousness. Through her blurred vision Yuri saw a bald man taking hold of her cheek.

"She's spitting blood! I told you we had to get here quicker."

It *was* the rude woman from the phone who liked to make Yuri feel small with her weird lectures. But she wasn't behaving like usual.

"She bit her tongue, but she won't die if she's treated immediately. It's not like she bit it clean off," the man muttered quietly in response to the woman's high-pitched voice as though to tell Yuri that everything would be fine.

"Sayuri, don't you die here!" the woman cried. She was no longer the voice that always made fun of her. Yuri felt something begin to surface through the chaos of her mind.

Ah, that's right. My name is Sayuri.

Just as she came to that realization, she lost consciousness.

Sayuri's body slumped in the man's arms.

7

Chu returned to his small, dimly lit chamber. The low thrumming of monitors and the ticking of equipment vibrated softly in the air. With the curtains closed, the pale blue gleam of the monitors seemed to meld everything together.

He realized something was wrong the moment he stepped in.

Dropping into a crouch, he peeled his eyes.

Someone's here.

He held his breath and continued into the room, his senses sharpened to their extremes. He stayed low as he moved in, ready to lunge at a moment's notice. He walked down the corridor, past the dining area, and into the main room. Someone was sitting in his seat. The person sat perfectly still, eyes fixed on Chu, a figure blended completely into the darkness.

The interloper didn't appear to be armed, and was seated. *If the fucker tries anything I'll rush in for a quick kill.* Chu's mind raced as he stared at the shadow.

"Some fortress you've got here," the shadow spoke. Chu's eyes gradually adjusted to the dark until he could make out the man's face.

It wasn't one that he recognized.

The man's complexion was pale, and he wore a gray suit. His long black hair fell in waves, half covering a chiseled face. Pitched against the darkness he looked like a stereotypical ghost, yet his eyes, glowing deeply with a purgatorial blaze, showed fierce determination.

"How did you get in?" Chu asked quietly, keeping his emotions in check. The Tower was protected by multiple layers of security measures. Breaking in from the outside was impossible.

"Your security is exceptional. Quite challenging." The man crossed his tall legs. "Perhaps because you had not suspected anyone on the inside, though, it turned out to be more fragile than we'd anticipated. Just a few moments ago, we achieved our objective."

"What are you talking about?" demanded Chu.

The man grinned. "The client data."

Chu's eyes opened wide. He made his decision in a split second. He had to eliminate this man.

He readied every muscle in his body, watching for the chance to lunge forth.

"Killing me will do nothing to improve your predicament," the man announced flatly but with absolute confidence. "The data is already out. You can put up all the fight you want, but it's done."

"Then why are you here?"

Chu took a couple of steps closer. The man remained utterly still, eyes on Chu.

Okay. Now I'm close enough to snap his neck. Chu regained a little composure.

"I wanted to convey our gratitude for the data."

What the fuck are you talking about, you stole it—Chu caught the words before they left his throat.

"This place really is a paradise for the rich."

"How do you even know about us?"

"*A certain someone alerted us to the existence and purpose of this place.* It was still quite difficult to pinpoint your location. Even with informants, it took a long time to get this far." The man smiled, but he sounded disappointed. "Not many people would think to commodify murder. I'm partial to *ikebana* myself, but to use people as flowers, well…"

"I don't know what you're talking about. This is a brothel. Sure, it's illegal, but murder? You're dreaming," mocked Chu.

"To call it prostitution is rather euphemistic, don't you think? You traffic in human flesh, parading lives as products. I think of the elite as goldfish with unbalanced diets; they're never satisfied. They lust for things that are difficult to obtain. Their appetites know no limits. I'm sure you understand that more than anyone."

The man's carefully paced speech conveyed assurance and an impression that he knew everything.

Chu considered his options. It would be easy enough to kill him here and now. But if the man had somehow managed to smuggle out the database, rubbing out a point of contact was unwise. The smart move was to grab the tail, negotiate with—or destroy—the organization behind this man. In order to do that, Chu had to regain control of the conversation.

Tap tap, he clicked one foot against the floor.

"So just who are you? How did you get in?"

"I employ a woman who specializes in *slicing up* systems. She is a master at severing links and reconnecting them someplace else. You recently accepted a new recruit, so we had her line connected to us and made contact."

Yuri. Chu silently cursed himself.

"We arranged it so that pressing '1' for an internal call would reroute to our slicer. We kept contact to a minimum so as not to raise suspicion, and for food orders and such we placed a separate call to the original line."

Chu had never thought twice about Yuri making lengthy phone calls, nor had he cared to know what she was talking about. The hidden cameras only relayed images and were not designed to pick up sound. It was too late now, but Chu was angry with himself for the error.

"But how did you pull that off?"

"It was easy. Your janitors work for me."

"The janitors?"

"Yes, the contractors that clean the lobby, the corridors. Of course they didn't have access to the *deeper* parts of the Tower, but it was enough. You kept staff to a minimum to protect the secrecy of the place, but that ended up being your Achilles heel. The lack of eyes on the ground meant we only had to shut down the security cameras in order to move around freely. We eroded your system, gradually and methodically, and today we finally succeeded in breaking through. We have your client database and information on all of your crimes. I'm glad we were able to make it in time."

"In time?"

"Yes. *Before we had any victims on our hands.*"

Chu clicked his tongue and, keeping his eyes on the man, took a deep breath to calm himself. "I'm impressed. You don't look like yakuza. Are you with Public Security?"

"No," the man answered, smiling. He wore a gray tie and gray waistcoat under his gray suit. A gentleman from some B-movie, in the real world he looked like he was cosplaying.

"Then you're an insane drug addict. With an awful fashion sense to boot. I'd be too embarrassed to dress like that." Chu did his best to put him down, but the man's face showed no reaction whatsoever.

"Insane… Yes, perhaps that is the best way to describe me at the moment."

Chu wanted to spit on him. He remembered an article he'd read somewhere about a man who had masterminded a series of robberies in August—a man who dressed in gray. *Could it be…*

"I'm sure it's a pain to chat standing. Please, take a seat," the man instructed as though it was his own room.

Chu ignored him and stayed where he was. Being unable to take the lead, in fact being controlled was making him feel disgusted, but he relaxed his fighting stance a little. His first task was to find out more about the organization behind the man.

"Say all of it was true. What do you plan to do? Are you going to threaten me? Kill me?"

"I'm only here because I wanted to convey my gratitude."

Just as the man in gray spoke, his cell phone began to ring.

It was true, then, that they had gotten the customer data out of the building. The Tower was equipped with a signal blocker that prevented the use of cellular phones. If the man's phone was ringing, then the blocker had been taken offline, and it was possible to transmit the entire client database out of the building.

"Excuse me."

The man pulled out his phone, had a short conversation, then hung up.

"We've only just met, but it's about time I took my leave." The man stood and gave Chu a bow. "The data you kept in the Tower is extremely valuable to me. Thank you."

"What are you going to do with it?"

The man slowly turned to face Chu. "Your client data. Your security camera records. All the crimes you videotaped. They are all intrinsic parts of my plan."

"I'm asking what you're going to do with them!" Chu raised his voice, nearly shouting.

The man stood stock still, smiling. "We have also discovered where you dispose of the bodies."

"Blackmail?" Chu felt ready to snap. He sucked in a deep breath and tapped his fingers against his thigh to try and calm himself.

Tap tap.

"Blackmail. How absurd." The man shook his head slowly.

"Then what?"

"I can't tell you. You will find out soon enough."

The man shrugged and began to walk slowly towards Chu until he was in arm's reach.

I could kill him now.

But Chu couldn't move. It was as if he were possessed. The man stopped directly before him. He was intimidating enough to make Chu's hairs stand on end, and he had to force himself to not back away.

"I will not get in the way of your business. I do not approve of what you do here but it is not my place to fix it. That is the job of our corrupt police force. Not that I can place much hope in that happening when the brass there frequents your establishment."

So he really does have the data.

The man's words served to further drive home the enormity of the situation. There was no way Chu could afford to kill him now. He had to let him swim free then decimate his organization.

Chu gazed at the man like a predator, and the man returned his stare, his grin unwavering.

"I have two points of counsel."

The man's eyes seemed to transfigure and pierce Chu's.

"First, you should probably stop the auctions."

"If I do that, the Tower is meaningless," Chu spat.

"It's for your own benefit. If you continue, you will effectively shorten your life. If possible, I would like you to put the business into hibernation while convincing your superiors that it is being run as before. Whatever you do, you mustn't create any more victims. I would like you to maintain the facade for about a year and a half. I will cover any costs if your setup requires that you forward part of the proceeds to some higher tier."

"And if I don't, you'll come for me?"

"*No, it won't be me.*"

The man was definitely with some organization or other. *I have to get more information. I'll have to stay in line, do as he says until I come up with a good plan.* Chu had the backing of a large organization himself. He would do everything in his power to find out about this man, then destroy him.

The man took Chu's silence as agreement. "I'm so glad I have your consent on this. Let's see if we can keep it up for the next point." The man paused, raised his seemingly bloodless right hand, and pointed a finger at Chu. "My second counsel is that you follow my orders and give me any information that I was unable to obtain."

Chu laughed like a balloon bursting, eyes opening wide at the man's coercive tone. "Now why do I have to do that?"

"Why? I hope you realize that the information I did obtain today means you're finished," the man replied, looking honestly puzzled.

"Don't fuck with me. I don't owe you anything, and there's no benefit for me in that."

"There is indeed a benefit."

The man parted his lips, handsome yet pale and bloodless. Chu felt fear for the first time in a long while upon seeing that smile.

"The benefit is that I wouldn't have you killed. Heed my counsel, and I guarantee your safety. I will be in touch again soon. Make sure you follow through."

You're fucking kidding me.

Blood rushed to Chu's head. He was taken with the sudden urge to beat the man to death. To kill him now, however, meant losing a lead as to the whereabouts of the stolen information. He'd find a chink in the man's armor one day. Moreover, he couldn't let his superiors find out about this. If they did, he was as good as dead. He had to find an out somehow, and he would have to do it alone.

The man nodded as though he could see Chu's inner conflict,

took a step closer, and rested a hand on Chu's shoulder. The hand felt deadly cold and Chu shivered as though he'd been frozen to the core.

"Oh yes, I almost forgot." The man raised a finger and pointed towards a bag in the corner of the room. "I'm going to buy one of your girls. The bag has twenty million inside. With it, I buy back her identity and her body. The original bidder, Togo, has of course given us his happy consent."

The man removed his hand from Chu's shoulder and left the room ghost-like, without making a sound.

Finally alone, Chu let out a loud sigh, picked up the monitor closest to him, and slammed it into the floor.

The man emerged from the Tower and got into the passenger seat of a nondescript car parked on the side of the street.

"Thank you," he said to the burly, wide-shouldered man in the driver's seat as the car pulled slowly away. Then he breathed softly and asked, "What's the situation, Takano?"

Over forty but built like a boulder, the driver answered, "We have successfully freed our target. She'd bitten her tongue in an attempt to commit suicide, so I treated her before bringing her out of the Tower with Kozue. Kozue hacked and destroyed their systems from the inside and deleted all traces of our visit. And of course all security cameras are offline."

"And the client data?"

"Transferred to multiple servers. We made another copy, just in case." Takano pulled a memory stick from his breast pocket and passed it to the man. "The data is on this drive."

"Good," the man said and fell silent, his eyes on the memory stick.

Takano looked at the man's profile and opened his mouth, but shut it again.

"You have something you want to ask?" The driver's heart jumped when the man, his eyes still on the memory stick, spoke again.

"Just wondering... What are we going to do about the Tower?"

asked Takano, his body shaking, his rage barely under control. He knew the Tower's exact *function*.

"What do you want to do?" The man smiled thinly as though he could read Takano's every thought. The driver was at a loss for words. "Do you want to kill them?" the man asked quietly.

"Yes." Takano nodded. His eyes briefly *went vacant like he was recalling something.*

"I understand your desire. But it's not time yet," the man said, turning to look at Takano, whose face hardened under the penetrating gaze. "*We need more time to achieve both objectives, yours and mine.*"

A voice like the earth rumbling. A growl that fumed with a deep grudge. An order from an absolute authority, impossible to disobey.

"I've taken the necessary steps to ensure there are no more victims. We will be watching."

"Of course."

Relieved, Takano decided to stop thinking about it and to concentrate on driving.

The man looked again at the memory stick. He muttered, as though trying to convince himself, "Almost all of the pieces are in my hands. Now we only need to wait for the right time. You were good for nothing, Lord Almighty. Neglecting to reform evil, you let it run free and even live in peace. Lord Almighty, you allowed a twisted world to run its course. You forsook me, un-merciful God. Hapless God, good for nothing. Look on in envy as you do nothing."

The memory stick creaked as the man tensed his hands.

"*Lord Good-for-Nothing, I shall be your proxy.*"

Bloodshot eyes opened wide like a beast's, the man gnashed his teeth.

CHAPTER THREE

1

November 29, 2013

Yuki Iwazaki hurried home in his designer suit, bracing himself against the biting wind. Carefully polished leather shoes. A leather briefcase worth over a hundred thousand yen. On his left wrist, a luxury foreign-brand watch. It was as though the man had covered himself with wealth in a bid to keep people from seeing his true character.

He had been busy with admin work and lost track of the time. He glanced at his watch—after 1 a.m. There was no one else around. It was almost December, and it felt more like winter each day. He had a slight headache from the bone-scraping cold. His wiry frame shivered. He cursed himself for not having worn a coat, but he would be home in five minutes. He rubbed his leather-gloved hands together to try and warm himself a little.

It was a fifteen-minute walk from his office to his apartment in the high-end housing block. Too close to drive, too annoying to take a bike. He had decided to commute on foot and now enjoyed it as a chance to exercise his out-of-shape body. Health came first.

As he expelled white breath, his hand subconsciously traced

over the left side of his chest, over the gold badge he wore on the lapel of his suit—his identity. He had passed the bar exam with flying colors and set up a legal practice with money from his parents. His personal history meant that he had wanted at all costs to avoid joining a big firm despite the chance to gain experience. A lawyer in the family had introduced him to some clients, and his practice was doing well enough.

He was amazed that he had been able to re-establish himself so well since *that unpleasant affair*. He had come close to losing everything, all because he had gone along with those fools.

His future. He knew perfectly well it would not last forever, but his future was so important to him he often tricked himself into thinking that it stretched endlessly before him. Nothing was more important to him.

The kidnapping and murder of a mother and child from Miyamae. Iwazaki was one of the accomplices, the criminals who had beaten someone's wife and child to death. The assault had been his idea, and he'd been the one to suggest they release photos of the act.

He clucked his tongue as he continued walking. The scandal had nearly caused his life to run aground. Those fools had taken the practical joke too far. There was no need to have killed anyone. His white breath streamed out as his thoughts raced.

The folly of youth. Unchecked libido and curiosity. A harmless prank.

Iwazaki wanted to wipe the memory clean away, but at the same time a part of him wanted to hang onto it forever. He would never be able to experience it again. He would live his new life to the full, forever keeping his treasured memory a secret. His job as a lawyer was going well and he had a wife and two kids. He had social standing and plenty of income. Just as each step now brought him closer to home, so too had he been able to take sure steps towards building a happy life. Of course, that was how it ought to be. He had the right. No one could get in his way.

His apartment came into view. The one he had bought at twenty-six. His parents had helped out, but it was still his hundred-million-yen castle. Everything was on track. His wife and kids were happy, probably sound asleep. The thought made him smile.

That was when it happened. He saw someone standing under the glow of a streetlamp. He seemed to be waiting for Iwazaki. He was utterly silent and seemed intangible, like a ghost.

Iwazaki came to an abrupt stop and strained his eyes. He saw a man plastered in gray. The man wore a hat that covered his features, but Iwazaki could make out the deathly pale skin around his mouth. It was as if the man had no blood.

"Sorry to disturb you at this late hour," the man in gray said, curling his nearly gray lips.

Was he smiling? As the thought crossed Iwazaki's mind, he remembered the gray man who had been all over the news. He sensed someone behind him.

The next moment, he fell unconscious.

2

December 2, 2013

Gakuto Namiki made his way unsteadily down the dimly lit street. He had been drinking alone at a pub since 6 p.m. After six beers he had paid a call to an outpost of the sex industry. Now he was on his way home. The alcohol helped relax his body after a hard day at work, and his body felt light *after the act.*

Whenever he was due a day off at the factory he went out drinking alone and visited the parlor. He liked one of the women there. She was cute, with a snaggletooth visible when she smiled. Born where it often snowed, her skin was so white it was almost transparent. She had blotches here and there, but that was to be expected from someone in her profession. She let him do more than the rules allowed. He wanted her for himself.

Since *that affair*, Namiki found he could no longer date *amateurs*, so he had his fun with sex workers. He had tried dating for a while, but he was only able to get an erection with prostitutes. Guilt-driven impotence. That could have been it. But more than that, Namiki had simply become unable to derive pleasure through normal means. Even the parlors he visited had to be BDSM-themed. Sometimes he liked to dominate, sometimes he liked to be dominated. Both got him excited.

He let out his aggressive side when he played the dominator, allowing him to relive the abnormal excitement he'd experienced that one time. When he was being dominated, he was able to put himself in his victim's shoes and revel in the immorality. He felt genuine regret for having committed murder. But the sensations he had felt at the time had taken root deep inside of him and twisted him.

He looked at his wristwatch. It was already after 11 p.m. Since he had the next day off he could drink a little more after getting home. Then he would sleep like a log. He rubbed his bulging belly and sighed heavily.

As he continued drunkenly down the street, he suddenly tripped on something. He lost his balance but managed to find his footing and stop himself from falling. He clucked his tongue and looked down to see what he had tripped over, but he couldn't see in the dark.

He looked up and huffed, his breath stinking of alcohol.

There was someone there, who hadn't been until just now. A man dressed completely in gray. Not just his clothes, but his entire appearance and presence seemed grayed out.

Namiki felt suddenly flustered. He didn't know why, but something told him that *he shouldn't let this man find him*. He tried to run but his legs didn't comply, only his mind rushing.

The man snorted lightly as though he sensed Namiki's panic and lifted up the brim of the hat that covered half of his face. Eyes smoldering with hellish intensity pierced right through Namiki, freezing his heart. He started to choke, like something had caught in his throat.

"I'm here to collect you."

With that somebody grabbed Namiki from behind and threw him into a car.

3

December 4, 2013

Makoto Goda sat with the laced curtains drawn closed, drinking wine in his dim abode—the penthouse of an eight-floor apartment building. Rain lashed against large picture windows that only revealed heavy rainclouds.

Goda gulped down some wine and took a mouthful of cheese. It was his third day on parole. He was frustrated, not yet enjoying his new freedom after a succession of annoyances. His parents had looked terrified, like he was some kind of monster. They'd told him they wanted him to look after the apartment building and literally begged him to leave. They didn't celebrate his release, instead kicking him out of home and forcing him to live in the apartment in Taito. They said they would send him money aside from the rental income in exchange for him never returning home. He had been disgusted, but he had stopped himself from doing anything more than kicking over the shoebox.

Who'd fucking want to live at home anyway, Goda swore in silence, tipping more wine into his glass. He missed and soaked the table, the red liquid spreading like blood.

It wasn't a bad deal. His parents managed a number of companies that turned over enormous profits. The Taito apartment they'd given him was a three-bedroom and rented for two hundred thousand yen a month. The design was high-end and it was close to the train station. Adding the money they remitted each month, his income was probably several times higher than the average salaryman's. As an ex-con he hadn't thought he'd be able to get a proper job, and his parents' offer was sweeter than he had any right to expect. Yet he couldn't stomach their attitude towards him. Treating him like a parasite. Tremulous, fearful looks. Barely deigning to speak to him.

"Why should I give a shit about them," Goda muttered, annoyed.

Even before *that affair*, his parents had always treated him like he didn't exist. Their idea of raising him was to shower him with money like they were watering a plant. They had never made him feel loved. They inhabited their own worlds and neither had made any room for him.

Not that that's why he'd done it, of course. He'd done it because he had wanted to. He had made the decision to abuse his status as a minor and commit the most atrociously violent crime he could imagine. He had been ready to accept the price of three years in a juvenile detention center. He hadn't anticipated the prosecution pushing to try him as an adult. He had pleaded diminished mental capacity, but even that had not resulted in the sentence being shortened as much as he had hoped. The prosecutor was skilled enough to collar him with a twelve-year sentence. He'd spent the last ten years behind bars. He regretted *not putting on a better act for the judge*.

But he was still twenty-seven. It wasn't too late for him to celebrate life. He had money—and with money he could enjoy life without ever doing a day's work. Goda poured himself some more wine, downed it like it was water, and furrowed his brows.

There was one more regret. He'd have loved to *enjoy that affair for longer*.

He hadn't thought they would be found out so quickly. And he hadn't expected women to break so easily. It had been disappointing to discover just how paltry human fortitude was.

Just recalling the affair excited him. Screaming, begging, despair, resignation, and finally, nothing. Each phase had been wonderful. The bereaved husband had sat in the public gallery during the trial. His despondent look had been a thing of beauty.

I stole everything from the woman you loved and made it all mine.

He had felt superior to the husband. He had been unable to stop himself from breaking into a smile.

Goda returned from the sweet reverie, opened his eyes, and laughed at himself. He had spent enough time reliving the past while locked up. Now that he was free it was time to start looking forward. He wanted to experience something like that again. But he was no longer a minor, and a repeat offense could earn him capital punishment. He had to somehow make sure he wouldn't be caught. Find a way to avoid discovery. Something to keep his crimes in the dark.

He remembered something he'd seen on the news. They'd discovered a place where you could buy women and do whatever you wanted with them. In Ikebukuro or somewhere. Police had seized the building in question, but the perps were still at large, and the authorities hadn't learned anything about the organization behind it. Goda licked his lips. If the perps were still alive, he hoped they'd build another place like that. Maybe another one already existed.

A place where money could buy *true luxury*. They lived in a society where money let you do anything. From the capitalist point of view of the strong exploiting the weak, there was nothing wrong with buying someone's life. If anything, it made perfect sense. It had to be shouted from the rooftops that the poor were fertilizer for the rich, that lip-service like "protect the weak" and "aid thy neighbor" were mere pleasantries to patch up society's surface. The weak were meat, and society only grew when they were consumed.

And I'm on the consuming side.

Goda repeated the phrase in his mind, violently gulping down another mouthful of wine. The blood-red liquid dribbled from the corners of his mouth. He used the back of his hand to wipe it away, then slowly turned to look out the windows. The clouded sky was showing signs of darkening.

Guess I should turn on the lights.

As Goda got up he noticed something odd. A something reflected in the window glass.

"Sorry to disturb your R&R," the something boomed in a voice that seemed to shake the earth. It took a step closer.

Goda instantly jumped up and swung around to face it. He cowered, instinctively sensing danger. The something was tall, pointed like a lance, and covered in gray. It wore a gray hat over half of its face and its long black hair fell in waves at the sides. It was the kind of get-up Goda would have usually laughed at, but he was so overwhelmed he couldn't even begin to find it funny.

A gray man. It was the only way to describe him.

"Who are you?"

Goda tried to sound threatening. He picked up the wine bottle and readied himself.

"Answer me! Who are you?" Goda shouted again. He could see that the gray man was unarmed. He had the advantage.

"My name is Gray," the man said, taking another step closer.

Goda measured the distance between them as his pulse raced, ready to bring the bottle down on the man's head at a moment's notice. The hat covering half of the man's face made it hard to read his expression, heightening Goda's fear.

"Never heard of you, jackass!" Goda yelled as if to obscure the fact that his body was trembling.

Gray wordlessly strode closer, forcing Goda to step back. "You don't know me? And I thought myself pretty famous."

"The hell? What are you, nuts?" Goda sneered.

Gray took yet another step forward; a leisurely, relaxed movement. Goda took another step back. Gray moved closer.

It's legit self-defense. I can kill the fucker.

Goda tensed his hand around the glass bottle. He was shaking from a combination of fear and vexation. Gray took another step. Goda gauged the distance between them.

One more step… One more step… Now!

Goda held his breath and swung the bottle upwards. Gray reacted with surprising agility, closing the gap between them in an instant. He stretched out a long arm and grabbed Goda tightly by the neck and smashed him to the floor.

Caught off guard, Goda had taken a strong blow to the back of his head. He muttered something unintelligible as his hand released the bottle. There was a crunching sound as his windpipe was crushed. He writhed desperately, struggling to free himself from Gray's hold. Then, unexpectedly, Gray relaxed his grip.

I have to fight back.

Goda managed to stagger to his feet.

You're dead.

He was drooling as he got ready to pounce. In that instant a pair of hands reached out and pinioned his arms behind his back and forced something into his mouth. Goda immediately lost consciousness.

Takano stood behind him, eyes burning with anger. He roughly stuffed Goda into a body bag then left the room with Gray as though nothing had happened.

*

Makoto Goda woke to see a dimly lit room. It took him a while to take in his current situation. He had been laid out on the floor. His head was heavy. He tried to bring his hands to his forehead but found he couldn't move at all. That was when he realized he had been tied up. He swallowed to moisten his parched throat, then attempted to trace back his memory, but he couldn't recall what had happened.

The room was lit by a single naked bulb suspended from the ceiling. It was dark but he could make out his surroundings. He scanned the room, moving only his eyes. There was an oversized bag near his head. *So I was brought here in that.* He could make out two larger lumps lying on the floor near the edge of his field of vision. He strained his eyes and saw that the lumps were people—people he realized he knew.

Iwazaki and Namiki. The partners with whom he had committed murder. They appeared to be unconscious, with their eyes closed and their mouths open and slack. Goda wanted to move, but his body was frozen with fear and he had no idea what was behind him.

Yet he understood everything once he saw that Iwazaki and Namiki were there, too. The man called Gray must have some connection with what they'd done. But who the hell was he? Goda couldn't recall ever seeing him before.

"Ah, you're awake," a voice dispelled the quiet.

Goda started, widened his eyes, and held his breath. As the

room fell back into frozen silence, he struggled to control his trembling and pivoted his eyes round and round on the lookout for sudden developments. He sensed someone standing next to his head, but when he strained his eyes to see, he was kicked in the abdomen and faced in a new direction, toward a human figure.

Pallid skin, jet black hair and eyes. Gaunt cheeks and a disproportionately large mouth. He looked so spooky Goda could have believed the man was a vampire. He was wearing a suit that was gray from top to bottom. He was tall, elongated, like a spear. His voice seemed to well up from the earth itself.

"How do you feel?" Gray asked, smiling from his chair. The dull light from the hanging bulb made him appear like a ghost.

"Where am I?" Goda spat. He moaned, his face distorted from the pain in his abdomen.

"Not your concern," Gray said, crossing his legs.

"What do you want?" Goda demanded.

Gray didn't reply.

"Please just tell me," Goda pled. It was evident that his life was in this man's hands. He had to be careful not to provoke him.

"Why is it not clear to you?" Gray's voice trembled slightly. "How can you not understand why the three of you are here?"

"Is it because of the crime we committed?" Goda offered immediately. Gray didn't reply, but the silence was confirmation enough. "I… I know it was wrong. I spend every day regretting it. It haunted me every day I was on the inside, in prison. Still does. I honestly regret what we did."

Goda forced himself up, still bound, sitting with his legs formally folded underneath him, supplicating to the man as if in prayer. As he did, he cursed the man for bringing up a crime from so long ago. *How's he connected? A relative? A cop? Maybe he's just some jackass who thinks he's some kind of defender of justice.*

Goda's thoughts raced as he continued to talk. "There was something wrong with my head. Really, I'd lost it. I was afraid of myself. To think I did something like that… I want to make amends to the family and relatives, to everyone affected."

Goda was amused by how easily the words spilled forth. Spouting promises he had no intention of keeping was as easy as breathing. Even back in court, it had been his silver tongue that had come to his aid. And now it would get him out of this. He opened his mouth, taking care not to reveal his true thoughts.

"I will regret it for my whole life, and I will make amends. I will live for people now. I swore that I would do so back in prison. In my heart I've offered penance to God. The fact that I committed such crimes makes me want to kill myself, to apologize through my own death. I mean it. You have to believe me. So please, don't do anything rash."

Gray rose soundlessly. "Untie him."

Takano, who stood behind Goda, sliced off the ropes without a word. Goda moved his hands to check they had been freed. *I win,* he thought. *Now I can escape from this freak.*

"Give him the knife," Gray said. Takano passed him the knife from behind.

Huh? Goda's mouth fell open. He stared at Gray.

"Gouge out one of your eyes with that knife."

Goda couldn't take in the words' sense.

"If you can do that, I will let you go," Gray said, still standing.

Gouge out an eye?! Goda silently wondered if the man was an idiot as the meaning of his words sank in. *How the hell can I do something like that?* Goda scanned the room, trying to take in as much information as he could.

He didn't know where he was, but he knew his opponents were two men. He could take out the one before him if he caught him off guard, then it would be one on one with the man behind him. He could pull it off. He had to gain the upper hand.

Gray paced towards him, carelessly it seemed. "You said that you were so full of regret you could kill yourself. I'd like to see some evidence of that. Now, stab yourself."

Goda staggered upright. Gray's words no longer reached him. He sensed that the man behind him had moved a little farther away. Gray was the closer of the two, and Goda was the one with the knife. He was being confined against his will. Anything he did would surely pass as self-defense.

"Okay, fine." Goda silently cursed as he raised the knife to his face, trying to work out this man's connection to the case. The knife glinted as it caught the light from the bulb, momentarily reflecting his own face, dyed the color of madness.

Goda dropped into a crouch and turned the knife to point at the man in gray.

"Yeah, right! Like you could order me around!"

He charged, closing the distance between them and thrusting the blade directly at Gray's heart. How he'd missed the feeling of knife sinking into flesh.

Goda's face contorted when the expected intoxicating pleasure was not forthcoming. The knife had been stopped. *A stab vest.*

"Motherfucker!" Goda yelled, sliding the knife upwards in a bid for the man's throat. Before he had the chance, Gray knocked the knife to the floor and wrapped both his hands around Goda's neck. The man's powerful fingers dug in with enough force to shred it to ribbons. Goda began to lose consciousness.

"If you'd gouged out your eye, we might have been able to proceed differently."

Gray's hold tightened. Goda's neck made an audible crunch. The whites of his eyes turned red as they strained nearly out of their sockets. Still the pressure on his neck mounted.

"Do you hold yourself that dear?"

Goda squirmed. He waved his fists blindly and drove a knee into the man, who didn't even flinch. He was solid as a tree.

Goda finally passed out.

"You will pay for your crimes once I've had my revenge on this country," Gray whispered as he released his grip. He turned to Takano, who stood by in silence.

He was gazing down at Goda as upon a worm.

CHAPTER FOUR

1

Takeshi Serizawa slumped his exhausted frame into the hard seat of the train. The soles of his shoes were worn down. His legs fidgeted. The hair by his temples was already graying—an outcome of his distress. He looked older than his thirty-seven years. His skin was still supple and he seemed to look after his appearance, but his air made him seem aged.

He gazed vacantly at the tabloid ads hanging from the ceiling. As usual the headlines were mostly an array of political scandals and celebrity gossip, but a few continued to run articles on the raid at the jewelry exhibition four months ago.

"Gray…" the word leaked through his dehydrated, chapped lips, only to be drowned out by the sounds of the train wheels against the rails.

The raid at the Grand Capital Hotel. Close to ten billion yen's worth in gems stolen. Witnesses had testified that it had been carried out by a man attired in gray, a girl in a school uniform, plus about ten others in face masks. The hotel's security camera footage showed them clearly. It was a bold heist of an exhibition with lax security. An escape route that was impossible to trace. A perfect crime.

It was just like the preceding case. The only difference was the involvement of a girl in school uniform. The police had tried to work out her identity by tracing the outfit she had been wearing, but it had apparently been specially made. The uniform as described by the witnesses simply didn't exist. The raid had taken place in August, four months ago to the day. The public intuited a recurrence of the serial robberies that had occurred just the year before.

Those four days.

The robberies, perpetrated by the gray man, had come out of the blue in August 2012. Naturally, such cases tended to be unforeseen, but those particular robberies had sent shockwaves through the entire country like a natural disaster. They'd left a powerful impression on society that lasted even now.

A total of thirty billion yen stolen.

A series of consecutive, nearly simultaneous raids on banks, armored trucks, and large jewelry stores and the like for their cash and gems.

A one-hundred-percent success rate.

And a zero-percent arrest rate. For such a thing to happen nowadays seemed like a dream or illusion. The robberies started on August 12th and continued until August 15th. The series of sensational thefts, dubbed the "August Raids," bred mass speculation. The key factors that piqued the public's interest were the lack of casualties and the fact that no one had suffered any personal financial loss since the attacks had only targeted top-level banks and jewelry stores.

In the wake a small theater company staged a play based on the events of the still unsolved case. Tabloids referred to the perp as Robin Hood, which elicited heavy criticism from the intelligentsia. Gray became a trendy color, and people were seen parading through town dressed entirely in it as though it were a costume. At first the police stopped them for questioning but their numbers became too great, and over time the cops left them alone.

Serizawa recalled a phrase that kept cropping up in relation to the robberies: *no leads as of yet.* It was rumored that the crimes had been committed by a single, unified organization. Not that anyone had any evidence; it was simply a surmise based on combining certain facts—the crimes had been perfectly executed, committed over only four days with no casualties, the criminals were all still at large, and seemingly outlandish witness testimony received mutual corroboration.

Yet everyone was *convinced* that the whole thing had been the work of one organization, mainly due to the witness reports. A consistent profile emerged from testimony given by the armored truck drivers, the bank clerks, the jewelry store workers, and a smattering of passersby. Plus there were the security camera tapes.

The gray man.

His outfit was gray, his skin was sallow, nearly gray, and wavy long black hair fell over half of his face. Sometimes he was seen in a gray hat, sometimes not. An anachronistic British gentleman. Dressed like a dandy, towering above the people around him. Slender yet solidly built. Witnesses said the oddly garbed man staged the raids along with accomplices.

He had not been present at every crime scene. There had been ten raids over the four-day period, but the man in gray was only reported to have been present at four. In other words, he had attended one raid per day. Reports from the other six cases all contained statements claiming that the assailants were all wearing "something gray," and footage from the various security cameras installed at the banks and jewelry stores backed this up. The police had conducted a thorough analysis of the footage but were unable to glean anything to positively identify the gang.

The raids, which had taken place in broad daylight, must have been planned out thoroughly, and were indeed executed so flawlessly as to be deflating. It had almost seemed as though the perps were simply taking back something that belonged to them in the first place.

The raids became a headache for the police. Why would a gang about to commit a robbery dress in a way that made them stand out? It practically guaranteed robust witness statements. Any talk of gray men would normally be dismissed as nonsense arising out of confusion, but the description from those who'd seen the main culprit at four separate locations accorded so well it was if they had conspired beforehand. Security footage of an assortment of gray men only made their statements harder to laugh off.

The police marked the man in gray as the ringleader and began to search for him. Based on his daredevil attire and crime, they profiled him as some type of fantasist with a desire for an audience. They tried to ascertain his escape route by checking footage from all security cameras in the vicinity of each site but couldn't find a single recording of any figure fitting his specific description. *It was as though he knew beforehand the location of each and every camera and its angle.*

On top of that, a large number of relevant wireless surveillance devices in the city had been hacked into and rendered inoperable during the raids.

The police next tried to follow the route exploited by the suspected hacker. They found traces, but it proved extremely difficult to pinpoint the origin. The hacker's skillfulness was worrisome. When they eventually managed to track down the route, it led them to internet cafes with loose ID policies or an empty room in an abandoned building where a number of computers used for the hacking would be recovered without yielding any new leads.

Investigations at the crime scenes had been rough-going, too. The police found the targeted banks and jewelers to be far from cooperative. Even after more typical robberies, there were always instances where the affected party was less than willing to cooperate, wary that dirty laundry would be exposed in the process. This was especially true with banks, where one could hit paydirt with a single tap. With the August Raids, however, this unwillingness came close to plain refusal. The attempts to keep the police away suggested that they were afraid, perhaps even under blackmail. As a result, the investigations stumbled from the outset.

Since there were clear signs of organized crime, it was only natural for Public Security to get involved. The Organizations Section carried out a series of thorough enquiries into a number of cults, ultra-nationalist and extreme-left organizations, gangs, mafia and foreign syndicates, but came up with nothing. Besides, the PS's country-wide network of informants would have tipped off the force if any of the organizations had been planning something on the scale of the August Raids. That there had been no tip-off could only mean that the organization was independent, self-sufficient with no external ties, and comprised of members who did not leak. Yet, such organizations simply didn't exist.

A man in gray. Like a character from a fairy tale. The public was utterly captivated by him. Serizawa was one of those people. He had read countless articles on the man.

The train pulled into Futago-Shinchi Station.

Serizawa trudged off the platform and left through the exit. He started to walk down a narrow, barely lit street. He walked for around fifteen minutes until a building appeared in the darkness, as if on a whim. The sign bearing the name "Chateau d'If" in gothic lettering wavered like a mirage thanks to the flickering bulbs behind it.

As he opened the door with its plate of frosted glass a bell announced his arrival.

Rokuzo's skinny frame was visible across the counter. He gave Serizawa a quick, indifferent look before turning away. His back was a little hunched, but his face was twisted in a stubborn look, warning the world he'd live another thirty years yet.

"Still alive, eh?"

Rokuzo snorted, holding a hand to his thick round glasses. "I can't help thinking you'll be the first of us to go."

"I'm still thirty-seven. I'd have to be caught up in a serious mess to die before you. The way of the world says you go first," Serizawa disagreed, taking a seat at the counter. As usual, there were no other customers.

Rokuzo had bought the place ten years ago, back when it

was still a rundown coffee house, wanting somewhere to die a dog's death rather than spend his last years in an old folks' home. Chateau d'If had been open for business every day since, but Serizawa had never seen any customers.

Rokuzo's background remained a mystery. Based on bits of conversation, Serizawa's guess was retired cop, but it was pure speculation as Rokuzo never seemed to want to talk about his past. Serizawa, for his part, had never asked point-blank.

"I'm just looking forward to bidding this shitty world farewell so that I can have a soak in the tepid waters of heaven. It'll be a darn sight better than a hot spring resort packed full of tourists." Rokuzo seemed to mean what he said—the man appeared to harbor no lingering attachments to the world.

"The world's a tough place. Maybe you'll set up shop in heaven, too. Just keep a seat for me for when I get there."

"If I find your seat I'll chuck it down for you, don't worry."

"I doubt hell would like having me around."

"Guess you'd better do your best to stay alive until they figure out which place you're headed." Rokuzo chuckled wheezily through his shrunken windpipe, poured whisky up to the brim of a heavy glass, and put it down in front of Serizawa.

"No ice?"

"This'll warm you up," Rokuzo said, jerking his chin towards the glass.

Serizawa looked at the dark whisky and took a small sip. He made a sound like a burp as his throat burned. He felt his body warm up as the liquid dropped into his stomach, as though someone had kindled a fire inside him. He felt a sudden pang of hunger and his stomach rumbled.

"Got any food?"

"Yup."

"I'll take whatever you've got."

"That'll be 3,000 yen."

Rokuzo gave him a shrewd glance and disappeared into the back of the bar. He came back almost immediately and put down a plate in front of Serizawa. It contained ten artlessly arranged slices of ham.

Serizawa frowned. "That it?"

"I've got some instant curry. No rice, though."

Rokuzo chuckled, adding that it would be another 3,000 yen, of course. Serizawa picked up a slice of ham, threw it into his mouth, and retorted that if he paid it would be in place of any condolence money at Rokuzo's funeral.

It was roughly five years ago that Serizawa, a detective for the Kanagawa Prefectural Police, had begun frequenting Rokuzo's bar. It more or less coincided with his increasing disillusionment with his job as a detective. He was exhausted by his job, having to constantly suss out trouble, and increasingly doubtful of the police system at large.

One day he had happened to find Chateau d'If and, after a while, Rokuzo had become his *ass's ears*. Serizawa was not allowed to discuss work or any investigatory leads, not even with his family. Yet, weighed down with resentment and exhaustion, he found it increasingly hard to hold back. His need to vent steam had eventually gotten the better of him until he found himself telling Rokuzo about his work. He had felt guilty for violating a taboo, but it was nothing compared to the sense of liberation that came with it. Besides, this loner Rokuzo, having turned his back on society, seemed unlikely to spread information. That assuaged Serizawa's sense of unease and further spurred his urge to talk. He felt that having someone to talk to helped alleviate his stress, so he came to discuss more and more cases, even the ones he was currently investigating. Any remaining traces of guilt had evaporated, and Rokuzo of Chateau d'If had played the *ass's ears* role for five years.

There was no music inside the dimly lit bar. Serizawa took slow sips of his whisky. Rokuzo seemed to have forgotten about playing host and sat on a stool behind the counter reading a faded old paperback. There was an ancient TV set behind him. Sometimes he had the news on but today it was switched off.

Silence reigned.

Serizawa replaced the heavy-bottomed glass on the bar

counter with a thump. "You've heard about the mess in Ike-bukuro, right? It's inhuman," he muttered, staring at the amber liquid that now filled just a quarter of the glass.

Rokuzo looked up, a token response. "Oh, the giant prostitution ring. Looked pretty rough."

"They'd rented out a building of luxury apartments and put runaway girls to work. 'Rough' doesn't even begin to describe it. They could have left it at selling the girls' bodies, but no, they had to go and sell their *lives*. It's the end of the world." Serizawa's voice dripped venom.

They had been running the operation from a luxury apartment not far from Ikebukuro Station. It was like something out of a tasteless horror movie. They lured in runaway girls—or girls who just spent many nights away from home—lured them into prostitution and paraded them as items for auction, where the winning bidder earned the right to kill them. A madman's paradise. The ages of the girls ranged from ten to eighteen years old. Their bodies, only six unearthed so far, had been hacked into small pieces. That information was yet to be released publicly.

"These were children, minors that had gone missing. You'd expect their parents to be desperately searching for them. But I heard the folks of three of the four girls we've been able to identify acted like they'd forgotten their daughters had gone missing in the first place. And we call these people parents? It's fucking laughable." Serizawa's eyes glowered at Rokuzo as he offloaded the anger that had lodged in his gut.

"Three… Meaning you haven't met the fourth one's folks yet?" Rokuzo asked, unperturbed by Serizawa's gaze.

"The parents of the fourth girl had been murdered."

"Murdered?" Rokuzo's eyes narrowed.

"We found the bones. It happened some while ago. It looks like the girl had been living with their dead bodies, commuting to school like normal. She was expelled when the school found out she had been making a killing working an extortion racket. According to her neighbors, the girl's parents had been arrested once over marijuana use, and they'd been forcing their own daughter to earn money *in all kinds of ways* since grade school. It's ugly. The other girls who'd been trapped in the building said she was in league with the perps. Anyway, she's dead now."

"Maybe a split with her employers?"

"Dunno, but that's a possibility. Her body was still fresh, killed with a single bullet to the head. The girls we managed to rescue said she was known as Suiren."

Rokuzo muttered some words of a Buddhist prayer. "And the identities of the other bodies?"

"Their limbs were severed, teeth and fingerprints removed. Then they were buried in concrete. I mean, what the hell kind of way is that to treat human beings? Their bodies had started to decompose. We'll get there, but it'll take a while to work out their identities. And I guarantee we're going to see more bodies before this case is closed."

"End of the world."

"Indeed. It looks like they'd been running the business there for quite a while. We were lucky to get an anonymous tip-off. We think there'll be more bodies." Serizawa used the whisky to moisten his throat a little. "We searched the areas the informant shared with us, but we only found the six so far. One of them was from our jurisdiction and the locals are abuzz about it. Do you know how many people go missing in a given year?"

"Including cases not officially recognized, about two hundred thousand?"

"Oh, you know."

"It was in a magazine I read the other day."

"Hm." Serizawa pulled a moody face at Rokuzo's nonchalant answer. "Whatever. It's not such a rare occurrence for disappearances to happen in Miyamae's jurisdiction. Add the number of kids running away from home and you get a pretty sizable figure. Now we've been buried under a mountain of requests to set up investigations for each of them, all because of this case. We don't have enough hands as it is. There's no way we can investigate them all."

"But one of those requests might end up being another victim.

Complaining that you don't have the manpower makes for a pretty poor excuse."

"Then they'll have to increase our ranks and our pay. It's all the useless politicians raking it in for getting nothing done that's speeding up Japan's decay." Serizawa's mouth curled into a sneer.

Rokuzo conceded the point and chuckled. "So, do you have any idea who the perps are?" he asked, yawning. His attitude made it difficult to tell if he was actually interested.

"Not yet. They did a thorough job of cleaning up behind themselves, to say nothing of info they had on their clientele. The only lead we have is a description of two people from the girls we managed to save from becoming corpses. A young man known as 'Chu' and some effete man who did their makeup, plus the girl called Suiren who used to recruit the girls. The girls we rescued unanimously identified the body we found as being the recruiter, so the police are only looking for the main culprit and the cross-dresser."

"Any leads on them?"

"The apartment was in Toyoshima Ward, so it's not really my business. I mean, the precincts are nominally working together because the victims came from such a wide area. But no, we've not been able to trace them. Whoever they are, they were able to set up something on that scale. They would need the backing of some huge organization. Chinese mafia have been flexing their muscles recently, but there's no evidence. If we scour everything and still don't find them, then either they've gone deep where we can't reach them, or they've been erased like that girl Suiren."

Serizawa pulled a pack of cigarettes from his shirt pocket and lit one, as if he'd just remembered they were there. He did not particularly like smoking, but it had become a habit during his years as a detective.

"All we know are the identities of the four victims. If we don't even know the names of the perps then we can't figure out the organization behind them. We don't even have details on the guy that fed us the intel. It's pitiful, even for us."

"Your informant's name's Gray, right?" Rokuzo quoted

information gleaned from the tabloids.

"I don't know if he's trying to intimate that he's some kind of unidentified creature, but hell if it doesn't feel like we're being toyed with."

The man behind the leaked information had apparently introduced himself as Gray. The call had come exactly twenty days after the man in gray had orchestrated a raid at a jewelry exhibition. Judging from the timing, it was not outside the realm of possibility that Gray and the man in gray were the same person. The media had jumped on that bandwagon, with some tabloids already publishing completely unfounded articles that claimed Gray as an accomplice in the Ikebukuro scandal. Serizawa, overwhelmed by the many uncertainties, didn't know how to wrap his head around the events, but he was sure of one thing—the man in gray whom some had claimed dead after a year's absence was still at large. And with that fact came the possibility of yet more incidents.

The investigation into the case of the gray man had previously hit a dead end, but the police were back on high alert. They pursued both Gray, the informant, and Chu, the man believed to be behind the Ikebukuro scandal, but were making no progress in apprehending either.

"There's word that PubSec is on the case, but I have no idea if they're making any headway."

"Sounds like our nation's police force is more impotent than I'd feared."

Serizawa gave a conflicted smile, half agreeing and half disagreeing with Rokuzo's statement. "The N-system allows monitoring of public transport, and they can install bugs wherever they want, plus there are surveillance cameras all over the city. Public Security can do as they please. If that doesn't bring about a result, then we're dealing with either a ghost or a real Gray alien."

"Perhaps you should try Area 51, he'll pop up there."

Serizawa nodded at the joke. "That would be perfect. Next time I see my superiors I'll be sure to let them know that they need to send a crime squad to America," Serizawa jested in turn, but his expression remained serious.

Rokuzo noticed and ventured, "Something on your mind?"

Serizawa sat slightly straighter in response. "It's just a hunch, but something tells me the police aren't really trying to catch them." He drained the rest of the whisky as though in need of a distraction.

"Not really trying? What do you mean?"

"During the serial raids last August, we went on full mobilization and searched frantically for the man in gray. But we lost. It was a complete failure. He's got the brains and the physical stamina needed to carry out his plans, computer system hacking tools, access to weapons you can't buy in Japan, and the perfect organization with zero traitors. No weak points, no links to other groups. Our informants had nothing. Us cops were left dazed. And now we have the jewelry theft, and public exposure of the Ikebukuro scandal. I became suspicious after the latter."

"Ho," Rokuzo hooted like an owl.

"Look at the scale of it. For the dignity of the nation we need to do all we can to apprehend Chu and this Gray who seems to be involved. But there's an abnormal amount of disruption coming from above."

"Disruption?"

"Investigation HQ is getting constant visits from Metropolitan Police Headquarters brass. At first I thought their involvement was simply testament to the horror of the case, but it was soon obvious that that wasn't it. They butt in, requesting updates every day almost like they're interrogating us, even extra-jurisdictional detectives like me. Then there's the rumor that special units have been assigned to the case, working independently of Investigation HQ. That's where Public Security, who follow their own special rules, comes into this. Kind of gives you the impression they're trying to nab the perps before we can, huh?"

"You're saying the brass knows something and wants to get to Chu and Gray first?" Rokuzo asked back, using his wrinkled fingers to massage his temples.

"Maybe I'm reading too much into it, but the idea's tempting," Serizawa confessed, stroking his chin with his right hand.

It was possible that someone among the ranks of the police—or with equal power—was connected with the Ikebukuro case. If such a thing came to light, it could topple the country. But he had no way to prove the theory.

"There's one more case that bugs me."

"Huh, quite the chatterbox today."

"I've got a lot on my mind. Shut up and listen."

"Ooh, scary. Never taught to respect your elders?" Rokuzo shrugged and poured more whisky into Serizawa's empty glass.

The detective stared at the contents of the tumbler before taking the last slice of ham and popping it into his mouth. "There was a string of bizarre cases not too long ago. Three men just disappeared: Yuki Iwazaki on November 29th, Namiki Gakuto on December 2nd, and Makoto Goda on December 4th."

"What's this?" Rokuzo cocked his head to the side, seeming not to have heard of it.

Serizawa continued at his own pace without addressing the question. "Goda was sentenced to twelve years in prison for committing murder while he was still a minor and was released on parole earlier this year on good behavior after only serving ten years. He went missing three days after his release. And get this, all three of them were partners in crime, all convicted for the same incident."

"That sounds pretty serious. You don't know where they went?" Rokuzo grazed his hand over his whitening stubble.

"We have no witnesses and no leads. I know I shouldn't say this, as a cop, but it's like they were spirited away. There is a potential suspect, however. Ever heard the name Kiyomi Takano?"

Rokuzo looked up to the ceiling. "Huh. Maybe, maybe not."

"How about a mother and daughter kidnapped and murdered in Miyamae?"

"Ah, that rings a bell..."

"Ten years ago, in 2003." Serizawa looked pained, as though someone had sliced open an old wound.

Rokuzo muttered to himself as he dug through his memories, eventually clapping his hands together. "Yes, I remember. Miyamae, where three minors kidnapped and killed a woman and her daughter."

"Exactly. The three that are missing were the killers."

"Huh…" Rokuzo nodded, lips pursed in thought.

"What's more, Kiyomi Takano was spotted tailing Iwazaki and Namiki two years before they went missing. They were a little sensitive to that kind of thing, being ex-cons and all, and came crying to the police. We looked into it and got plenty of witnesses reporting a suspicious character loitering around."

"A suspicious character? You mean Kiyomi Takano?"

"We weren't sure in the beginning, especially as he'd been missing since 2006. But one of the officers we sent in to keep watch happened to know Takano by face, and that was how we identified him. That being said, plenty of people know him, so we'd have figured it out sooner or later."

"Is he famous?"

"Among cops, he is. Kiyomi Takano has an impressive amount of mistrust and hatred for the police. He went berserk inside a station once. Tough guy."

"Part of some yakuza group?"

"No, the bereaved party from another murder case."

Rokuzo looked surprised by the answer. He was quiet for a moment while he collected his thoughts and reframed his question. "You looked into him anyway, right?"

"We were lucky to make the match, but it didn't help us track him down." Serizawa sighed, then sucked in a deep breath. "Goda went missing three days after he was released on parole. It was clearly planned. Iwazaki and Namiki went missing right before him, as if it was all prearranged. Iwazaki's married with kids and Namiki has stable work and an income, so it seems unlikely the three of them would get together for another crime. Our only lead is the witness statements on Kiyomi Takano."

"Are you working on that case?"

"No. But I worked on the Miyamae kidnapping, so it's pretty

heavy on my mind."

Serizawa clicked his tongue and exhaled sharply. Then he fell silent, the gesture marking the end for now of Rokuzo's role as confidant.

It was after twelve by the time he left Chateau d'If.

Serizawa rode the nearly empty weeknight train to the final stop at Kajigatani, where he got off with a crowd of tired salarymen. He exited through the ticket gates and stood waiting for the crosslight to change, glancing sideways along a street devoid of recreational buildings. The roads were empty so most people ignored the lights, but Serizawa waited until it turned green.

When they did, he clenched his hands inside his coat pockets, shivered, and began to walk home on unsteady feet. His sense of balance was suffering after those shots of whisky.

The sleeping neighborhood was dark, and there was something lonely about the light shining down from the equidistant street lamps.

Serizawa tried concentrating on the cases through the fog in his brain.

The sensational serial raids one year ago. The jewelry heist four months ago. The appalling Ikebukuro incident. Three missing persons.

Serizawa had read every item, every bit of information available on each of them, clipped articles, and kept notes, writing down everything he learned about the progress of the investigations. He did this out of a different sort of passion than what was called for in the line of duty. Yet, he still felt no closer to the truth. It was irritating that he had yet to even stumble across the entrance to the labyrinth.

There was only the one lead. Kiyomi Takano. Infamous for going wild in the police station, screaming about police negligence.

Serizawa narrowed his eyes as he shivered against the cold wind and grit his teeth together. The cold had helped clear his head of the whisky from Chateau d'If, sobering him up as his warm body was chilled to the bone.

He was almost home. Hunching over, he picked up his pace.

Every now and then he would pass a streetlight that was colored blue. The blue lights were said to have a calming effect and had been rolled out in a hurry with the hope of reducing crime. Now they served only to accentuate the frigidity of the air.

How many more blue lights before I get home?

Serizawa lived alone. All that waited for him was a room as frozen as the wind outside, but he craved his bed nonetheless. He couldn't wait to get into the futon and warm up.

Suddenly, he sensed a presence under one of the streetlights ahead and strained his eyes. Bluish light fell on a man. He was tall and wore a gray suit and a gray hat.

It was the gray man. The moment he realized, Serizawa stopped dead, unable to move.

"My apologies for disturbing you at this late hour." The man bowed politely.

"Wh-Who are you?" Serizawa stood stock still. His voice was weak and trembling from fear. He could only see the man's mouth since the rest of his face was hidden under the brim of his hat.

The mouth smiled. "These days it appears I must call myself Gray."

Serizawa felt every muscle in his body clench. The tension was almost unbearable. "Why are you here?" He tried to pull himself together as he spoke, but his voice was thin enough to disappear in the wind.

"I'll be brief, if you don't mind. I'm a wanted man, after all," Gray said, ignoring the question. "There is a man who owes you a debt of gratitude." His tone was flat, yet each word was full of spirit. "When you worked as a detective on the Miyamae kidnapping case, you hounded the perpetrators, helped the prosecution, and did your utmost for the victims. The bereaved party is most grateful for your work."

"Th-That…"

No, that wasn't it, Serizawa said to himself.

He had been unable to let such evil go, that was all. He wanted to smash a world where criminals were rewarded. He wanted to consign evil to oblivion.

He had never put himself in the victims' shoes. He had been relentless because of his hatred of evil, of injustice. That was why he had started to doubt the police force. As an organization it had begun to exhaust him.

Gray chuckled, as though he was privy to Serizawa's internal conflict. "Whatever the reason, your principles remain exceptional. You deserve commendation for so persistently fighting evil until the bitter end. It falls to me to offer thanks, as proxy for the man whose gratitude you earned."

"Thanks?"

Gray nodded and glanced off into the darkness. Another man came into view.

Serizawa flinched instantly, but Gray spoke softly, disarming his caution. "Please do not be alarmed, he is a colleague of mine."

"A colleague?"

Gray said nothing. The younger man was holding a handled bag, which he placed in front of Serizawa before retreating into the darkness. Serizawa wordlessly looked at the bag, then back towards where the man had disappeared.

"It contains roughly one billion yen in gems. Legitimate and clean, of course. I'm offering them to you."

"Wh-Why?" Serizawa was unable to absorb the meaning of Gray's words.

"As I said, consider it a token of gratitude. We have also taken the liberty of setting up an offshore bank account in your name. It holds deposits of one billion yen. You can use this card to access the account." Gray stepped closer and handed Serizawa an envelope. "Inside, you will find a slip of paper with the PIN and a ticket to Dubai, valid for two months."

"Dubai? What are you talking about?"

"Feel free to choose somewhere else. Northern Europe, perhaps, or the south of France. If you limit your extravagances, and if you so desire, there should be enough money to spend the rest of your life traveling. I'd imagine that would be an agreeable way of life."

"I mean… Why should I leave the country?" Serizawa managed to ask through the chaos rattling his mind.

Gray was silent for a few moments, but it seemed like forever. Serizawa could feel sweat on his back even as he stood in the midst of the biting winter wind.

Gray laughed softly. "Because Japan's end is near," he said. "Now, there is a favor we would like to ask before you leave."

"A favor?"

"We will be in touch again regarding the details. This might sound rude, but it'll be a little test to see what decision you make."

Gray began to step back into the darkness, utterly silent.

A test? What the hell does that mean?

Serizawa could do nothing but stand in a daze. He shivered as he snapped out of it and called out, "Just what the hell is it that you plan on doing?!"

His voice echoed in the darkness, but Gray did not come back.

Two days later, Serizawa happened to be looking at the flight ticket to Dubai when he received an unexpected visit from a stern-looking bald man.

Serizawa recognized him straight away.

The man introduced himself as Kiyomi Takano.

2

December 14th

It was four months since Ryotaro's involvement in the raid. He had quit his job at the jewelry store immediately afterwards. As per Gray's instructions he'd spent the next month doing nothing, just relaxing. After that he began to work for Pharaon Logistics. Gray had provided the introduction.

In the midst of the recession, a small venture business had bought up the debt-riddled sixth-ranked company in the freight industry. Soon afterwards the venture took over the likewise poorly performing third- and fourth-ranked firms. The newly merged company went on to take the lion's share of the market. The venture business that had orchestrated the M&As was Tomosun Corporation. Pharaon was a subsidiary.

Ryotaro was assigned to the year-old Nihonbashi No. 2 HQ of Pharaon Logistics, whose operations consisted mostly of supervising various branches around the country. The Nihonbashi No. 1 HQ was in a building dating from before the mergers and handled the company's day-to-day business.

Most of Ryotaro's work at the No. 2 HQ concerned inspecting the branches belonging to the Tokyo Office. The job could hardly even be called "work," as he only needed to make twice-weekly visits to nearby outlets to carry out a basic inspection and email reports to the Tomosun Corporation. He stayed on-call for the three remaining days in the week in case there was a problem and one of the branches needed him, but this had never happened. His job was not vital to operations. Ryotaro felt a little inferior seeing how busy his colleagues were, but he stayed with the job regardless.

He reached Ikebukuro after having finished his inspection of the Nerima office and went into the emptiest cafe he could find. Over half of the tables had been set up outside; the place's main attraction seemed to be terrace seating, though no one was interested in sitting outside at this time of year. It was warmish when the sun was out, but he decided to sit inside, ordered a coffee, and began to put together a straightforward report.

His reports required little effort. If there was something unusual, he'd write that down, and if there was nothing in particular, he simply noted that everything seemed to be humming along. The report was finished inside of fifteen minutes. Ryotaro sighed and placed his laptop back in his briefcase.

All he had to do now was return to the Nihonbashi office. It was eleven in the morning, but he had already finished the day's work. He was completely relaxed. He thought he might order lunch and was just opening the menu when his phone buzzed in the inside pocket of his suit jacket. It was Sayuri.

"Hi, what's up?" Ryotaro kept his voice down, mindful of his surroundings, but he was the only customer, perhaps because of the hour.

"Oh, Ryotaro? Got some time?" Her voice was a little high-pitched, but it echoed pleasantly in his ears. The question was not something adults asked each other at lunchtime on weekdays.

"Actually, it just so happens that I do."

"Great. See you in a minute," Sayuri said and hung up.

Ryotaro pulled the phone away from his ear and stared at it. "Huh," he muttered to himself. *See you in a minute? How do you know where I am?*

Just then he felt someone tap his back. He turned around to see Sayuri standing there, smiling. She was in her school uniform, as usual, and carrying an oversized gym bag over her right shoulder.

"Whoa!" Ryotaro gawked at her, blinking in confusion at the sudden appearance of the girl who had just been on the phone.

"Surprised?" Sayuri narrowed her eyes like a cat as she took the seat across from him at the round table. "I'm hungry. Mind if I order?" She called over the waiter without waiting for his reply and ordered a ham sandwich with tea.

"How did you know I'd be…"

"I was just passing by when I saw you."

"Why are you in Ikebukuro?"

"Work," Sayuri answered flatly.

"Dressed like that?"

"What do you mean? This is what I always wear. I like the uniform. Well, there are *various things* it's not appropriate for, of course, so my work clothes are in the bag." She pointed to her bag with a serious look on her face and took a sip of the water the waiter had left.

And what work do you do? Ryotaro refrained from asking out loud. It was the unwritten rule among those in Gray's employ: Don't discuss your job. There was also an understanding among those rescued by Gray not to probe into one another's backgrounds or work history if the other person didn't want to discuss it. This was out of a desire to avoid opening old wounds, yet it went beyond that courtesy.

They already knew how the other person felt.

Suffering that tears through the body. Pain like a crushed lung. Despair arising from the awareness that the world does not need you. Anger that burns through every cell of your body. Grief from being constricted by that anger. All-consuming self-hatred.

Everyone that Gray saved had suffered such emotions first-hand, so they had a natural empathy for one another. The understanding came like breathing, subconsciously, on a different level from pity or any rational patterns of thought. It was the reason that they felt closer than blood relatives and worshipped Gray more selflessly than they might God.

It was not dissimilar to religion, but Ryotaro didn't think they were the same. With religion, people sought benefits. Prayer expressed the desire to fulfill one's desires. Even a suicide bombing was predicated on the devotee's own salvation.

Everyone rescued by Gray simply lived for Gray. Without him, their lives had been forfeit.

Ryotaro had never discussed this with the others or asked what they thought. He knew it would be the same for everyone Gray had rescued.

Pharaon Logistics was a mix of those who had been saved by Gray and others who had worked there previously. Ryotaro was able to pick out the former. They always stood out when he made his rounds to the branches.

Undulating pupils that knew despair—the air of a person who had witnessed bottomless darkness came through at some moment.

He knew Sayuri was on *this side* even as she ate her ham sandwich before his eyes. She always put on a positive show but on occasion flashed pupils that held such darkness. Ryotaro didn't know the scale of whatever trial she had undergone, but the flashes of darkness were evidence that her wounds had not yet healed.

She was only able to act as she did thanks to the grounding Gray provided. That was only speculation, and he had nothing concrete to back it up, but he'd believed that ever since *that one time.*

That time. It was three months ago—a month after his involvement in the jewelry raid—that Sayuri suddenly asked him out on a date.

"Gray suggested we take a breather, go on a date, goof off," she'd said bluntly, averting her gaze, when they'd met at Yokohama Station.

Ryotaro noted that Sayuri had taken to calling the man Gray, but the way she puckered her lips in embarrassment was funny, and he'd felt a little shy himself.

She suggested, to his surprise, going to Kamakura. He said he thought it a little old-fashioned for someone her age, but she told him to shut up with a pout on her face.

They took the Yokosuka line to Kita-Kamakura. Heavy clouds swept across a dark sky, and it felt like they might burst into rain at any moment. Ryotaro let Sayuri lead the way. Maybe because the weather was still humid, she wore shorts and a t-shirt. Her elegant body line and pure white skin were enough to draw his attention.

The two of them had hiked silently up the hills surrounding Kenchoji temple up to Hansobo, stopped to eat purple sweet-potato ice cream in silence, and tasted agonizingly spicy rice crackers at a specialty shop.

It was proving difficult to start a conversation. They passed the hours awkwardly distant. Neither of them was used to going on dates, so both were building a wall between them. The heavy clouds got heavier and eventually broke into rain.

As the rain came down Sayuri said, quickly, "There's a place I want to see," and scampered off towards an art museum next to Kita-Kamakura Station.

The museum was a converted red-brick building. The white entrance was left open and the reception area was to the right.

"Welcome!" the female receptionist greeted, looking up from a paperback. She looked bored, there seeming to be no other visitors that day.

"Two adults, please." Sayuri paid for them both and took the tickets.

She led Ryotaro through the dividing curtain and went into the exhibition space.

The room was large, like a living room, with two sofas and a square table on which sat a mountainous pile of picture books.

"Picture book artist?" Ryotaro asked, admiring a large painting hanging from one of the walls. Most of the canvases on display were simple, dominated by large swathes of sky and land with a lone subject detailed in the center. The light colors gave a gentle impression like they had been drawn with crayon.

"That's right," Sayuri answered.

She hopped lightly up the stairs to the second floor and Ryotaro followed. There were more paintings, equidistant from one another. There was another sofa plus a desk. Sayuri perched herself on the sofa at the top of the stairs and caught her breath.

"Have a seat." Sayuri tapped the space next to her.

Ryotaro did as he was told, sitting next to her on the two-seater. The room's temperature was comfortable, and the lack of other people left the room so quiet they could hear the clock ticking. The furniture on display was smart, with warm wood and pure white wallpaper having a distinctly calming effect.

"It's nice, right? I come here a lot."

Ryotaro made a noncommittal nod in response.

"You don't like it?" Sayuri worried as she peered at his face.

Ryotaro hurriedly shook his head. "No, it's definitely nice. It's just, why would a girl like you like it?" It didn't quite fit; Ryotaro found it hard to get his head around the combination of the still innocent-looking girl before him and the museum.

Sayuri responded with a subdued sigh. "It's because I never had a place of my own. So I went ahead and made this my own special spot." The soft tone of her voice was a perfect match for the room.

There was a long silence. Then words rolled off his tongue of their own accord. "I…I might be a lot like you, Sayuri."

That had been enough. With that single exchange, they had confided in each other. Ryotaro had been salvaged by the overwhelming person called Gray, given a place of his own. He thought that Sayuri had probably gone through a similar experience, too.

"I had some awful things happen to me," she said as she leaned back into the sofa. "For a number of reasons, for better or worse, my memory is hazy. But I was at rock bottom when Gray rescued me. That's when I thought, 'Hey, there's someone who can fight back against this rotten world. Wow.' So I chose to stick with Gray. I'm still all about taking revenge on this sucky world, but I also want to know what he'll do, what he'll be from now on."

"You mean…"

Sayuri finished his thought for him. "It's probably just curiosity."

She laughed, but the sadness was there concealed beneath her features.

"What's wrong?" Sayuri asked, peering up at Ryotaro. He seemed to be lost in thought in his seat in the cafe. She furrowed her brows slightly, looking worried.

"Uh… I was just thinking that looks pretty tasty," Ryotaro responded smoothly as he found himself hauled back from the ocean of memory. He ordered a bacon and egg sandwich and a refill of coffee.

"Getting used to your job?" Sayuri asked, glancing at his briefcase.

"It's a cake walk. Easy work, lots of pay. Treated well enough to make anyone jealous." Ryotaro was very aware that his compensation was too high for the amount of work he actually did. Plus, the staff at the Nihonbashi No. 2 HQ exclusively consisted of people who had been rescued by Gray, so his co-workers gave him zero stress.

"Oh," Sayuri remarked, sounding disinterested despite having asked the question. Her eyes flicked over her wristwatch; Ryotaro thought it looked expensive. "What time do you finish today?"

"If nothing comes up, five thirty." No one would bother him if he left earlier, but he was making the effort to stay at work for the entirety of his stipulated hours.

"Okay, then let's have dinner tonight," Sayuri suggested, brushing the crumbs from her hands.

"Sure, sounds good," Ryotaro nodded. They had gone out for meals a few times before, so there was nothing particularly surprising about it. He was secretly thrilled but was careful not to let it show.

"Expect a car at your place at seven."

"A car? Yours?" Ryotaro tilted his head to the side. She shouldn't have a license as she was still a minor.

"No. Today is Gray's invitation." Sayuri had fallen into the habit of calling the man Gray, and it wasn't just her. Everyone the man had saved had taken to using the name. Ryotaro suspected it was because Gray had begun to use it himself.

"Gray's invitation?" Ryotaro felt his heart jump. *I get to see him again.*

Ryotaro could easily count the number of times they had seen each other since his rescue. When he had, it had only been in passing, with only enough time to exchange greetings—there was no chance to have a proper conversation.

Ryotaro had no means of contacting Gray and absolutely no idea of where he was or what he was doing, but Sayuri was different. Apparently she seemed to be meeting him on a regular basis since she was always the one to relay his words and work directions.

As a result, Ryotaro and Sayuri had come to see each other fairly often. Only three months had passed since he'd started at Pharaon Logistics, but he already felt closer to her than anyone else.

"Gray asked me to bring you with me, actually. I thought

about calling, but then I saw you sitting here. So, how about it? You'll come, right?"

Ryotaro's eyes were wide open. *Gray wants to see me.* It was enough to make him shiver with joy. "Of course," he mumbled to keep his excitement in check, nodding repeatedly.

Sayuri chuckled in response. "You're acting weird."

"Shush," Ryotaro retorted as he blushed hotly.

He was unable to stop himself from trembling. A doubt suddenly flickered in his mind.

"Why does Gray want to see someone like me?"

Sayuri had been enjoying his curious behavior, but now she pulled a serious expression. "I wonder."

Her reply deepened Ryotaro's anxiety. He didn't consider himself worthy of Gray's time unless the man wanted something from him. Given that, what would spur Gray to call on him now?

"Why not ask him when you see him?" Sayuri's tone suggested she already knew the answer.

After parting ways with Sayuri in Ikebukuro, Ryotaro took the subway back to the No. 2 HQ at Nihonbashi. The eight-floor building, a ten-minute walk from the station, was originally owned by another company, which had put it on the market due to the recession. Pharaon Logistics had purchased it and implemented major renovations.

Ryotaro almost choked on the sudden rush of warmed air as he came through the glass-paneled entrance. The brightly lit interior was welcoming but lacked a reception area as they never had clients visit. The place was empty and the lobby was perfectly silent. Ryotaro swiped his IC card at one of the three elevators and the doors slid open. There were no security guards in the building, but the place was rigged with every kind of security system imaginable.

The elevator stopped at the fifth floor and the doors opened slowly. There were ten or so people, some at their desks, others pacing the floor.

"I'm back," he called out.

Everyone reflexively welcomed him back. Ryotaro was still unused to this routine.

Back then…

Back at the jewelers in Okachimachi he was treated like garbage, and the only time anyone spoke to him was when they wanted to heap abuse or ridicule. They never welcomed him, only harassed him relentlessly, with the sole aim of getting him to quit. Recalling it was enough to make him feel dizzy even now.

"What, is, the matter?"

The face that appeared before him was Sasaki's. Ryotaro gathered himself, mumbled, "Umm, uh, nothing," and took a seat at his desk.

"Did, some, thing, happen?" Sasaki sat next to Ryotaro, putting a hand on his shoulder. "Gotta, get, worries out." The colleague smiled as he struggled to get the words out, causing the bridge of his nose to wrinkle up.

Their desks were next to each other, so they often chatted.

Sasaki was short, baby-faced, and gelled his hair and dyed it brown, making him look like an oddly colored sea urchin. He was a high school dropout but was now employed by Pharaon Logistics. Although he sat next to Ryotaro, their jobs were completely different. Whereas Ryotaro had one computer, Sasaki had three on his desk plus another in a room on a different floor. Sasaki referred to what he did as "infiltration, inspections," and he spent entire days glued to his computers.

Although Gray's flock didn't pry into each other's backgrounds, Ryotaro made sure to be very attentive when such information was volunteered. He had known Sasaki for a week when his colleague first told him about his past.

He had been raised by a single mother. They never had much money so he took a part-time job delivering newspapers starting in middle school. While helping out with household finances, he barely managed to get into high school. He was not a particularly zealous student but was smart enough to easily grasp ideas after hearing them just once, allowing him entry to the prefecture's best school. Once there he joined the computer club, where he exhibited prodigious levels of talent.

Hacking.

Using information gleaned from websites and reference books in the library, he figured out how to hack through the security firewalls of weakly protected companies and extract information from their systems. He picked up programming skills effortlessly and became proficient enough to be interviewed on TV. At one point he was lionized at school.

But it didn't last long.

A group of three students, irritated by his popularity, began to bully him. Because they were pivotal figures in the school's social milieu, the bullying spread like an infection. At first it was mostly indirect. They would hide his shoes or shove his desk to a corner of the classroom. Sasaki wasn't particularly bothered by such harassment. He had never been particularly timid, and thanks to being generally sociable, not a few friends stuck to him behind the scenes. His relaxed attitude, however, only served to spur the bullies to step up their attacks. A group of eight kids with the original three at the core isolated Sasaki by threatening his remaining handful of friends and started demanding money. He resolutely refused to give them any, which caused them to resort to violence.

They continued to demand money on an almost daily basis. Each time, he would refuse, and they would attack him. He resisted but the odds were against him. He was no match for their numbers. He never mentioned anything to his teachers since he feared that the information would get to his mother and he didn't want her to worry. He took care to hide his bruises and act as though everything was normal.

One day, he got called out as usual by the group of eight to the roof of an abandoned two-floor factory. Saying they wanted to practice wrestling, they assailed him one-sidedly. As they laid into parts of his body covered by clothing—carefully avoiding leaving any visible marks—one of the leaders said he wanted to practice flying kicks. A couple of the guys grabbed Sasaki's arms and pulled them wide so he stood as though crucified. The leader ran up and launched a flying kick at the defenseless Sasaki's abdomen. The kick was so forceful it sent him flying backwards with a loud thwack into the rusted fence, which creaked and groaned. Instead of rebounding, Sasaki's body collapsed backwards along with the fence and tumbled off the second-story roof as though in slow motion.

The concrete holding up the fence had been full of cracks, so it had only been a matter of time until the fence collapsed. It had ripped clean off under the impact. The eight students peered down at Sasaki, who was as still as a corpse, and bolted from the scene; none of them tried to help. An ambulance was called by a passerby who had seen the kids and, suspicious, run in to inspect the scene.

Although Sasaki had miraculously escaped with his life, the full-body impact had left him with severe injuries including six broken bones. His scalp required twenty stitches. The wounds healed over time, but he had fallen head-first, and the damage to his brain left him with a speech disorder.

It had been serious enough to qualify as aggravated assault, but the case ended with no indictments as the offenders were minors. There was talk of a civil trial but the family didn't have the necessary funds or time.

Hearing the truth from her son and beside herself with anger and regret over his speech disorder, the aggressors' recalcitrance, and not having noticed the bullying, Sasaki's mother cried until she ran out of tears. Only five of the kids' families came to visit; three didn't even try to get in touch. The five that visited hardly did or said anything and offered none of the expected apologies. It was hard to tell why they had come at all. One had been rude enough to imply that Sasaki's disability was his own fault and that they had been put out by the whole thing, as though the kids were not to blame at all. One parent had even blamed Sasaki for getting his son involved in something that could have an impact on the son's future. The father of the leader of the pack, he was a policeman.

Sasaki sat listening next to his mother as she trembled with rage and bitterness. The father's words made him resolve to kill the kid and the father and then commit suicide.

At that point in the tale Sasaki had laughed, telling Ryotaro that he had probably gone slightly crazy. Killing himself would only have caused his mother even more grief, but he had been so consumed with the will to destroy the source of his mother's wrath that the withholding thought had never occurred to him. He had even prepared a will.

Sasaki bought a knife from an outdoor equipment store and got ready to ambush the kid, waiting at a spot where he thought he could get him alone on his way back from cram school. He would kill the kid, then go after the father.

The guy appeared on schedule, walking towards him, alone. He carried a shopping bag from a convenience store and was stuffing his face with a meat dumpling. Sasaki quieted his breath in the shadow of a telephone pole. It would be easy, he thought, to kill someone who was nothing more than a target of hate. He saw an image of his mother, briefly, but hardened his resolve, rationalizing to himself that he was about to wipe out the source of her suffering.

The kid drew closer. He was in striking range.

It happened just then, as he readied the knife, tensing his trembling legs so that he could lunge forth. He felt something chilly on his shoulder, his body went rigid, and he froze to the spot, unable to move.

Sasaki locked eyes with the kid. The kid gaped as if he'd seen a ghost and bolted away, wailing. As the kid ran away, Sasaki just watched, his mind focused on whoever was behind him.

"You won't get anywhere like that," the presence behind him chided. The voice was soft but had a force that brooked no opposition.

Sasaki's breathing was shallow. He tried to speak but the hand on his shoulder stopped him.

"Allow me to avenge you in your place. Delay your plans for thirty days. If you are not happy with what I have done by then, you are free to try again with that meager instrument. If you find that you are sated by my actions, however, I would like you to offer me your assistance."

It was like the whispering of a devil, an offer one would reject under normal circumstances, but Sasaki could only nod. The words' force had left him with no alternate course of action. The figure behind him laughed softly, sounding satisfied, and took his hand off Sasaki's shoulder.

"In thirty days, then."

The voice drew away. Sasaki swung around as fast as he could but there was no one there. Only darkness extended.

The events of the following month were bizarre enough to make him shiver even now. The three families that had not visited came first, turning up at his house in rapid succession. They proffered all the money they could scrape together and begged for forgiveness, foreheads bowed to the floor. Then four of the five families that had visited returned. This time their attitudes had taken an about-turn. They'd sold their houses and brought the proceeds.

Sasaki and his mother were completely baffled. What could have caused the sudden change? *Why did they all seem afraid of something?*

The ringleader and his policeman father came to see Sasaki one week after the other seven families had visited. The kid had a broken leg and arm, both in casts, and his head was wrapped in bandages. The father looked like a different person—weak and frail, as if he'd lost weight. He had sold the family cars, their home, and even taken out a consumer loan. They had brought close to fifty million yen in total. When the father handed it to Sasaki's mother, *he apologized as though he were begging for his life.*

Sasaki's mother was spooked by this abrupt change in their attitudes. Sasaki was the same, but he was also barely fighting another emotion that made his blood rush. His body trembled with fear and reverence for the invisible but palpable power stunningly on display before him.

It was on exactly the thirtieth day when the man behind the

voice appeared. Sasaki was on his way home from school, the outlines of the city seeming to float in the twilight. The man stood in a deserted alleyway. He was completely gray, smiling as though he could see right through everything.

He told Sasaki that he wanted to borrow his expertise in hacking, data cracking, and server infiltration.

Sasaki didn't think to ask why. He nodded without hesitation, completely entranced by the overwhelming power of the man before him.

"Defi, nitely, wrong." Sasaki peered at Ryotaro, trying to read his thoughts from his expression.

Ryotaro looked away and considered what he should say. After hesitating, he looked back at Sasaki and said in a near-whisper, "I'm going to have dinner with Gray tonight."

Sasaki's eyes grew wider. Finally he made a loud croon of admiration.

"Hey, keep it down!" Ryotaro felt like putting a hand over Sasaki's mouth but managed to stop himself from actually doing it.

"That's, amaz, ing." Sasaki's cheeks were rosy and his mouth was twisted with envy.

"I know," Ryotaro said with a sigh. Just the thought of seeing Gray again made his heart beat so hard like it might tear open. It was hard to breathe.

"What? You're seeing Gray?" Kozue Kirishima butted into the conversation.

Her almond eyes and straight nose gave her a slightly harsh look, but she had the body of a model. She always wore lean jeans and a smile that seemed to ridicule the world.

"So where are you meeting him?"

She leaned forward and brushed up her straightened hair. Something about the gesture made Ryotaro turn red.

"They're, gonna, have, dinner," Sasaki answered, looking away, also turning red. He had a secret crush on Kozue.

"Wow! A date, huh?"

"Sayuri's going to be there too."

"Oh, the brat's tagging along?" Kozue made a disappointed face.

Kozue and Sayuri were like cats and dogs—or rather, with the power balance overwhelmingly favoring Kozue, the better comparison was a lion and a mouse. Her total dislike of Sayuri was a little puzzling. Kozue said it was because she "didn't like ignorant brats." Whenever the two were in the same room together Kozue poked endless fun at her and Sayuri started screaming at Kozue in response.

"That brat trails after Gray like crap on a goldfish. Well, if she's going to be there, it's probably *that dinner*," Kozue said suggestively, giving Sasaki a conspiratorial wink.

That dinner? Ryotaro wanted to ask what she meant, but Kozue's bristling tone made him hold back.

"Why the hell does Gray want some brat barely out of diapers following him around?"

Though Kozue's words were harsh, oddly she didn't give an impression of ill will. The saying that fights are evidence of a good friendship seemed made for her and Sayuri.

Like Sasaki, Kozue's main skill was hacking. The difference was that she called her job "social hacking" or "behavioral hacking." She declared that her immaculate beauty was perfect for social hacking, wherein she used her looks to *trick people into divulging information*. Ryotaro wasn't sure exactly what kind of hacking this was or where she hacked into, but whenever she got a call on her cell she'd board herself up in her private office and set to work. Sometimes she went out, but aside from that she seemed to have little to do and killed time reading magazines.

Kozue's parents had abused her, one time so badly she almost died. They suffered from personality disorders that made them think of her as a piece of property, and they mistreated her whenever they felt she had disobeyed their will. They never applied direct violence like punches or kicks; instead, the abuse took on various twisted forms, such as not letting her sleep, not feeding her, or locking her in a room with deafening noise.

Kozue did her level best to bear their punishment. She never tried to get help and prayed that one day her parents would change and show her kindness. Kozue relinquished both thought and action and simply tolerated the status quo.

She just barely managed enough attendance to graduate from high school, but that was when her mental state began to disintegrate. One day, while she was locked in the house, she caught her parents off guard, stabbed them with a kitchen knife, and fled. She spent the day wandering aimlessly before climbing to the roof of a mixed-purpose building in order to jump to her death when Gray appeared as though he'd been waiting and called out to her. He told her that both her parents had survived, promised to obliterate them socially, and guaranteed they would not press charges; and he did exactly as promised. He told her he valued her brains and sent her to study abroad, where she received schooling in electrical engineering, communications technology, information theory, and such.

Kozue never told anyone about her past. Back then she'd been lost in self-hatred, but witnessing Gray's power had given her the will to start a new life. She had also resolved to erase her past and never speak of it. Until she met Gray, she'd cursed every moment of her existence and hated the whole world as intensely as her worthless self. Rescued by Gray, she was able to interact with others like her, people salvaged from the bowels of the earth. Gradually she came to want a role in changing the world. Being able to serve someone for whom she had the deepest respect and affection was rare happiness. She'd do anything for that.

"You, really, hate, Sayuri," Sasaki laughed, watching Kozue frown.

"From the moment I met her, with a passion."

Kozue didn't say Sayuri disgusted her because it was like seeing her younger self. She'd first made contact with the girl in the Tower; Gray had tasked Kozue with hacking into its systems. He had also asked her to keep watch over Sayuri until they'd finished collating the necessary data. As she witnessed Sayuri's drug-induced descent via the miniature cameras, Kozue had entreated Gray to get her out, but he had refused. They needed all of the data as evidence and would not be able to save Sayuri until she was driven to the brink. Gray's attitude was somewhat revolting to Kozue, but she had obeyed him simply because he'd given his word that the girl would be rescued. And he had kept his promise while also driving the Tower to ruin.

"When did you first meet her?" Ryotaro asked. Kozue remained silent.

Picking up on their conversation, more and more colleagues gathered around, each expressing their jealousy. They were all people who'd been abandoned by those around them, by society itself. They had resolved to end their own lives; as they reached their personal nadir, Gray had saved them. They were happy to be his shields and swords.

Having nothing in particular to do, everyone on the floor gossiped gaily until clock-out time came at 5:30. The staff at No. 2 HQ all had positions in Pharaon Logistics, but none were vital to the running of the company. The No. 1 HQ, on the other hand, kept on staff from before the merger and took a more active role in steering the firm.

In other words, no one at No. 2 HQ performed duties integral to Pharaon Logistics. Each had *other work* unrelated to the company and carried out *that work* without interfering with one another. This made it impossible for any single worker to glean the full scope of what they were contributing to, of what their precise role was in the grand scheme. But it was satisfaction enough to know that they were helping Gray. *Why does No. 2 HQ exist? Why am I working here? Why was I saved?* Such questions naturally arose but didn't lead to misgivings.

The workday over, Ryotaro walked the five minutes it took to get to his high-rise apartment. He paid close to five hundred thousand yen a month to rent it, but it had been a natural choice since his salary more than covered the expense and many of his colleagues from the office lived there too. It was just before six by the time he got back to his apartment. He still had an hour before he was due to be picked up. He had nothing in particular to do so he made some coffee and switched on the TV.

He flicked to a channel showing the news and sat watching a rapid succession of brief, gloomy reports on murders, political scandals, and various diplomatic issues. They went through each story quickly as though they didn't want the information to stick in people's minds. After the muddy stream of ghastly news, they took their time on sundry features to create a smokescreen for the viewers.

There was nothing on the August Raids or the jewelry heist that Ryotaro had taken part in. Japan wasn't halcyon enough for the news to dwell on cases that were getting nowhere even if they had yet to be solved.

As he sipped his coffee, Ryotaro reflected on how hard it was, even now, to believe he had actually been part of the raid Gray had orchestrated. What was it that Gray wanted to do? Ryotaro had lost count of the number of times he'd considered the question but he was still no closer to an answer. He just knew that *something was going to happen.*

The buzzer rang, interrupting him in mid-thought. He went down to meet Takano, the bald man who was always with Gray, in the lobby.

"I've come to pick you up," Takano said, bowing his robust, gym-trained upper body before ceding the way to the car stopped outside the entrance.

Ryotaro felt uneasy around Takano. The man always wore a fixed expression, and the way he trained his knife-like gaze and narrowed his eyes to assess a person was exactly a predator's. Perhaps because he was aware of how intimidating he looked, Takano made an effort to keep his eyes lowered when talking to people. Every now and then, however, his eyes came up and met Ryotaro's and made his flesh crawl.

Ryotaro began walking to the car with Takano directly be-hind him. Despite his huge bulk, the man was able to efface his presence and moved without a sound.

"Sayuri is waiting at the destination." A disembodied voice in the darkness.

"Okay," mumbled Ryotaro.

"Are you all right?" Takano inquired, his voice like a sudden draft of cold air, making Ryotaro shiver. "You're sweating," the man observed detachedly.

"I'm fine," Ryotaro answered without turning back and sped up. He wanted to be free of the stifling air as soon as possible. When he reached the car the back door swung open, revealing Gray.

"It's been a while," Gray said, stepping out of the car.

Ryotaro felt immediately calmer as the man looked down at him. He attempted to return the greeting, but Gray preempted him by continuing to speak.

"I realize it's a little irregular for the host himself to pick up a guest, but I have a policy of accompanying first-time visitors. Shall we?"

Ryotaro climbed into the car. When he had settled into his seat, Gray slowly lowered himself back inside. The elegance and overwhelming self-assurance with which he carried himself was enough to instill a sense of inferiority in anyone who saw him.

"Let's go."

The car slid forward in silence as though in direct response to Gray's request. Takano had somehow gotten into the driver's seat without Ryotaro noticing.

They drove through Nihonbashi, weaving through the confusion of streets. The interior was completely quiet as if soundproofed. It hardly felt like the car was moving at all.

"Sorry for the abruptness of the invitation. I hope you can forgive my neglecting to let you know well in advance," Gray apologized.

"Not at all. I want to thank you for the invitation," Ryotaro answered, shaking his head.

Gray let out a sighing chuckle in response. "Please, try to relax a little."

It was only then that Ryotaro realized his body had gone tense. "Sorry… I'm a bit nervous," he admitted. The first time he had met Gray, the man had just been a stranger who'd put him on guard, and they'd been able to chat more or less like equals. But now Ryotaro owed Gray his life, and he was all too aware of the awesome power the man wielded. There was no way he could maintain his calm before such a figure.

"Ryotaro, you christened me. If anything you're the parent, and I'm the child. Please, do relax," Gray urged, attempting to soothe Ryotaro's nerves.

"That is utterly inconceivable."

"I am indeed quite a bit older than you, Ryotaro, but in my mind I'm still just an innocent little boy," Gray shared in a jesting tone. "*I relish the name you gave me—Gray—like a toy from Santa Claus that a child has received, frolicking with joy.*"

"R-Really?" Ryotaro had not meant to say anything so significant when he had blurted out the name——it had merely been his first impression of the man. He felt a little guilty.

"It's a wonderful name. Now everyone calls me Gray," remarked Gray, looking straight into Ryotaro's eyes.

It seemed that he hadn't had any proper name before Ryotaro had called him that. Since then, Gray had spread the word that he wanted to be called thus. The fact helped Ryotaro believe that Gray was telling the truth when he said he liked the name.

"This pains me, as you are my godfather, but I have a single favor to ask."

"Yes?" Having relaxed somewhat, Ryotaro was able to let his voice reflect his affection for the man. He was happy to listen to any favor Gray might ask him.

"We are heading to my private residence. My secret lair, in other words. I'm not the most sociable of people, so I place a high premium on having somewhere I can be by myself. My ideal hideout is one where no one else can intrude."

Gray paused, and when he spoke again his voice was a little deeper.

"I'm ashamed to ask, since I'm the one who invited you,

but would you be so kind as to put this on?" Gray requested, holding out a blindfold. "It's not that I don't trust you. It's just another one of my rules. I'm afraid I can't break custom for you, so please don't be offended." Gray's eyes narrowed as he made a remorseful face.

Ryotaro glanced at Takano for a brief moment, then nodded. "Of course, I understand," he promptly replied, taking the blindfold and placing it directly over his eyes. "Is this okay?" he asked, turning to face Gray, blindfold in place.

Gray sounded surprised at Ryotaro's unhesitant manner. "Perfect. My apologies for the indignity."

"It's no problem at all. I'm happy to do whatever you ask of me."

"Just remember to call me Gray."

"Of course, Gray. If you ask me, I'll do anything." Ryotaro bowed his blindfolded head.

"You're too kind. Thank you," said Gray after an interval of silence.

Ryotaro couldn't see his expression, but he was sure that Gray looked happy.

The car seemed to get caught up in traffic for a while after Ryotaro had put on his blindfold, repeatedly lurching forward and coming to a stop. Thirty minutes into the ride the car shook as though crossing over something before finally pulling to a halt.

"You can remove the blindfold now."

Ryotaro obediently took the cloth from his eyes and looked around. Everything was obscured by the smoked glass windows, but they appeared to be in an underground parking area. The space was small, room enough for maybe three cars, with nothing else of particular note. It was almost too nondescript. It was impossible to tell where the entrance or exit was.

"Allow me to lead the way," Gray invited as he took the blindfold back. Ryotaro's door swung open to reveal Takano— Ryotaro had thought he was still in the front—who motioned for him to get out of the car.

He squinted at the light in the ceiling. Combined with the unease of being in an unknown place, the bright light in the otherwise dim area gave him a mild case of vertigo.

"Are you okay?" Takano's voice came from behind. Ryotaro felt a chill run down his back.

"Yes," he answered curtly and took a deep breath. He looked around, trying to get a feel for the area so he could regain his equilibrium.

There seemed to be no heating in the obscure, rectangular space and it was icy cold. A single bulb in the center of the ceiling burned dazzlingly but failed to illuminate the corners. The contrast between light and dark was unnerving. Ryotaro felt like he'd come to the end of the world.

A sharp contrast, black and white—standing there, Ryotaro was struck by the illusion that everything had suddenly turned gray. His visual center instinctively sought *a balance between the vivid light and the abyss of darkness and created impossible shades of gray.*

"Okay, let's go," Gray said cheerfully as if to dispel Ryotaro's nervousness, footsteps echoing along the floor.

He reached one of the walls and extended a hand to a knob that Ryotaro had not noticed, opening a door.

It revealed a flight of stairs descending into the ground, just wide enough for a single person. While each step was clearly lit to minimize the likelihood of tripping, the ceiling was shrouded in a cloud of darkness.

Their three sets of footfalls echoed randomly along the tall, narrow stairway. There were only forty or so steps in total, but it felt like more to Ryotaro.

Once they reached the bottom, they came to a featureless door. Gray kept his eyes on Ryotaro as he quietly pushed it open.

"Welcome to my little hiding place."

The door opened to a simple room. It was large, enough to fit thirty or so people, but hardly impressive. At the center was a large, rectangular table that could seat over ten people. There were four doors in total. That was it. An unexceptional room with nothing particularly odd about it.

If there was anything that stood out, it was the wooden table placed in the center. It had been laid with knives and forks. This was probably where they'd eat. A stout vase holding a bouquet of flowers sat in the middle. Ryotaro felt disappointed. He had expected something palatial.

"A little unexpected, perhaps?" Gray asked as though he had read Ryotaro's thoughts.

"Ah, just a little."

"Everyone has the same reaction when they come here for the first time. The ominous parking area, the concealed staircase. Anyone would imagine the awaiting chamber to be quite splendid. But you get here and it's just a room. That is fine, I say. Isn't it much more interesting to have a plain room take you by surprise than be greeted by the predictable grandiose hall?" Gray opined, obviously enjoying himself.

He sat at the head of the table in a mahogany chair that matched the table's design.

"Please, take a seat," he gestured to his right.

Ryotaro sat down awkwardly and cast his gaze over the tabletop. There were five sets of cutlery and wine glasses, so there would be at least two more people joining them.

He looked at the large vase decorating the center of the table. It contained a neat arrangement of flowers of varying colors.

"I arranged those," Gray divulged, noticing Ryotaro's interest. He scrunched his eyes slightly, looking a little self-conscious.

"It's amazing," admired Ryotaro.

The vase contained blooms from every season: plum blossoms, cherry blossoms, sunflowers, zebra grass, cosmos, narcissus, and tree peonies. The flowers were clearly real but curiously seemed to have no scent to them.

"Given my personality, I tend to go for eccentric arrangements. I never learned any particular school so my style is rather idiosyncratic. I'm not skilled enough to merit an audience, but I like to put something out when I have guests. I have the fragrances removed so it doesn't interfere with the food. My little hideout has an underground garden where I can grow flowers all year round."

"It's a little surprising," Ryotaro said honestly. He found it difficult to imagine Gray dabbling in *ikebana*.

"I would imagine so. I surprised myself. I also enjoy preparing tea. I'll take the liberty of making you some later."

It was the first time Ryotaro had seen Gray look so shy. It was refreshing.

"You're late," a familiar female voice spoke as though it had been waiting for a gap in the conversation. Sayuri came through from one of the other doors and took the seat to Gray's left, without hesitation, so that she sat facing Ryotaro. She sighed loudly. "I got tired of waiting. I'm starved!"

"We were a little behind schedule, the roads were a bit jammed," Takano explained, sitting beside her. The only remaining seat was next to Ryotaro.

"Well then, shall we start?"

Gray checked his wristwatch and, as though on cue, one of the doors opened and food came streaming in, several male and female servers setting down plates of French cuisine before disappearing again into the back room. Ryotaro guessed it was the kitchen. The servers were dressed in suits, each with a unique appearance, and looked more like office workers than waiters.

For hors d'oeuvres, they had set out guinea fowl and a galantine of chicken breast, paired with white wine. The room filled with succulent smells that whet the appetite. Ryotaro swallowed as his mouth watered.

"Bon appetit." Gray lifted his wine glass in his right hand and tipped it to the others. Ryotaro copied the gesture. "I would like to offer thanks for us being able to dine together like this."

Gray gently wet his lips with the wine before putting it back on the table. Then, without showing any signs of touching his food, he concentrated his jet-black eyes on Ryotaro. Prompted by his gaze, Ryotaro took a sip.

A sweet bouquet spread inside his mouth. The wine was so beautifully smooth that he almost sighed with appreciation.

The elegantly prepared soup and plate of fish that appeared

next were so well prepared Ryotaro couldn't help but smile. Just as he finished the fish, the servers brought out the meat dish, perfectly on time. Each was a joy for the palate.

As he worked his way through the food, Ryotaro observed the others. Gray took occasional sips of wine as he engaged his guests in casual conversation, hardly touching his plate. Sayuri was clearly enjoying the cuisine, while Takano carried it mechanically to his mouth, not speaking unless spoken to. Once the staff was done serving, they prepared their own dinner and sat eating together at the same table. There were eight of them in total, and they all smiled and chatted merrily.

The seat next to Ryotaro remained empty.

As he looked around while working his knife and fork Ryotaro felt suddenly uneasy and put his cutlery down. *Why was I called here? For what reason and purpose? What's going to happen next?* He listened to Sayuri conversing in high spirits, an antithesis to his growing unease.

"Ah, I feel revived," she declared, looking thoroughly happy as she drained her glass.

"Aren't you underage, Sayuri?" Ryotaro asked as he stabbed at his foie gras.

"Don't be such a bore!" she accused, her voice brighter than usual. In her uniform as ever, Sayuri picked up the nearest bottle, poured herself another glass, and emptied it again. Her eyes drooped; she was probably already drunk. "Can't let you keep something this good to yourselves, can I?" she chirped, leaning her head to one side.

"Drinking is nothing compared to a raid," Gray pointed out amusedly.

"That's true." Gray's words stirred up the guilt that had settled like sediment in Ryotaro's heart.

As if to put him at ease Gray continued, "There is no need to look put out. It bears remembering that you have chosen to follow me now, not the law. And I don't consider myself bound by such puerile tricks. The law exerts no influence over my actions or thoughts. From what I have seen, the law is utterly ineffective.

It is no more illegal for Sayuri to drink alcohol as it is for me to steal because there is no such thing as law." The words had rolled off his tongue. He looked completely self-assured as he turned to Sayuri. "Even so, it is a little painful to watch people drink to the point where they begin to lose control of themselves," he scolded, chuckling.

Sayuri pouted like a naughty child but immediately put her wine glass down and pulled her water glass closer. Gray nodded approvingly, then looked at the others around him.

"We're still one short, but it's time to move on to tonight's business," Gray began, his eyes flashing briefly over the empty seat next to Ryotaro. "Ryotaro, do you know why I have called you here tonight?"

Ryotaro shook his head in response. He couldn't even begin to guess.

Gray nodded slightly. "I am going to let you in on a secret."

"A secret?"

"Yes. But before I do, I have a few questions. May I?"

"Of course," Ryotaro nodded as he felt Gray's eyes bore into his own.

"Ryotaro, are you willing to follow me?"

The question was vague, but there was only one possible response. "Of course."

"Well then. Would you be willing to put yourself in danger for me?"

"Yes," Ryotaro answered instantly.

"Even if it meant possibly losing your life?"

Ryotaro felt a moment's hesitation. "Yes," he blurted out his response, embarrassedly compensating for the delay.

"I see…" Gray smiled, but only with his mouth. "The next question will be my last. *If I were to ask Ryotaro to kill someone, what would he do?*" Gray's eyes sharpened as he sounded Ryotaro's thoughts.

Ryotaro's mouth went dry, and he fell mute.

Kill someone?

His body flushed and he began to sweat. He stiffened as

extreme tension spread through him. Gray sat waiting for his reply, a smile still on his face.

"In what—"

"Please answer the question." Gray's voice was soft but forceful, peremptory.

Ryotaro considered it. There was no way he could kill someone.

Kill someone…

He had contemplated the act. Back when he had been working at the jewelry store, he'd lost count of the number of times he'd killed his manager Yoshimura in his mind. But he had never actually planned on doing it. He was a coward. Unable to rid himself of his enemies, he had ended up choosing to end his own life. That, too, suggested that he could never kill someone.

Even so… Ryotaro's dry lips began to move. "If you wished it, Gray, and if I were happy with your reasoning, I wouldn't shun murder, even," Ryotaro answered. He felt dizzy and nauseous, but he had kept his eyes on Gray's the whole time.

"That will do," Gray stated readily. He narrowed his eyes, encouraging Ryotaro to relax.

Ryotaro inhaled sharply as though he had forgotten to breathe and put a hand to his chest to try and calm himself.

"Please accept my apologies for the rather malicious questions. Rest assured, I will never ask you to kill anyone. In fact, my request is the opposite."

"The opposite?"

"Indeed, I would like for you to assist me in saving people."

"Saving people." Ryotaro turned the words over in his mind, but he was still too confused.

"Are you aware of how many people in Japan commit suicide each year?"

Ryotaro's mind raced, trying to remember. More than thirty thousand, he thought. He had told himself at one point that if thirty thousand others would be doing it then he could too.

"Somewhere around thirty thousand, I think…"

"The official figures tend to be around that. But another two hundred thousand go missing each year. It is safe to assume that many of them commit suicide without other people ever finding out. It is therefore quite easy to imagine the real number as close to twice that reported by the government," Gray calmly argued, resting his elbows on the table. "Say we were to accept the publicly reported statistic of thirty thousand. That would still come out to eighty people taking their lives each day. It is difficult even for terrorists to kill eighty people at once, except in acts on a scale to shake an entire society. But in Japan, eighty people—in reality, over a hundred people—succeed in ending their own lives every single day."

Ryotaro had never thought of the annual number of suicides as anything more than a statistic. But now, reframed by Gray, the figure was large enough to make him think that the nation was at war. He felt his body shake from fear; he had come so close to becoming a statistic himself.

Gray continued. "The reasons vary, but the majority of suicide cases stem from money problems. Put differently, suicides, in the main, stem from problems that can be solved with money. Of course there are other misfortunes such as grave illness, but it is clear that the overwhelming majority of cases originate with money." Gray paused, his eyes asking if Ryotaro disagreed; Ryotaro shook his head. "So what needs to be done to stop these suicides? I have pondered this question. Here is the answer I have found: *We must, to the utmost of our abilities, minimize money problems.*"

Money problems? Ryotaro felt he didn't quite understand. Gray went on.

"Suicide due to crushing debt. Suicide due to your company going under. Suicide due to being laid off. Then there are those souls who cling to the jobs they have just to survive, who become depressed and are hounded to suicide."

Ryotaro felt his heart contract painfully on hearing the last bit. Gray was talking about him.

"There's even suicide from bullying. If you have enough money, transferring becomes a viable option. Perhaps there would be no need to attend school in the first place. With money enough to last your whole life, you wouldn't have to be a part of a system of education that's designed only to benefit the upper classes. You could work part-time when you felt like it without committing to a vocation. I don't see any reason why kids should be forced to go to schools that can't keep reckless bullying in check. Some would hold that running away isn't the answer, but when we are talking about children choosing to end their lives, that dictum doesn't seem universally applicable. Run away if you are bullied. Throw money at bullies to make them go away. When children kill themselves from bullying, that tragic outcome is due to their having had nowhere to run. Money allows you to avoid all kinds of problems. You can escape from the violence of the strong. Sometimes you can even *gain total control over them.*"

Gray put particular emphasis on the final phrase, then smiled quietly.

"I have dirtied my hands with crime for a reason. I have stolen back riches as part of a process of *redistribution.* I will accomplish this, whatever the cost. What do you say? Will you offer me your assistance in helping reduce the number of casualties in this country?"

Gray fell silent and sat perfectly still as he waited for Ryotaro's reply.

What does he mean by "redistribution"? How does he plan to carry it out? Can he really pull it off? Questions flashed through Ryotaro's mind but vanished in an instant.

"It would be my pleasure, if I may be of assistance."

Ryotaro had no reason to ruminate over the method to be employed. There was no need to consider whether or not it was possible. Gray said he would do it. And if Gray believed it was possible, it was as good as done.

"Thank you." Gray finally looked away from Ryotaro and drained his half-full wine glass.

"I'm glad you didn't refuse," Sayuri injected gaily from across the table. Ryotaro looked up and saw that everyone was smiling at him.

Gray continued. "Our organization is composed of over one hundred people. They work tirelessly every day in support of my selfish goal. I have been inviting to dinner a select few members who will help with my plans of redistribution, as I have done tonight. Unfortunately, Shindo appears to have been unable to join us on this particular occasion, but she, too, is a member of the team."

Ryotaro remembered Kozue having mentioned "that dinner" back in the office. That meant Sasaki and Kozue, the two professional hackers, had already attended one of Gray's dinners. And Shindo, the woman he'd met in the Tomosun building who helped Gray launder money, was also on board.

"I wanted to gain Ryotaro's assistance in the redistribution project. That's why I called you here tonight." Gray's eyes narrowed into a pleasant smile.

Ryotaro, on the other hand, felt a growing sense of apprehension. *What kind of assistance could I possibly offer?*

"I... What would you have me do?" Ryotaro asked timidly.

Gray put his hand to his chin. He eventually replied, "Nothing difficult. Ryotaro can take on *the role of seeing it through.*"

That was all Gray said about Ryotaro's duties. He went on to outline the methods he would employ for redistribution. The plan he outlined sounded preposterous. Gray went through it all with a smile on his face, not once letting Ryotaro see whatever emotions lurked behind his eyes, except the apparent enjoyment.

The dinner ended after Gray treated them all to some Earl Grey.

3

Three days since Ryotaro attended dinner with Gray, his daily routine hadn't undergone any significant change. As usual he went to his utterly unnecessary job, left the office at 5:30, and went straight back to his apartment. He received no new instructions, no fresh tasks, and there were no signs to suggest coming changes.

Meanwhile, others in the redistribution scheme interacted with him at work. It seemed many team members were based in Nihonbashi No. 2 HQ, including Sasaki and Kozue.

That interaction, however, was limited to people sidling up and greeting him with a whisper: "We're counting on you for *Christmas.*"

The member would say this in a hush so as not to be overheard, give him a meaningful glance, then just go about his or her business.

December 24th was just seven days away. That was when Gray planned to carry out his redistribution.

Redistribution. The operation that Gray and the others called *Christmas.* The day, to wit, that they planned to break into the Bank of Japan and the National Printing Bureau.

No matter how often the logic or the viability of the scheme was explained to him, the whole thing was far beyond the limits of his imagination. He sat at the four-seater table in his apartment, scribbling in a large notebook he bought at a convenience store, trying to sort out everything Gray had told him.

Gray had carried out the August Raids in preparation for Christmas, in order to raise and operate the funds necessary for his plan.

He had bought up a small trading company on the brink of bankruptcy and injected huge amounts of capital into it. He named it Tomosun Trading and used the company to import necessary goods. For example, the computers manufactured abroad that Sasaki and Kozue used were veritable miniature supercomputers. The guns they used were also sourced from overseas. Gray had also bought up mining rights in Mongolia, securitized the rare earths uncovered, and directed Tomosun Securities to sell them as a financial product to the wealthy. This was apparently a key part of amassing funds. Even the government was investing large sums in the excavation of rare earths.

Pharaon Logistics was similar, set up to provide Gray with a vast freight network to facilitate the flow of goods, personnel, and stolen money. The vans and uniforms were an everyday sight, always on the streets, so no one thought them suspicious.

Ryotaro went over the roles people had been given.

Ten, including Sasaki and Kozue, were assigned roles in hacking, data cracking, server infiltration, and social hacking. They had each played important roles during the August Raids, disabling security systems and cameras, leveraging sensitive information that *banks—and individuals working at these banks—wanted to keep from public scrutiny*, forcing them to become unwitting collaborators and thus ensuring the smooth execution of the heists. In the case of the jewelry exhibition they had not required these methods since Ryotaro already functioned as their insider, but for every other raid their preparations had been exhaustive.

There were a number of buyers who negotiated with foreign countries for items to be shipped into Japan. They traveled to places like Russia and secured goods through untraceable routes.

There were many others, each carrying out their roles every day. Sayuri had told him that all of them apart from a small minority were people who had decided to die but had been rescued by Gray.

The minority included people like Shindo, who handled Gray's money laundering.

Strictly speaking, her work stance differed from that of members personally saved by Gray. She had worked at a bank where she'd been lining her own pockets helping the yakuza launder their proceeds until the police got wind of it; she had been about to receive a prison sentence when Gray stepped in. That was when she started at her current position, but Gray was not forcing her to work for him. Of course she was indebted to him for saving her from prison, but he paid her a significant sum for her help with laundering money. Theirs was more of a business relationship.

Ryotaro tapped the nib of his ballpoint pen against the notepad with his right hand and massaged his heavy head with his left. This issue of *redistribution* had short-circuited his thinking process.

He closed his eyes and took a deep breath, then exhaled

heavily, readying himself for another round of notes. Just then the intercom's low buzz echoed through the apartment and made him recoil. He looked to the monitor by the door and saw a face he recognized. Someone he had met only once.

Ryotaro rushed to his feet and picked up the receiver by the monitor. "Hello?"

"There's something I'd like to discuss with you," Shindo said high-handedly, glaring at him through the screen.

"S-Sure, just give me a second," Ryotaro answered, sounding terrified. He rushed to the entrance and opened the door.

"Hurry it up, it's cold out here," Shindo spat. Her coat was trimmed with fur that nearly covered her face. She nearly knocked him over as she strode into the room.

Ryotaro followed behind, dumbfounded. Shindo took off her coat in the living room, revealing a lustrous, tight-fitted black suit with a blue camisole underneath. It showed off the curves of her body, just like the white suit she'd worn before.

"Don't you get depressed being all alone like this?"

"Uh…" Ryotaro muttered, not knowing how he was supposed to respond.

"A textbook case of a hopeless man-child. A woman comes to visit you through frozen gales yet you're totally tactless. You should offer me something warm to drink."

"How about some…coffee?"

"I'm chilled through, but that'll do. Hurry up," she demanded.

Ryotaro hurried into the kitchen and boiled some water, readying two drip filters. As he poured the water onto the grounds, he began to worry over Shindo's sudden call.

"Sorry to barge in like this," Shindo apologized in an arrogant tone, perching herself at his table.

"It's fine," Ryotaro said quickly, looking up. Their eyes met and he hurriedly looked back at the coffee cups. "Why the visit?"

"Do I need a reason? Am I in your way?"

"No, that's not what I—"

"I've got something I want to discuss," Shindo announced

with her back to him.

"Discuss?" Ryotaro carried the cups over to the table.

"Yes, about *this*." Shindo held up Ryotaro's notepad. He almost dropped the coffee, just barely managing to maintain his grip.

"You saw?" Ryotaro gave her a reproachful look as he put the cups on the table.

"Just skimmed through them."

"Please, don't read other people's things without permission." He already knew that Shindo was involved so he did not feel too shaken but wasn't thrilled to have someone rifle through his notes unbidden.

"Ah, got you angry?" Shindo joked as Ryotaro snatched the notepad from her.

Instead of answering he pushed one of the cups to her and sat across from her. "So you want to talk about *Christmas*?"

"Yes, about *Christmas*." Shindo took a sip of her coffee, not showing any reaction to Ryotaro's bad mood. "By your notes I assume you went to Gray's dinner party."

"I did. You didn't turn up."

"I don't care for those kinds of events. Besides, I don't believe what Gray says."

Ryotaro felt wariness take root as his body stiffened. At the same time, he was a little surprised to hear Shindo call Gray by his new name and not just refer to him as *that man*.

"Relax. I'm not going to betray him or anything. I haven't told anyone, and I don't have any intention of doing so." Shindo brushed her wavy hair up and laughed quietly. "I have my own sense of obligation to him, you know. I would never do anything to disadvantage him. It would also become my disadvantage, after all."

If what Sayuri had told him was true, Shindo received a substantial income from Gray. Ryotaro's monthly pay was over ten million yen and he wasn't even doing anything important, so it was easy to imagine Shindo receiving over ten times that amount.

"But this *Christmas* thing is different. What you wrote here, that's all stuff Gray told you, right?"

Ryotaro nodded. Gray had said that breaking into the Bank of Japan and the National Printing Bureau was how he wanted to kickstart *redistribution*. He hadn't been told all the details but it appeared that the others, including Sayuri, knew everything.

"I'm not really sure what he meant, but he said it was for redistribution."

"He hasn't told me anymore than that, either, although the others seem to know. But I've got a pretty good idea of what he's trying to accomplish. He's going to raid the Bank of Japan at the end of the year when it has the most assets on site to secure a vast amount of money. At the same time he has five hundred billion yen in financing from the government for Tomosun Trading's rare earths project, plus around two hundred billion from rich investors and various companies from selling securitized rare earths via Tomosun Security. My guess is that he plans to use Pharaon Logistics' freight infrastructure to disseminate the money across the country. It's quite possible that Gray has other sizable assets to his name, so we should expect a ridiculous amount of money to be released. That's what I think Gray's so-called redistribution is."

Ryotaro nodded as he listened. "I had no idea what it actually meant."

"It's a hypothesis, nothing more," Shindo said with contempt in her voice. "Steal huge sums of money from the government and redistribute it among the poor and middle classes. Tomosun Securities, on the other hand, functions to rob the rich. If the plan succeeds, it could result in a temporary dissolution of gaps in wealth. But, no matter how you go about it, the logic fails."

"Why?"

"Have you heard of inflation?" Shindo asked, peering hard at him.

"That much I know," Ryotaro answered flatly, then jerked his eyes open. Indeed, if money were recklessly redistributed, the economy would be flooded with cash and naturally suffer from inflation.

"How could you not see?" Shindo continued, sounding amazed. "Let's assume the redistribution succeeds and each and every citizen gets, say, a hundred million yen. Then what? Everyone's suddenly rich and can afford anything. But if demand rises, prices soar. Something that's a hundred yen today becomes ten thousand yen. The over-abundance of cash in the market leads to the depreciation of the yen. Even if he manages to redistribute a hundred million yen to everyone, inflation would drive prices into disarray and force an adjustment. The result is that the wealthy, their riches increased further, would survive."

Shindo sighed, looking tired, and took a sip of coffee. She made a face that suggested she didn't care for the taste, then tossed a question towards the speechless Ryotaro. "So you just accept what Gray says at face value. Are you that *head over heels* for him?"

"Okay, then what do you think Gray meant?" Ryotaro felt his face turn red.

"I don't think that Gray is too stupid to recognize inflation as an issue. So either my theory is way off or Gray *has another goal in mind*."

"Another goal?"

"You won't find out by asking me. But his desire to hit the National Printing Bureau as well as the Bank of Japan bothers me." Shindo flicked her long nails against the coffee cup.

"He wants to stop them from printing new money?"

"Exactly. Even if he spread the BoJ's cash among the masses, it's quite possible that the government will be able to track the money as stolen funds. I don't know the extent to which the BoJ has their stuff in order, but cash is printed with serial numbers. They might try to find a way to print completely new bills and have them traded with legal tender that wasn't stolen from them."

"To stop them from doing that, you have to take away their ability to print money. I guess it makes sense. It's possible."

"Exactly, it makes sense. But following Gray's logic, he would have to make sure that it stays that way. He'd have to set up camp inside the National Printing Bureau or destroy the printers."

"Destroy," Ryotaro muttered, realizing she was right. A temporary occupation would have no meaning, but it would be pretty much impossible to keep the presses under siege over an extended period.

"Well, my thoughts are strictly within the realm of speculation. Perhaps Gray has a perfect formula in his head, something I can't even begin to imagine. It's just... I get angry when I think about this *redistribution*."

"Why?" Ryotaro asked.

Shindo furrowed her brows in response. "If I knew why it'd be easy. Just..." Shindo swallowed, wetting her parched throat. "It's suspicious. There are too many unknowns to just trust him. I get the feeling Gray's not giving us the whole picture. I think he's keeping *his true goals* hidden."

In the wake of her assertion the already quiet room sank into a whirlpool of silence. Ryotaro looked down at his coffee. It had stopped steaming. The black liquid dimly reflected his face.

"You know Sayuri, right?"

"Yeah, sure..." Ryotaro recalled their date in Kamakura. He remembered the sorrow he'd glimpsed through her smiles. It had left a deep impression.

"Do you know what her role is?"

Ryotaro shook his head. He'd wondered about it, but the unspoken rule among those rescued by Gray was not to probe unless the topic was volunteered.

Shindo's eyes narrowed behind her glasses, and she opened her captivatingly lip-glossed mouth. "You should ask her directly. You want to know, don't you?"

"No..."

"Liar," Shindo laughed. "I know the two of you went on a date to Kamakura."

"Huh? How..." Ryotaro was agitated. It was nothing to hide, but they had not been public about it either, so he hadn't expected Shindo to know.

"Sayuri told me. At any rate, I know you like her. You want to know what kind of amazing tasks Gray asks her to perform,

185

don't you? If you find out, you might learn more about the kind of man Gray is. For someone who worships him so blindly, it might just be the perfect medicine. Well? You wanna know?" Shindo closed her mouth and fixed her eyes on Ryotaro like a scientist watching a guinea pig.

He came close to telling her that he did but managed to swallow his words. He dropped his eyes to the table, bowed his head, and drank his coffee.

"Well, whether you ask or not is up to you," Shindo quickly stated, turning serious. "So what's your role for Christmas? That's actually what I came to ask."

Ryotaro faltered, hesitant. His head was full with thoughts about Sayuri's role, but his own task troubled him nearly to the same degree.

"What's wrong? No reason to be coy. My job, by the way, is going to be money laundering and to create a number of absolutely undetectable hidden bank accounts. In other words, nothing directly related to the bank run. I'll be helping post-event." Shindo smiled before assuming an inquisitive expression. "And you? Don't tell me you're going to be on the attack squad?"

"I..." Ryotaro hesitated.

"Don't put on airs—let's hear it."

Her spiky tone finally compelled Ryotaro to speak. "He asked me to *see it through*."

Shindo's mouth dropped open as she gave him an idiotic look. "What the hell is that?"

"That's what I want to know," Ryotaro threw back.

"See what through?"

"I don't know," Ryotaro answered without pause.

"You didn't ask?"

"Of course I did. But Gray wouldn't tell me. He just said I needn't worry until the day of. So, basically, I don't know what I'm supposed to be doing."

"Huh," mocked Shindo. "You sure you're not going nuts?"

"Uh, I don't think so," Ryotaro replied without confidence.

"No, no, this is a problem. Doesn't not knowing your role

make you anxious? No matter what anyone says, what we're about to attempt is illegal. This isn't some game. We're not playing house."

"I know. But if Gray gave me that role, it's because he thinks I can do it. That's why, even if I don't know the details of my part, I still plan to do what I can as best I can. If Gray says I don't need to worry about the details, then it's best to take his word for it."

"You're so naive. I wonder if your brain is actually functioning properly. You're like some kid who's ignorant of the ways of the world," Shindo admonished, amazed. "Just like one of the Forty-Seven Ronin. Do your best, then."

Shindo got up and began to walk towards the door but turned back as though just remembering something. "It's not like me to say something like this, but you tickle *the sadist* in me so I'll give you a warning as a reward. I'm only rear support and won't be taking a direct part in *Christmas*. But you should know that many of those on the front lines are ready to die."

Ryotaro did not so much as flinch on hearing her words.

"Oh, you already knew that," Shindo knotted her brows and looked worried. "So you're ready to die, too."

Ryotaro didn't speak. Shindo took his silence as affirmation and shook her head in exasperation.

Ryotaro sensed that everyone that had attended one of Gray's dinners was literally prepared to die. The majority of the front line consisted of members who had secretly traveled to the United Arab Emirates to train with PMCs in the use of guns as well as raid and suppression tactics. If they barricaded themselves inside the bank, it was likely that special teams would be mobilized alongside the police. The opposition would be heavily equipped to halt the scheme. All in all, they needed to brace themselves for the worst-case scenario.

"I owe Gray my allegiance. He hushed up my dealings at the bank and saved me when I was on the verge of heading to prison. And he pays me a salary I couldn't hope to earn from a lifetime of honest work. He keeps me busy with exciting work. I enjoy it, even. But…" Shindo gave a tiny, almost inaudible sigh. "He didn't save my life like with the rest of you. My debt is different. I don't owe him my life. If the worst happens and Christmas fails, I'm heading overseas right away. I'll sit back and watch the aftermath from afar."

Shindo's tone seemed to contain a measure of animosity for Gray. "He saved your life and now you're offering it right back to him. But think about it. Sure, he might have saved your lives. But you're about to throw away the very life he saved. Can't you see you're just headed towards the same terminus? Sorry if it sounds like I'm lecturing here, but *your very life isn't something you ought to let a stranger meddle with.*"

Shindo looked away.

"You weren't part of his plan. By the time he'd completed the August Raids he had enough personnel, enough money, enough preparation. Hell, *he had enough money even before then—he didn't need to resort to stealing in the first place. But he went through with the August Raids anyway, putting himself at unnecessary risk. And then he got you involved. He carried out another raid that wasn't in his original plan just to reel you in.* He's cooking up something. And I think he brought you in to help with that, to do something different from whatever the rest of his band of ronin will be doing." Shindo hesitated briefly before continuing, "I guess I'm kind of a bystander in all of this, but I believe that, as someone directly involved, you really need to think this over for yourself, make your own decision. And…"

Shindo suddenly fell silent, squared her shoulders, and started walking. She left the room, opening the door and disappearing into the world outside.

A rush of frozen air billowed through, stabbing Ryotaro in the cheek.

Click, the sound of the door closing disturbed the silence.

Ryotaro stared at it and vaguely wondered if Shindo had picked up on something during her time working for Gray.

CHAPTER FIVE

1

The city overflowed with Christmas illuminations and decorations. The area in front of Mitsukoshimae Station was gorgeously decked out. It was a weekday so many people were still in suits, but the area filled with shoppers as soon as Mitsukoshi department store opened. The streets were awash in smiling faces. The sounds of a Christmas song floated in the air and the whole city seemed to be restless. Ryotaro was swept along by the crowds, unable to resist the muddled current.

It was December 24th, just after ten in the morning.

The morning sun made the wintry sky seem ever more translucent as the air fairly sparkled. Ryotaro sat with Gray, Sayuri, and the hackers Sasaki and Kozue in one of Pharaon Logistics' distribution vans. They drove past Mitsukoshimae Station, turned onto Sotobori Road, and came to a stop at the curb in front of the Bank of Japan's main branch. The newly constructed building was ten stories tall and almost completely surrounded by a high external wall with black wrought-iron bars. There was an automated barricade to the north where through-traffic was screened. A number of police were stationed around the building and all key angles were covered by a web of security cameras.

There were so many people coming and going, however, that the cops on duty didn't appear to be checking everyone. There was no sense of heightened security.

Ryotaro gazed up at the bank through the van's tinted windows. Gray was dressed as usual, but Ryotaro and the others were outfitted like a special military force with radios in their vests and guns they had received training in fitted to their belts. Kozue sat in the driver's seat, blowing smoke from a cigarette as she took in the scene outside.

Three other delivery vans were lined up along the street. Another two were parked on Edo Sakura Street, near the entrance to the old bank building that was open to the public. The Pharaon vans did not appear to be raising any signs of suspicion among the suited workers or the officers manning the gate.

"Okay, go," Gray spoke into his radio. Groups of masked men simultaneously jumped out of the other vans.

The armed men jogged in a straight line towards the main bank building's interior. It was a bizarre scene—the men were clearly armed and carrying armored briefcases. Some of the men carried bags large enough to fit a person inside. Passersby and bank workers watched in a daze as twenty armed troopers suddenly appeared, yet no one made to run away. If anything, everyone was totally calm.

This can't be happening.

That was what was probably going through their minds. No one attempted to alert the police.

The cops on guard themselves seemed to have lost the ability to think, their eyes peeled open at the sight of the troopers. Gray's men seized the chance to ram shotgun-like tasers into them to neutralize any potential threat. That was when the first civilians began to scream.

The men, dressed completely in jet black, instantly disappeared as if sucked through the entrance. Once Gray confirmed they had made it in, he pulled his hat down over his eyes and handed Ryotaro a black face mask.

"Put this on, just in case."

By the time Ryotaro had the mask in his hands Sayuri was already wearing a hunting cap. Sasaki and Kozue were hidden under their own masks, too.

"Does it, suit me?" Sasaki asked, struggling to speak from under the mask.

"You'd be happy if the answer was yes?" Kozue asked in amazement.

"I think it suits you," Ryotaro muttered as he put his own on.

Sasaki scratched at his head, scrunched his eyes together happily, and reciprocated, "You look, cool too, Ryotaro."

There was a distant sound, like the banging of a small drum. Immediately afterwards, screams and footsteps broke through the calm. Ryotaro looked outside to see a flood of people emerging from the bank's main building like water from a broken dam. Five minutes later there was a voice on the wireless.

"Assault Team. We've secured the interior," the report came in through the radio in Gray's hand. The voice, sharp and tense, was Takano's.

At almost exactly the same time, a younger voice sounded from Kozue's radio.

"Hacking Squad Beta. Surveillance temporarily neutralized. Commencing physical destruction of cameras. Locations mostly in line with blueprints. A walk in the park. You can come in now."

"Hacking Squad Alpha. Roger," Kozue said and turned to face Gray. "The cameras have been taken care of."

"Right, let us proceed." Gray opened the door and quietly exited the van.

The street, which had been overflowing with Christmas cheer, now looked like a scene from a disaster movie. People were fleeing in all directions, faces stricken. Screams gave rise to more screaming, fear to more fear. Ryotaro caught the gaze of some of the panicked people. They bolted out of his way with a terrified look on their faces.

Gray walked against the flow of bodies and into the bank's main building. They reached the business area on the first floor without meeting any resistance. There was no one left inside apart from their armed comrades. Business had been going on as usual until moments ago, but the echoing footsteps of the armed men erased that atmosphere.

Some set up computers. Some dragged three-seater sofas over to barricade the entrance. Some sprayed the glass windows to prevent anyone spying from the outside. Some rolled barbed wire over the exits and barricades. Some scanned the room to check if anyone was hiding and some scouted for any movements outside. Everyone worked with perfect understanding of their roles and executed them flawlessly. Sasaki and Kozue had opened their computers and were typing away at breakneck speed. Sayuri was scurrying around in her hunting cap, watching everyone work. Apart from that she didn't seem to be doing anything in particular.

Ten minutes since initiation.

They heard sirens. Huge numbers of police would be on them at any moment to eliminate Ryotaro and the others.

"Is there anyone left inside?" Gray asked one of the nearby men from Assault Team.

"There were just a few workers who had been slow to leave. We sent them straight out."

"Fine. Continue searching the building, and if you find any staff make sure to remove them immediately."

"Roger." The man relayed the instructions over his wireless set.

Gray turned to face Sasaki and Kozue. "Vault security?"

"Under control, successfully neutralized," Kozue answered with a smile without stopping her typing.

Gray nodded and looked down, concentrating on the sound of the sirens. He took out his wireless receiver. "How's the vault looking?"

"Vault Squad. Just as the blueprints showed. Ready to set nanother-mite explosives to commence melting of door."

"Good. We've got control of the security systems. Make sure to stay clear from the explosion."

"Roger and out."

The line went dead, and Ryotaro went pale.

Nanothermite? We're going to use explosives?

Gun in hand of his own volition, he thought he'd had an adequate understanding of what was going on, but the mention of explosives made his heart beat faster.

"You can take your mask off now. I'm sure it's quite uncomfortable," Gray said.

"Yes," Ryotaro responded, but he hesitated to remove the mask.

"Please, don't worry. All the security cameras have been destroyed."

Ryotaro looked around. No one else was wearing a mask. He breathed in rapid, shallow bursts of air as he peeled his off. The room was warm, but not hot, from the business area's heater. Even so, Ryotaro's nerves had left him drenched in sweat.

"You're worried about the nanothermite?" Gray asked as though he'd read the cause of Ryotaro's unease.

The question caught Ryotaro by surprise. He straightened up and tried to hide his shaking voice by tucking in his chin. "Yes…"

Gray nodded slowly and hoisted himself onto a counter and sat with his legs crossed. "You're familiar with the terrorist attacks on America in 2001?"

Ryotaro nodded.

"Two passenger jets were hijacked by Arab men. Both planes crashed directly into the World Trade Center. The buildings collapsed and a large number of people died. The incident helped stoke extreme levels of anti-Iraqi sentiment among Americans and the U.S. government declared war. The long war ended after countless casualties, America having taken on the terrorists and eliminated the threat," Gray spoke matter-of-factly, his mouth slightly twisted in a sardonic grin. "But you may not know that more and more people have come to doubt the motives behind the war, even the terrorist act itself. Some claim the government had been an accomplice or turned a blind eye."

"The U.S. government?" Ryotaro shook his head.

"Indeed. A number of theories were debated across the

country, each backed by various kinds of evidence. Conspiracy theorists flock to such incidents. Now, I cannot say whether or not the U.S. government was in collusion in this instance. There was, however, one compelling argument among all the theories and evidence presented. The assertion was that there was no way a collision, even one as large as from a passenger jet, could have sufficed to cause the World Trade Center buildings to collapse as they had."

Gray chuckled quietly. "One of the building's architects was quoted as saying that the buildings had a net-like steel fence wrapping around them and that the impact from a passenger jet would be *like sticking a pencil through a wire screen*. He also said it was impossible for the buildings to collapse under the weight of the crushed steel. In other words, something else had to have caused the buildings to fall."

"And this something else was nanothermite explosives?"

"Bingo. Inspections of the remains revealed several places where the steel had melted and snapped. Yet the heat generated from burning jet fuel is nowhere near the temperature needed to melt steel. Still, the buildings' supports had been mysteriously melted and the towers collapsed as neatly as if it had been a planned demolition. Firefighters on site said they heard a number of mysterious explosions.

"So perhaps the terrorists set off explosives that had been planted in advance. But could a group of terrorists really gain access to such closely guarded buildings and set explosives in all the necessary places on their own? Unthinkable under normal conditions. With insiders, however, it would be a different story. Before 9/11, workers in the building complained of noise from inexplicable renovations."

Gray's analysis sounded like a story about some faraway world. For Ryotaro, the events of 9/11 had been someone else's problem or like a development in some piece of fiction. Conspiracy or not, it had had no impact on his life.

"I don't have much interest in arguing for or against the innocence of the American administration. But if it is true that a government destroyed the buildings and forsook the lives of its own citizens in order to launch a profit-generating war—well, I can't think of anything more fascinating than that." Gray paused to take a breath. "Sacrificing your own citizens for war profiteering. Were that so, don't you think nanothermite is *eminently suitable for a collapse?*"

Just as Gray finished speaking, the floor rumbled and shook hard enough to cause Ryotaro to stumble and almost lose his balance. The nanothermite had been detonated underground.

"Anyway, I have talked too much. I have some business to attend to, so please make yourself comfortable," Gray said before walking across the business area. Takano stood waiting at the other side; the duo disappeared into the depths of the bank.

The whole building echoed with the wailing of sirens. There were shouts outside. The rushing of footsteps. The thrumming of helicopter blades. Each sound was an attempt to drive Ryotaro and the others into a corner.

With nothing to do, Ryotaro sat down on one of the chairs that wasn't appropriated for the barricade. It was in the corner of the room. No one else was nearby, and he couldn't even hear any conversation. He heard intermittent detonations. Nanothermite explosives, designed to generate temperatures hot enough to melt steel. That was how they were currently breaking through the Bank of Japan's vault. Ryotaro gazed up at the ceiling of the business area and its myriad of lights. *I'm barricaded in, in here.* He was so tense it made his skin ache, but everything still seemed unreal. Just like the 9/11 attacks, the events seemed to be unfolding in some faraway land.

He turned to look at his comrades as they bustled around. Each pressed on towards a goal that remained a mystery to him. Redistribution. That was all he had been told. He felt alienated, like he'd been cast out from the group.

His role was *to see it through.* What exactly was he supposed to be doing? He knew that thinking it over wouldn't help, but he thought about it nonetheless.

He closed his eyes. The indoor lighting filtered through his eyelids.

When he opened his eyes, he saw Sayuri's face.

"Are you tired?"

"I don't think I'm stout-hearted enough to be able to sleep through something like this."

"Right?" Sayuri came to sit next to him, smiling. "Everyone's working hard," she said, looking around.

"Don't you have to do whatever you're supposed to be doing?" Ryotaro asked coyly.

Sayuri gave him a blank look and inspected one of the plants on the service counter. "I already finished my role before Christmas. Right now I'm just a woman of leisure with no job to do." She flashed a smile, and there was something of Gray in the expression. "You wanna know what kind of job Gray gave a little girl like me?"

"Not particularly."

The unwritten rule: people saved by Gray did not pry into each other's business. But Ryotaro couldn't help but wonder what kind of work Gray could have given a woman as young as Sayuri. Shindo, Gray's money launderer, had seemed to know, and had suggested that Ryotaro ask Sayuri directly.

"I can tell that you want to know. It's written on your face." Sayuri teased her lips into a cruel smile as she looked at a flustered Ryotaro out of the corner of her eye. "My job was exploiting the weaknesses of men in power."

"In what way?" Ryotaro felt his chest tighten.

"I tricked them."

"Tricked?"

"I used *my allure* to come into their secrets."

"You mean…"

"Exactly what you think it means. I sleep with the old guys Gray targets and use the fact that I'm underage as leverage. I grab them by their weakest points, threaten them, manipulate them. We record them with bugs and hidden cameras. A classic badger game. We were able to get in here so smoothly because an old bastard I coerced provided us with guidance and blueprints. No matter how excellent their position, men are all very simple creatures," Sayuri scoffed like a grown-up.

Ryotaro's mind had gone blank. He couldn't believe Gray had Sayuri do those things.

"Don't get the wrong impression, though. We didn't go *all the way*. We'd go to a hotel, I'd let the guy touch me a bit, make him say a few pervy things, and that's it—mission accomplished. No need to go any further. We would already have enough photos, videos, and sound bites for blackmail."

Sayuri's tone was light, but Ryotaro's heart was still heavy.

"There were a few others with the same job, it seems. In many cases it's thanks to them that the bank robberies and jewelry heists went as swimmingly as they did. Gray rescued me in September of 2012, after the August Raids, so I don't know the details too well."

"You didn't…hate it?" Ryotaro asked, regretting the question the moment it left his mouth.

Sayuri had instantly narrowed her eyes, giving him an angry look. "I don't need your sympathy, if that's what it is. Gray saved my life. I have to do at least that much to repay my debt to him. That's all," Sayuri concluded firmly.

As she spoke the sound of a news broadcast filled the business area. *"Police cars have surrounded the main building of the Bank of Japan. We can also see mobile troops moving in…"*

The newscaster's voice was coming from Sasaki's computer. Others stopped what they were doing and gathered around to watch the screen. Gray was among them.

"Looks like it's about to start," Sayuri said cheerfully, her face totally different from just a moment ago. She scampered off to where the others stood. Ryotaro dithered for a moment, then followed after her.

He peered at the screen in front of Sasaki showing footage of the Bank of Japan—exactly the building they were barricaded in.

"The perpetrators are as yet unidentified, and we do not know of any hostages or what kinds of demands are being made. Eyewitnesses suggest that this may be the work of the Gray Man…"

Gray glanced at the clock on the wall of the business area, confirmed the time to be 11:00 a.m., and looked back at the monitor.

"Let us see what their first move is," he quipped happily.

2

December 24th, before dawn

Data leaked to media outlets via a source requesting anonymity contains damning video footages and documents implicating a number of influential men across various industries and sections of government—high-level bureaucrats, police brass, directors of large corporations, doctors, lawyers, and celebrities—in the Ikebukuro Scandal, the unresolved incident involving an organization that auctioned off the lives of girls.

8 a.m.

An investigative committee is formed among the media to debate whether or not the information should be made public, but a small online magazine has already posted the leaked info. The government responds to the resultant furor by imposing a press blackout, but any restriction proves difficult to enforce as video hosting sites enable *the incriminating footage* to spread around the world. The source of the leak remains unknown.

The same hour

A document is leaked to media outlets purporting evidence that the areas in Mongolia held by Tomosun Trading are yielding only a modicum of rare earth minerals. The information goes straight to press and results in huge losses for private investors and companies in need of the resources that have invested funds via Tomosun Securities. Total damages rise to over two hundred billion yen. A total of seven hundred billion yen, including five hundred billion in government-backed funds, is unaccounted for. Since the Minister of Economic and Fiscal Policy had decided virtually by fiat to invest public funds in Tomosun Securities, an investigation is opened into likely links to the Ikebukuro Scandal and the possibility that he was blackmailed.

10:30 a.m.

An anonymous group barricades itself inside the Bank of Japan. Police response is delayed in the midst of the scandal reportage that morning, but they manage to surround the building within ten minutes of the break-in.

11:00 a.m.

Factories owned by the National Printing Bureau in Takinogawa, Odawara, Shizuoka, Hikone, and Okayama are attacked by anonymous persons. The attacks occur simultaneously and in each case the same explosive materials—high-temperature nanothermite used to melt steel—are employed to destroy the factories. It is theorized that the attacks have been orchestrated by a single group.

The police learn that vehicles used in the attacks belong to Pharaon Logistics, the largest company in the freight industry, and launch an investigation into the company's involvement. Workers on each targeted site report that the assailants were composed of groups of seven or eight heavily armed individuals who required only thirty minutes to destroy the factories with explosives and make their escape. The police put on a search for the perpetrators. Nobody has been injured during the attacks, all staff having been allowed to exit the premises. The attackers' whereabouts remain unknown.

There continue to be no signs of activity from the group barricaded inside the Bank of Japan since 10:30 a.m. They make no demands and no channels of negotiation are established. Witnesses report the group to be armed, resulting in the Riot Police and Special Assault Teams surrounding the building. The Metropolitan Police Department continues attempts to ascertain the raiders' identity and whether or not they have hostages.

The simultaneity of these developments, originating with the exposure of the Ikebukuro Scandal, lead the police to conclude that these are acts of terror orchestrated by a single organization.

Identifying the perpetrators becomes the police force's top priority.

3

SAT officer Takashi Saeki carefully went through his equipment check as he listened absently to the angry roars flying back and forth among the commotion outside. One tactical vest, Eagle-made; one trauma pad, ceramic armor, one black balaclava, a kevlar helmet, a gun strapped to his thigh, special-grade MP5 flash-bang grenades strung over his chest.

After one final pass to make sure that everything was in order, he looked up and focused on his surroundings. He saw other SAT members, all wearing the same uniforms—maybe their personalities were uniform as well—all sardined into the mid-size bus. He looked through the vehicle's tinted-glass windows. Outside, other police hurried about frantically.

"Word is it's the Gray Man? What is happening to this country?" Yuya Kawakami, also on the SAT, muttered to Saeki as he peered out of the window. At twenty-four, he was four years younger than Saeki, and his face retained vestiges of innocence though his eyes were sharp and confident.

"Who knows," Saeki, Alpha Team's captain, replied disinterestedly. From the scene outside it was clear that this was nothing to sneeze at.

Kawakami's voice was full of emotion in stark contrast to Saeki's reticence. "First, all that footage gets leaked, then those attacks on the National Printing Bureau, and the Bank of Japan. These terrorists want to bring down the state."

He was right, this was not some half-baked terrorist ploy. The five factories attacked contained the machines used to print bank notes. Their destruction meant that, for the time being, Japan had lost the ability to issue new printed money. And now the Bank of Japan, the fulcrum of Japan's economy, was under siege. The nation would suffer an immeasurable blow. Saeki wanted to scream out loud, asking what the hell the police, which should be protecting the nation, was doing. But then he remembered he was an officer himself and suddenly felt awkward.

For a while they had heard intermittent explosions, probably as the terrorists blasted their way into the vault. But the content of the leaked videos was more alarming than finding out that the BoJ was under siege. The videos showed people at the very core of the state apparatus engaged in criminal acts. There was, of course, the possibility that the images were forgeries, yet the quality was such that a simple denial would not suffice.

"That scandalous footage. Our family are in it," Kawakami spat.

Saeki had not yet seen it, but some members of the upper echelons of the police force had been caught on tape. That was likely part of the reason the police had stepped up the search for the ringleader—the Gray Man—with such murderous, red-eyed intensity. The Gray Man was currently barricaded inside the Bank of Japan.

It was after 10:00 p.m., nearly twelve hours since the attack had commenced. Yet the Gray Man had issued no demands, and the police had no idea of how many were barricaded inside or whether or not they held hostages.

A cold snap of winter air billowed in as the door to the bus swung open, revealing Superintendent Akizuki. He was heavily built, especially for someone on the elite track. He was in charge of the current operation. He'd risen through the ranks due to his excellent memory and reliance on cold logic. Pencil-pushers with little field experience were often put in charge of leading SATs, a fact that was hardly popular among team members. Kawakami looked at the man with open aggression.

Akizuki cleared his throat, as though trying to dispel the tension in the air. "We're still in stalemate, but we have new witness reports that suggest about twenty inside. There are confirmed sightings of a man in a gray suit and a girl in school uniform. We're assuming that they're the same ones involved in the raid at the jewelry exhibition four months ago and that the Gray Man is their leader."

The superintendent looked around. It was all information the SAT team already knew, so no one raised any questions and he continued.

"They've yet to issue any demands, and we're unable to establish negotiations. Tech Team has set up concrete microphones to get intel on the situation inside. Apart from the explosions we have been able to discern footfall and a number of voices. We've picked up some chatting but nothing of core value yet. They're probably prepared for bugs and are using written instructions. They have destroyed every single security camera so we have no means of visual surveillance."

"How about hostages?" Kobayashi, Bravo Team's leader, challenged.

"Unconfirmed. For now all BoJ staff are safe and accounted for."

"That doesn't mean they don't have hostages. Yet you want us to go in? It's still too early."

They had just received orders to charge in.

"Instructions directly from the Commissioner. Granted, we don't know the situation inside, but we cannot allow the Gray Man to escape."

"So you're more concerned with covering your asses than with saving hostages?" Kawakami snorted derisively.

"How dare you," Akizuki rose to the bait.

"The leaked footage showed us the brass is involved and now they order us in?" Kawakami barked back. "It's obvious they're trying to hush something up. It would be reckless to go in without any intel on the situation. We haven't even made contact. They're putting themselves before the hostages."

Akizuki glared at Kawakami in silence. Kawakami spoke even louder, determined not to give in to intimidation. "And what about you? Will you give up on hostages and prioritize your superior's orders and advancing your career?"

"I seem to recall that SAT's prime directive is breaking deadlocks during crises," Akizuki retorted flatly.

Kawakami's hands curled into fists. "As an organization, yes.

But we're still human. We can't just ignore the lives of innocent people. People like you and the Commish can just sit back and issue orders in the background, but we front-liners deal with people's lives. Whether it's gunning down criminals or watching hostages die, it all happens right in front of us. Not that I'd expect a suit like you to understand."

"Knock it off," Saeki growled, immediately diffusing the heated atmosphere in the transport.

Akizuki stared at him *as if demanding reparation* for what had just transpired. Saeki glared straight back.

"I am responsible for the lives of my men, but as long as I remain part of the force I have to treat orders as absolute. So I will lead us in even though it's reckless. We will follow the fundamentals of your orders and do our best to apprehend the criminals. But we will not forget that the hostages are our first priority."

"Even if it means failure in your duty as an officer?"

"This is a question of our humanity, not our titles as policemen," Saeki countered, pressing his lips into a thin line and directing a steady gaze at Akizuki.

Akizuki stood completely still as he listened, then brought a hand up to scratch his crocodile-like chin. "I don't intend to argue with you. But orders must absolutely be followed." Though the superintendent himself wavered between his sense of duty and the recriminations of his conscience, he inhaled deeply to hide this and breathed out, "According to intel, the front and rear exits have been barricaded with barbed wire, making it difficult to breach. We have, however, identified an unmonitored emergency exit on the east side. I believe this to be our best chance of entry, assuming their numbers are small and the perps are mainly located on the first floor." With his eyes he sought Saeki's input. "What do you think?"

"Is it barricaded?"

"We're not sure, but if no one's on guard it should be possible to remove any barricade undetected."

"Should we be committing ourselves to a single access point?" Kobayashi of Bravo Team questioned.

"We could enter from above simultaneously, but all viable upper access points have been laid with barbed wire. I judged it would be better to surge through the first-floor entry, which is closer to where they're holed up, and take control rather than waste time taking down barbed wire."

"It's too risky. We can't dismiss the possibility that they have hostages upstairs. And it's doubtful that they're camped on the first floor. It's a ten-floor building—surely they could be anywhere," Kawakami spat.

Akizuki turned to look at him. "Granted, it seems reckless. If they have hostages on the upper floors things could become dangerous. But the decisions and instructions of our superiors are absolute. And it is *their view that there are no hostages*. In other words, we can act without worrying over the predicament of any. This allows freedom to charge in as we see fit," Akizuki quietly informed, one side of his face strained as though he had a cramp. "We go in at 2400. Your orders are to shoot to kill, not apprehend the perps. In other words, a search-and-destroy operation. Our sniper team has not been made aware of this. It's up to you to see this through. Once you're in, the riot police have orders to follow if the situation demands, but the brass wants you to complete the mission before that's necessary. I hope you understand what this means."

The orders were to clean it up before the riot police barged in. The brass clearly wanted the matter swept under the rug using the SAT—a small team from an organization that was still largely unknown to the public. Saeki felt so disgusted he thought he might vomit.

"To reiterate. This is a search-and-destroy operation. You are to eliminate everyone inside the building. Under no circumstances are you to discuss this with anyone outside the team. I'm sure you're all aware of what will happen to you if you do. Over." Akizuki glowered at the men through narrowed eyes.

The expression only served to irritate the team members. The atmosphere inside the bus remained heavy even after Akizuki left.

"Search-and-destroy? We don't have the authority for this," Kawakami spat.

"It appears that our superiors wish to get rid of the Gray Man no matter what," Saeki murmured with a pained expression.

These terrorist acts had delivered a blow powerful enough to put Japan's ability to function as a nation into doubt. The value of the yen had already plummeted, sending the populace into panic; moreover, the leaked info incriminating many of Japan's higher-ranking officials had precipitated a widespread drop in public confidence in the government. Unrest had not yet reached the level of disaster-movie hysteria, but Japan had been knocked down to rock bottom in a flash, and citizen anxiety could explode at any moment.

The nation regarded this man in gray, who had brought it to the brink of ruination in the blink of an eye, with something akin to terror. And now those at the top had authorized a search-and-destroy, thinking it better to suppress evidence rather than arrest the Gray Man and solve the case.

Saeki grimaced, stood up, and looked over the faces of the storm troops in the bus. "We will carry out our mission as per our orders. We go in at 2400. However, if you come across anyone you think may be a hostage, your first priority is to secure his or her safety. Assistant Inspector Kobayashi, do you find this acceptable?"

Beta Team's Kobayashi stood up and nodded slowly. Saeki looked at his legs.

The sight of them faintly trembling gave him pause.

*

As Akizuki left the bus and made his way back to the command center, he continued to ponder what he had said. No matter how he looked at it, it was obvious that someone had pushed through the search-and-destroy operation for his own benefit.

Police had a principle—absolute obedience. The system of law enforcement was founded on discipline, on following regulations.

Adherence to such rules was how Akizuki had risen to where he was today. He had thought his orders unreasonable on a number of occasions but had shut up and followed them, writing them off as a necessary evil. Yet could he do the same for this search-and-destroy operation? Akizuki was wracked with doubt.

He could see the Commissioner's face even now. "*If you make this happen I will personally guarantee a promotion.*"

Someone *above* was obviously pulling the Commissioner's strings. His words were a tempting enough carrot for an ambitious man like Akizuki, but it came poisoned.

Akizuki recalled the faces of the SAT members. They were younger than him, but their eyes had gleamed with a force of will greater than his. They would be going in ready to sacrifice their lives for their country.

If, having forced himself to pass on orders he was unhappy with, they ever did end up sacrificed, would he be able to bear it?

He knew that years of being tussled by society and the organization had weakened his conscience. But he still took pride in his belief in justice. Japan had been thrown into a maelstrom of chaos. If they were not careful, the government could collapse. The Gray Man's removal may well be an essential part of preventing that from happening.

But…

Akizuki's head ached, and he wanted to rest it in his hands.

The Gray Man's actions were clearly illegal, but so were the antics in the *incriminating footage* he had leaked. It was easy enough to see the operation as an act of self-preservation.

Akizuki pulled a face as he came to a stop outside the Mitsui No. 2 building where the temporary command center was situated.

The HQ on the other side of the door was aswirl with ulterior motives.

Was he to side with justice—with what he knew to be correct—or silence his inner voice and let himself become another cog in the machine? He let out a deep sigh, his features stern as he entered the building.

4

The stalemate continued beyond the twelfth hour. The terrorists still hadn't issued any demands. The only change was that the intermittent explosions had ended after the tenth hour; they had most likely succeeded in breaking into the vault. That only served to fuel the unease of the officers surrounding the building.

The SAT bus pulled up right outside the emergency exit on the east side and the troops bundled out without making a sound. The first four comprised Alpha Team, the latter four Bravo Team. The eight shadows slid into the darkness. They wore black balaclavas that totally removed any individuality. It was 24:00 on the dot. Just moments earlier, a fax had come in from the Metropolitan Police Department authorizing the strike.

Saeki was the point man. His eyes swept around their surroundings as he moved forward, towards the access point. The door was old and there were no signs of recent use. He used the recently installed concrete microphone to listen inside. He confirmed it was clear and tried the handle. Locked. The air was bitingly cold, but Saeki's hands were utterly steady when he inserted the spare key to the emergency exit. The lock offered no resistance and opened with a neat click.

"Alpha Team—entry point successfully breached. No other developments," Saeki reported to Akizuki in the command center, depressing the button of his L.A.S.H. intercom that processed the vibrations of his vocal chords and converted them into speech.

"Okay, there are no lights on inside, so it's going to be pitch black in there. Use flashlights and execute the operation."

"Roger."

"We're confident that you will succeed. Commence surge in thirty seconds. Repeat, commence in thirty seconds."

The words sounded in the ears of each member of the teams. Saeki turned around, exchanging glances with the other troopers.

"Counting down. 29, 28, 27…"

They all knew the mission was absurd, but they had to follow orders. If they were going to do it, they would make every effort to complete it as ethically as possible.

"3, 2, 1, 0. Go, go, go!"

Saeki opened the door. It creaked from rust. The sound was tiny but it echoed in the hearts of the men.

Alpha's Kawakami moved swiftly, getting a visual on the inside with a flash-bang grenade in hand. Another trooper leveled a gun towards the inside of the building. There were no signs of the terrorists. Bravo Team's captain, Kobayashi, padded soundlessly into the building as the rest of his team followed behind. In moments they had completely disappeared into the darkness.

Kobayashi moved forward, riot shield in hand, as the other three took formation behind him, scanning each direction. The formation allowed them to stay aware of a full 360 degrees. Saeki led Alpha Team in behind them.

They continued into the depths of the building, resting their bodyweight on their back feet as they stepped forward in a technique known as "stalking."

The emergency exit opened onto a wide corridor. Heading right would be the shortest route to the business area, but that would mean crossing a stretch where they expected lookouts to be posted.

Their orders were to kill, not to extract hostages. They headed to the right without hesitation, pacing quickly down the corridor without making a sound. The inside of the building was pitch black, but the flashlights fitted to the barrels of their guns made it easy to mark their line of sight. After a while, they came up to a door noticeably larger than the others. They were already at the business area. It had been too easy.

"Isn't this weird?" Kawakami whispered.

"Yeah," Saeki had to agree. The inside of his assault suit was already drenched with sweat. Something was off.

Tech had told them to expect the terrorists to be spread around the business area of the first floor. They had passed directly through a stretch where they expected resistance, but the corridors were empty. Perhaps the terrorists had relocated. But even if that were true, there was something unnerving about the total lack of people.

"We're going in," Kobayashi signaled behind, opened the door to the business area, and hurled in one of the flash-bang grenades at the same time.

The eight of them stormed in as the hall flared under a 2.4-million-candela flash and filled with a blast of 170 decibels.

Saeki immediately recognized the anomaly.

The barricades were arrayed as though the terrorists were prepared for this strike. On top of one barricade stood a life-sized Santa mannequin wearing a broad grin. In its hands was a placard welcoming the SAT.

The text read: *HELP! Santa's been taken hostage!*

It took them completely by surprise. They swept their guns around, scanning for signs of the terrorists, who had cleverly hidden themselves inside the barricades. The SAT stalled, breaking the principle of "shooting on move."

"Welcome!"

The room's lights came on like a crackle of lightning, revealing a man dressed in a gray suit. He held a pair of flash goggles in one hand and discarded ear plugs with the other. The SAT members trained their guns on him as they made an instant assessment of the situation and scattered in all directions so as not to provide a cluster of targets. More of the criminals appeared, surrounding the SAT from across their barricades.

Saeki knew he was now at a disadvantage but demanded the terrorists' surrender. "Drop your weapons!" he shouted.

If it came to a shootout, there was no way to avoid heavy losses.

Gray unguardedly took a step beyond the barricade. "I believe you are here to slaughter us. We can't possibly surrender our weapons."

That one utterance revealed that the details of the SAT mission had been leaked.

A mole? The word "despair" flickered through Saeki's mind.

"Surrender! You can't escape."

"Escape? We didn't come here just to run away. Actually, I think it would be in your best interests to lay down your own weapons," Gray proposed.

"I see. No deal, then."

After confirming there were no signs of any hostages, Saeki retrained his gun on Gray. The other SAT troopers targeted other terrorists. The SAT were the lesser in numbers, but they had the advantage in skill. With the anti-ballistic shields, they could put up a good fight. Even so, they were at an overwhelming disadvantage. Their own "barricade" consisted of a couple of anti-ballistic shields and there was no other cover nearby, while the terrorists were spread out and mostly bunkered. And they seemed to have MP5s, special-force-grade weapons similar to those wielded by the SAT.

"Surrender your arms if you don't want to die." In contrast to the harshness of his expression, Gray's tone was that of an appeal. "You have things to live for, that you need to protect. People who are important to you. We don't have such things. Therefore you have no chance of winning."

It was dangerous to listen to him. Saeki's finger hovered over the trigger, but it had already stiffened.

"We have been deprived. We have been forsaken. We have been abandoned by our country. We have stared death in the face," Gray continued flatly. "Perhaps you remember a man by the name of Kiyomi Takano?"

Sounds familiar, thought Saeki.

"A father whose son was killed in 2005 in Kanagawa Prefecture."

Saeki remembered. Someone had carted around a twenty year old for close to a month before finally beating him to death. The victim's father was definitely called Kiyomi Takano; the case had been followed by the whole nation. Takano had appealed to the police over ten times, claiming that his son had been abducted, that his life was in danger, yet the police had paid no attention. It was only after the mass media reported on Takano going berserk inside a station that the police finally dragged themselves into taking action. It had already been twenty-seven days since the son's abduction. Even then the police failed to take the case seriously, and when the carelessness of some officers on the case led to the victim's death, they were only subjected to a light punishment.

"The kidnapper dragged his twenty-year-old son all over before finally killing him. Inconceivably, the case was shelved before a motive was ever established and the criminal was still at large. It wasn't until I heard the truth about this from a certain person that I realized how disgustingly deep the corruption in this country runs."

Saeki was silent. It was true that the police response had been unnatural. The investigation had ended abruptly despite the fact that the criminal's identity remained unknown. There had been an outcry from the detectives in charge.

Even so…

"What has that got to do with this? Is this about revenge?" Saeki yelled. "Society would break down if everyone went around taking revenge."

"So you suggest we bear it? Cry ourselves to sleep?"

Saeki didn't know what to say. Gray's forceful tone seemed to preclude argument.

"No consideration of the victim's perspective. No consideration for the weak. That is our nation as it is now. Put up with it. What's done is done, you can't bring back the dead. Put aside your anger and get on with your life. Look forward, move on. That's what onlookers say, wheedling the bereaved and the weak, treating them as though nothing happened. The weak put up with it, and if they kill themselves it's their own fault. People want to file away the misery, the poverty, and the crimes of the weak as something they brought upon themselves." Gray's voice was becoming heated. "The strong always receive protection, the weak are cut off."

"That's not true. Japan—"

"There was a man by the name of Rei Yuzuki," Gray said, drowning him out. "His wife and child were violated and killed in cold blood. But that was not the end of his trials." He audibly ground his teeth. "After the murders, Rei Yuzuki fought without reserve. He collected all the damning information he could find on the criminals and pushed for the death penalty. But the criminals avoided capital punishment. People of influence spoke in their defense since the criminals were minors. At first, the mass media were quick to criticize the criminals but gradually became more sympathetic to their predicament, and eventually Rei Yuzuki was shunned for making a fuss. That's not all. The case spawned pieces in the style of lurid novels. The minute the photos the perps took of their crimes spread across the internet, the case was exposed to the public's malicious curiosity. Rei Yuzuki became distrustful of people, fearing others' gazes. His face became twisted from despair and hatred, his voice changed, and he stopped stepping foot outside of his home and turned bloodlessly pale, and for a while he wasn't even sure whether he was alive or dead. He became suspicious of, and hostile toward, everything. Eventually one thought subsumed all other emotions—revenge. Not just against the perpetrators of the crime but also against the structure eating away at this nation. That thought became the only strength that kept him alive."

Gray was breathing so heavily it looked like he was having a seizure. He scratched at his chest.

"Rei Yuzuki followed the advice of a detective in charge of the case and attended a therapy group for bereaved victims. That was where he met Kiyomi Takano. That was when he heard of *a system called the Tower*. His son had become involved, and it had led to his death. The two men came up with a plan, deciding to use the Tower as a tool for their revenge," Gray revealed, holding up his right hand. "When this hand falls, you will die. All of us here have, in the past, come to the decision to end our lives. We are dead soldiers. You all have family, people dear to you. We say this for your sake. We wish you to surrender. We have nothing to lose, therefore you cannot win. Nothing can prevent us from attaining our goal."

"Which is? What do you want from our country?" Saeki asked in a trembling voice.

"Redistribution."

"Redistribution? You plan to hand out the money you steal?"

"That would be pointless. I considered that, once. But it's simply not feasible."

"Then what kind of distribution are you planning?"

"I am going to destroy Japan," Gray answered simply. "I am going to destroy the nation and drag down those at the top."

"Ridiculous. Even if you ruin the country, the rich will survive while the poor become destitute. Isn't that the complete opposite of redistribution?"

"Destruction—is redistribution. Tearing down the strong is redistribution."

"What're you saying?"

"Japan—no, the world—is irrevocably structured as the survival of the fittest. We exist in a chain where the rich get richer while the poor get poorer. The strong grow fat as they feed on the weak, their crimes are defended, and their victims—the weak—are forsaken. Do you know why it has come to this?"

Saeki did not respond, but he could guess what the man wanted to say. But if he answered, he would be showing understanding, and that would mean defeat.

Gray smiled as though he had read Saeki's thoughts. "The top is too well-protected. They have nothing to fear, skipping about without a care in the world, their every whim forgiven. So they stop thinking about the weak, seeing things only from their positions of power, and forge a society designed to keep themselves safe and to strengthen their positions."

"That's just the way society works," Saeki objected. "That's how it's always been, people at the top ruling over others. Japan can't be that bad compared to the rest of the world."

Gray responded by narrowing his eyes. The look he gave Saeki seemed to penetrate right through him. "People say Japan is a good country, that her people among the world's fortunate.

Tell me, then, why does the suicide rate never go down? We know that over thirty thousand people end their lives each year. If you add in those who go missing, it's two hundred thousand. That's how many meet their deaths. This country is at war. Why does no one look more closely?"

"So you think that makes it okay to drag down the wealthy by raiding the central bank? Do you really believe that's going to solve anything?"

"I would not be barricaded in here if I did not." Gray's narrowed eyes shone with an abnormal light.

Saeki was fast becoming overwhelmed by Gray's argument, but the SAT had begun their mission. They were cogs in a wheel. Their job was to put their lives on the line, to carry out orders.

Saeki swallowed. His throat was dry. A single word and the room would descend into mayhem. The heavy gloom pressed down on his shoulders.

He breathed in, filling his lungs, and was about to open his mouth when he heard Akizuki's voice in his earpiece. The man sounded agitated by the fact that there had not been a single gunshot.

"Report your situation."

"We're surrounded. They've got MP5s, all guns are pointed at us," Saeki answered, focusing on his breathing. The vibrations of his vocal chords reached Akizuki as words.

"How many?"

"About twenty. Including the Gray Man."

"Is that certain?"

"Presently he's right in front of us. I have a clear shot, but if I take it…" his words trailed off. If he did, it would most likely result in the obliteration of his team.

Akizuki's reply was a whisper. He had understood what Saeki had neglected to say. *"Put down your weapons and surrender."*

Saeki could not believe his ears.

"This is an order. Surrender, now." Akizuki's voice was tense.

To put down their weapons could mean throwing away their lives.

"I can't do that, sir," Saeki's response hammered Akizuki's eardrums through the wireless microphone.

"What is this now? You'll all be killed if you don't! You want to throw away your men's lives?"

"I can't do it! Requesting backup!" Saeki shouted.

There was a metallic clanking behind him. He turned instantly to see that Kobayashi had thrown his firearm to the ground.

"We surrender," Kobayashi said, looking at Saeki. "We're throwing our lives away otherwise."

"Assistant Inspector Kobayashi!" Saeki yelled.

Kobayashi just shook his head. "I've got a family." The man's expression was hidden behind his goggles, but it was clear from his shaking voice that he had lost his will to fight.

"Shit…"

Saeki nearly lost himself to anger, but at the same time the realization hit him that they had lost. Kawakami's eyes were wide open as he struggled to work out what was happening. Saeki cast his own weapon to the floor.

"Good decision," Gray said, as though praising a child.

The remainder of the SAT members surrendered. When their radios were taken, they lost their only means of communication with the outside.

Ryotaro watched the troopers as their bullet-proof vests were removed. He looked towards Gray. *What was next?* Ryotaro had no idea.

"All right, everybody. We are short on time."

They had removed all the troopers' equipment and piled everything together.

The SAT members' clothing was also removed and they sat in their underwear, hands and legs bound, with another rope tying them together. They resembled a giant centipede.

"We are leaving here as scheduled. How are we doing with the hacking?" Gray asked Sasaki and Kozue. They had been furiously typing away for a while now.

"Perfectly. We finished distributing the copies of phone

exchanges between the police brass and the field commander across the internet. We even got a pretty choice soundbite: *'Wipe them out, the Gray Man and all his associates.'* It's stirring up quite a response," Kozue said, clearly enjoying herself.

Sasaki nodded the whole time Kozue spoke and continued to type away.

Gray gave the two of them a nod before turning to face Takano. "And the cash from the vault?"

"We have finished destroying the doors with nanothermite. We also succeeded in taking out the National Printing Bureau's factories, so the government's just lost a vast sum of money as well as its ability to print more. The one hundred billion yen we didn't destroy is piled up in the major shippings hall."

"It sounds like everything's in place. Listen up, everybody. Please destroy all electrical devices and anything else that might be traceable. Remove the barricades to ease access."

Everyone burst into action, doing exactly as ordered.

Gray drew a deep breath and spread his hands out. "Time for the finale."

He glanced at the SAT members before turning to face the tight besiegement that awaited them outside.

5

The officers surrounding the Bank of Japan and the bureaucrats monitoring the situation from their places of safety were not only getting frustrated but also denied means with which to express their increasing impatience and anxiety. Twenty minutes had passed since the SAT's insertion, but they had heard nothing back, not even a gunshot. The last communication had been the exchange between Superintendent Akizuki and Alpha Team's Assistant Inspector Saeki.

"Requesting backup!"

That was the last they heard before a powerful jamming wave fried their communication devices and all radios went dead apart from bursts of static that sounded like a sandstorm. Akizuki sighed deeply. The voice of the Commissioner, shaking with anger, still rang unpleasantly in his ears.

"What were you thinking, giving that order to surrender?!"

He had apologized over the phone and been immediately relieved of his command. He was prepared to be demoted and sent to some backwater to live out the rest of his career. But he knew his order had been correct. No matter what, it was not a mistake to prevent eight men from throwing away their lives. Still, it was too early to jump to conclusions since the men were now hostages inside the bank. The brass had already begun fresh preparations, still committed to search-and-destroy. The new commanding officer was on his way and due to arrive any minute. A second insertion. The Metropolitan Police Department approved the decision as soon as the first SAT had gone in. Instead of the riot police they would use another SAT unit.

The advent of the Gray Man had caused the police to suffer a total loss of face. He had made a mockery of the government of Japan, yet the police had made no progress towards apprehending him. Now, finally, he was in reach. Their desperation was understandable.

No, that's not it, Akizuki reframed his thoughts.

It was still odd that they wanted to go straight for the kill rather than arrest him. There had to be some reason for it. *Personal* reasons, on the brass's part.

They were scared of the Gray Man. Instead of arresting him to get to the root of the matter, they were trying to cover up evidence by killing him.

Akizuki clenched his teeth. He was no longer in charge. The second SAT detachment, now on site, was an execution squad directed by the Commissioner himself.

Gray had nowhere to run. The police had severely tightened their net around the Bank of Japan. In three minutes they would storm the building. Once they were in, many would die. The Gray Man would end up a corpse—or rather, they would not let up until he did.

Akizuki squeezed his eyes shut. All he could do was pray for the survival of the eight SAT troopers inside. He breathed out slowly, trying to ease his heart, which felt about ready to crunch into itself. His sigh was filled with suspicions about the force.

There was a sudden communication from SAT positioned on the roof of the Mitsukoshi department store. *"Sniper support reporting in. They've thrown up a smokescreen!"*

"Wh-Where from?" Akizuki stuttered, blindsided by the unexpected development.

"We can't tell. It appeared out of nowhere to cover the BoJ. It's some kind of tear gas… Officers down! Sir, we need gas masks, now!"

The command center was suddenly inundated with a flood of similar reports. Akizuki was seized with an acute urge to get outside since he couldn't parse what was happening from where he was. The report coming from officers stationed at the south gate made him doubt his own ears.

"W-We have an emergency! The whole area is covered in a ton of smoke. We don't know the source, but it seems like it's coming from the Metropolitan Expressway."

Akizuki's eyes opened wide. The Metropolitan Expressway curved past the Bank of Japan, crossing over Sotobori Street. He ordered his officers to scramble to the ring route.

On the expressway, *which they had neither manned nor blocked off,* one of the lanes was closed for construction with no notice.

Gray had considered wind direction for that day and set up a mass of smoke generators along the expressway across from the roadworks and directly upwind from the Bank of Japan complex. The buildings around the bank caused a tunnel effect through the area, effectively spreading the smoke and taking down the wall of police.

By the time the police noticed, it was already too late. The first reports of the smoke coming in were instantly followed by a flood of communications from the riot police stationed towards the north side.

"Riot Unit Bravo. We have visual on what seems to be the Gray Man!" the unit leader desperately tried, through a tear-choked and gas-ravaged voice, to communicate what he was seeing.

"What?" Akizuki jumped up impatiently. He was confused by the inundation of new information. "Where is he now?"

"*They're… koff… outside the police blockade, sir.*" The voice sounded agitated. Akizuki could hear the commotion in the background through the wireless.

"What are you saying? The Gray Man's still barricaded inside the building."

"*B-But…*" the man's voice was shaking. "*I can see them…*"

"Huh?" *Them?* Akizuki couldn't understand what he was hearing.

"*Riot Unit Alpha, sir! Visual on a large number of men in gray behind our lines!*"

"*Perimeter guards reporting in…*"

"*South gate guards reporting in…*"

The command center was buckling under the overwhelming number of incoming reports. The voices, most of them tear-choked, told of a sudden gas attack and the emergence of a huge number of men dressed in gray.

The helicopter pilot on watch was momentarily rendered speechless. The smoke had thinned enough to make out details on the ground. He saw the streets, lit up by Christmas illuminations, overflowing with gray. The gray mass pushed forward like a wave, surging towards the Bank of Japan from every direction. The pilot wasn't sure if he was hallucinating, since the change was so abrupt.

The streets, at first twinkling with lights, suddenly filled with smoke, and subsequently everything turned gray as if an unannounced rainstorm had passed through. There was no warning. The pilot did wonder that there seemed to be a lot of people on the streets, but at first he dismissed it as part of the Christmas bustle and paid no further attention.

Coming back to his senses, he picked up his wireless. "Air Patrol Big Bird 8 reporting in. Visual confirmation of a mass of gray men—uh, people dressed in gray. Can't confirm actual number but enough to fill streets."

Even after making his report, the pilot still found it hard to believe the scene under him. It was as if the police surrounding the bank had taken a blow from behind; there was practically nothing they could do. Most were incapacitated by the smoke. They had focused on encircling the bank and were completely unprepared for action from their rear. The lines quickly collapsed under the avalanche of gray men.

The detachment of uniformed officers posted to keep civilians away from the scene had grown suspicious when the onlookers suddenly took off their coats. But they did not call it in. If they'd bothered to report rubberneckers stripping off winter wear, they would have been laughed at. Soon they noticed the onlookers were all wearing the same outfit, but even then they didn't make a report. They had no idea what was about to happen and were distracted by the sudden appearance of billowing smoke. By the time they realized that all the onlookers who wore gray suits and hats were donning gas masks, it was too late. It was all the cops could do to keep breathing.

The gray mass of people charged through and overwhelmed the police's barricades and faltering lines. Officers had done their best to keep them back but had no riot gear and couldn't fire their guns. The cordons were destroyed in a matter of seconds while the officers struggled to breathe. The odds were against them. The blockade consisted of six hundred or so personnel; the masses of gray were tens of times that number.

The command center descended into chaos. Until they had a better grasp of what was happening, no one could give the order to fire. They also had to keep the eyes of the media and the public in mind.

The commanders on the ground requested immediate reinforcements and issued directions to try to regroup and suppress the infiltrators, but it was all in vain. The officers on the streets were too busy trying to avoid getting crushed by the onslaught. Only a few minutes after the first visual confirmation, the streets surrounding the Bank of Japan were awash with gray.

Having rammed through the blockade with ease, they stormed into the bank. Once they'd accomplished their *objective* the crowd dispersed, escaping every which way. Their unregulated movements, like so many baby spiders scattering, worsened the confusion of the police on the ground.

Gray and the others waited for the right moment then made their exit, unnoticed amidst the surge flowing in and out of the bank, blending perfectly with *the maelstrom of gray*. Sirens blared from every direction as the police gradually regrouped. They started arresting the gray masses, desperately hoping to catch *the real Gray*. But it was no easier than spearing a specific sardine among a whole school of them.

Gray was long gone when reinforcements from stations across Tokyo finally arrived. Frenzied police scoured the area, detaining a large number of suspects. Body searches revealed they all carried rolls of bills, but no one had any weapons or anything to link them to Gray. The bills were all stolen from the Bank of Japan.

6

Ryotaro and the others had donned gas masks and made an easy escape. It took no time at all to blend into the smoke and mass of people in gray suits and to make their way through the police lines. It had been anti-climactically straightforward.

Their car was far away by the time the police had set up road blocks. There was a chance that another ring would be set up farther afield, but Takano was perfectly calm, navigating the streets at an almost leisurely pace, giving no sense that they were on the run.

The car carried Gray, Ryotaro, Takano, and Sayuri. Everyone else had made their escape independently. Ryotaro felt discomfited by the fact that he wore a gray suit identical to Gray's. He looked at Takano and Sayuri in the front. They had on the same gray outfit, yet somehow it looked better on them.

"Who were all those people?" Ryotaro asked, still quite

unable to believe the surprising succession of events. Gray had once mentioned that he had nearly a hundred people working for him, but there must have been at least ten thousand in the crowd that swarmed the bank.

Gray laughed self-deprecatingly in response. "They represent the current state of Japan." He leaned back in his seat next to Ryotaro and turned to face him. "They are people so choked with debt that they had decided to end their lives or were at least considering suicide. There are around ten million people who live in poverty here in Japan. That poverty drives a large number of them either to suicide or to crime. We approached such people, assessed their ability to take action, then made a little request. We told them that they could get free rolls of cash if they came to a certain place at a certain time. Of course, they didn't believe it straightaway. But handed five hundred thousand yen each plus a gray suit and a gas mask, they guessed right—*that I was behind it.*"

Gray chuckled. "I mixed in a few people to help stir up the mood and told them to meet at Tokyo Station. I wanted to reveal the location, the Bank of Japan, only at the last possible moment. They were told to wait displaying a gray string on their wrists. That way they could tell who was there for the same reason. The knowledge that you're in it with ten thousand others does a lot to lessen any pangs of guilt. And dressing up in an anonymous uniform may make you a little braver than usual. If the uniform was a gray suit and hat, suggesting that the Gray Man that routinely flummoxed the police was behind it, well, you might be tempted to take the chance. After all, you're getting an invitation from *a superlative criminal organization that boasts zero members arrested to date. The August Raids were never for the money, they were preparation to help fashion my little proposal—propaganda to convince the populace that our organization is invincible.* My scouts are quite talented, and these are people with no economic future, so it was an easy assumption that they'd be willing to take the gamble. I imagined ten thousand Grays would be feasible enough, especially if we hid them from view under a smokescreen that also neutralized the police. To be honest, I was a little worried they might not be able to get through the blockade, but the agitators I'd inserted into the crowd plus a few cooperative policemen did a great job of making it happen."

"What would you have done if they hadn't made it through the blockade?" Ryotaro raised the possibility, thinking himself foolish even as he spoke, but Gray nodded as though he considered it a good question.

"In that scenario we would have dressed up as the SAT they sent in. We detain them, some of us put on their clothes. The rest of us would pretend to be hostages and be led outside. I had an insider waiting with instructions to point our way," Gray answered without hesitation, looking out the window. "It is easy enough to create insiders. You just need to take hold of vulnerabilities that could potentially destroy their lives, then use that as leverage. If they have none, you simply guide them into creating one. The police are sworn to protect our country, but most would sell it out if it meant protecting their derrieres, without even understanding the consequences of their betrayal."

Gray's profile stood out hazily against the gleam of streetlights. He despised his country from the bottom of his heart, and was sadder for it. Such was the impression Gray's conflicted smile gave.

Their car reached Kanagawa Prefecture. The streets were obnoxiously decked out in Christmas decorations, but there were hardly any people as it was 1 a.m. The roads were empty, affording them a clear path. Sayuri sat watching the news on her phone in the passenger seat. She was wearing earbuds so the others couldn't hear, but Ryotaro could make out the perplexed face of the newscaster. Footage streamed in the background, of the Bank of Japan engulfed in a sea of gray.

The destruction of the National Printing Bureau's machinery together with the raid on the Bank of Japan had resulted in fears for the yen's stability abroad. At the same time, footage incriminating many of the country's leaders had fomented public mistrust of government. Its precarious position was exacerbated by the revelation that the publicly funded rare earths project had been a sham. The myriad private investors who found themselves with significant losses on their hands were foaming at the mouth.

As he watched the images flashing across the phone's screen, Ryotaro wondered what might become of Japan. The series of events Gray had orchestrated were a substantial blow to the state apparatus. Considerable international censure was also to be expected. Even so, he didn't think it would bring about total collapse. Japan had stood back up from the ashes of World War II. She wouldn't be so easy to crush. At the same time, maintaining its current position and value system might become a challenge. Was this what Gray had meant by *redistribution*?

No...

"You never wanted redistribution. Your goal was to strike fear into the hearts of those in power," Ryotaro found himself saying.

Gray's eyes widened with surprise. Like a naughty kid caught redhanded, he flashed a smile that asked for forgiveness. "Call it a *redistribution of power*, and the term would not be off the mark. It wasn't the redistribution of money that I had envisioned. Nor was I talking about Japan's physical collapse when I talked of its destruction. Essentially, I had wanted *to grant the weak the possibility of resisting the powerful and to plant the seeds of fear in the strong*, thereby evening out the lopsided seesaw. In its current state, society forces the weak to yield. The strong levy restrictions on the weak, they intimidate, steal, and remove all means of resistance. The result is a society built for their own comfort. There are strong individuals, of course, who manage to climb into positions of influence through their own efforts, breaking through the status quo. But these people enjoyed their own privileges. Maybe they were raised in a good environment, perhaps they met the right people, maybe their gift was intelligence or good fortune. But the world is full of the truly weak. Saying that it is their own fault, for not trying hard enough, merely means that you have never been in a similar position yourself."

"The government must fear us for what we did today,"

Takano said quietly from the driver's seat. "And imagine their surprise when they learn it was the weak who delivered the blow."

"Many of the ten thousand who pretended to be Gray will be taken in by the police. They will be recognized as society's losers, and at that moment our aim will become clear. The arrested will have my sympathy, but their charges are unlikely to be very serious. After all, anyone who chooses to dirty his hands in crime has to pay some price, sooner or later."

The last bit sounded as though it was meant for Gray himself, too.

Ryotaro turned to Sayuri in the front passenger seat. She had stopped watching the news and seemed to be desperately fighting the urge to fall asleep. She resembled a child worn out after a round of excitement.

They pulled up to a plot of land alongside the Tamagawa river. Squinting into the darkness it was possible to make out a building, some sort of abandoned factory. According to Gray there was a network of secret passages underground. This was where Ryotaro had come for the dinner party.

Sasaki and Kozue were waiting for them in front of the factory. They had both changed out of the gray suits back to their regular clothing. Gray instructed only Sayuri to get out of the car. Takano began to drive quietly away before Ryotaro had the chance to wonder. Sayuri's unhappy face disappeared from view.

Ryotaro took a couple of slow, deliberate breaths. "Where are we going now?" Against the low thrumming of the engine, his voice sounded too loud.

"To where those who set all of this in motion await the conclusion of our play," Gray stated softly, seated beside Ryotaro, his voice harmonizing with the surrounding quiet. Something about his tone told Ryotaro that the man had nothing more to add, so he kept quiet.

The car maintained an even pace on the Aqua Line Expressway into Chiba Prefecture.

They continued along near-empty roads for close to an hour and drove through a fishing port and onto a dark mountain road.

They followed the narrow, winding road, passing through a number of short tunnels.

Ryotaro noticed a sign on the way that read "Ubara Utopia," but it was gone in an instant. There were no other visible landmarks along the sparsely illuminated route.

They drew to a halt after turning onto an unpaved pathway. Takano killed the headlights. They were plunged into total darkness. It was totally silent apart from the sound of distant waves.

"Let's go," Gray said, opened the rear door, and got out. Ryotaro followed.

The three of them hiked up a steep mountain path. The way would have been quite hazardous if it wasn't for the moonlight, but Gray walked as easily as he would over any paved road. They crossed another, smaller path that overlooked an inlet of water, then traced a route along a cliff face before entering a narrow, cave-like tunnel. Inside, the tunnel looked precarious, dug into the earth and held up by log frames. A small bulb hanging near the entrance provided the faintest of light. They carefully made their way through the tunnel, eventually coming out to another small path that resembled a beast trail.

"This way," Gray said, gesturing towards a tall thicket that blocked the way.

When he reached out and brushed the fronds, the thicket slid rightward to reveal a hidden slope. Gray and Takano continued in silence, watching Ryotaro's disbelief through the corner of their eyes. Ryotaro hurried after them, not wanting to fall behind.

They walked down the well-kempt and fairly negotiable path to a building that looked like a warehouse. Gray swiped a card through the reader on the door. There was a digital ping and the lock opened with a metallic click.

"Now you can perform your role of seeing this through to the end," Gray informed Ryotaro as they opened and went through the heavy door. "I assume you know by now that everyone I gathered together has been rejected by society. You fell into depression at work and were ready to commit suicide. Takano's son was murdered and the police suppressed the truth. Sayuri came close to losing her life to auctioneers of human flesh. *My wife and daughter were murdered, the media and public trampled on us, and everything I had was destroyed."*

Ryotaro subconsciously massaged his chest, which constricted painfully as he listened to each word spoken by Gray, by Rei Yuzuki. The deep lines of pain covering Gray's face communicated the unimaginable depth of his anguish.

"I put together a group of people with similar experiences. Why? It was partly out of a desire to become an agent for their revenge, to save them from their grief, but that was nothing more than a pretext. *I helped them—I helped Ryotaro—to license my own revenge."*

Gray traced his fingers along the hard, cold concrete of the walls as he continued deeper into the building. "Our rights as men have a framework. We have established the law to ensure we don't stray too far from that standard. It forbids theft. It forbids murder. Such actions are beyond the definition of our rights. Yet, some people are able to step beyond the framework of the law, and I do not mean regular criminals. The powerful are able to break the law, calling it morally justified. Killing during wartime is a good example. Or, closer to home, business owners lining their pockets while they work their staff to death. Those who practice deception for profit. They are no different from criminals. Only, they hide behind some greater good."

Gray's eyes met Ryotaro's. "Three criminals took away people who were dear to me, so I swore revenge. Of course, I am aware of whether or not this decision is just. I have cause to exact revenge but not the right. Yet I must have it. For that, I sought license. I sought to compensate."

"And so...you saved us from suicide?"

"Yes. Exactly," Gray confirmed, staring into Ryotaro's eyes. "I swore to exact my revenge on the monsters who killed my family, on the media and the countless citizens who trampled on us by relishing the gossip, on the government that tacitly accepted the crime by failing to punish evil. It was with that purpose in mind that I rescued the weak. With each person saved, I lessened the weight of my conscience and spurred myself to believe that my good deeds were compensation enough, that I was gaining the right to avenge."

Ryotaro could not utter a word. The fact that he and the others had been used made his mind go blank.

"Performing good deeds to talk myself into, what? Revenge. Absurd, don't you think? Understand that I am not a strong man. I have a firm grasp of right and wrong, and I know that revenge is not permissible. Yet it must be permitted. Of this, I had to convince myself. I had to rationalize driving the country into chaos and taking human lives."

Gray fell silent and continued deeper into the building. His back looked slightly sorrowful.

The inside of the building was solid, far more so than the exterior suggested. It was, essentially, a prison. The airtight space was streamlined, its only function to contain a secret, to hold captives and keep out prying eyes.

They walked down a dim corridor surrounded by concrete-reinforced walls until they came to another door made of steel with a handle in the center. A portal meant to lock away all secrets, to intercept all intrusions.

Key already in hand, Takano unlocked the door. His whole body strained as he turned the handle and pulled the door open to reveal jet-black darkness.

"Why d'you kidnap them?" a coarse rumble suddenly made Ryotaro's eardrums vibrate.

"I don't really know," a younger voice followed.

"Ya think kidnapping for no reason makes any sense?"

"...Yes."

"Never thought about getting a ransom?"

"..."

"Spit it out!"

"I don't know myself..."

The voices, both accompanied by hisses of static, seemed to have been recorded on low-quality equipment. It was immediately clear that they were not *live*, but Ryotaro couldn't guess why the recordings were being looped.

"You didn't just assault them, you killed them, okay? That's a helluva crime. Don't think your fucking age will let you off." The tense outburst was followed by a period of silence.

"I know." The response was feeble.

"Okay, then. Now spit it out, everything about your role in this case. Starting from where we left off yesterday. You raped her, what did you do next?"

"I strangled her... Then, I think... I used a knife to cut her all over."

"The fuck do you mean, you 'think'? You're the one who did it."

"Yes... But I really can't even tell if it was me."

Takano paused the recording with a remote control and the voices stopped.

He pushed another button, flooding the room with light. It was a featureless rectangle. Three handcuffed men sat in chairs. One was overweight with thinning hair. Another was in an expensive but worn-out suit. A golden badge flashed on his lapel. The third man, his eyes darting about, looked like a cornered beast that had to be handled with care.

All three were gagged. They looked towards Ryotaro and the others. Their eyes were bloodshot from terror, and they were shaking.

"These men killed my wife and daughter."

Gray walked into the room. Ryotaro's legs threatened to buckle, but he forced himself to follow. The air in the room was stagnant, too warm, and Ryotaro's ears ringing slightly perhaps because sound was shut out by the heavy walls.

"They stole everything that was important to me, throwing me into an abyss from which I found no escape. My tears dried up long ago. All my joy was wiped out, my hope extinguished, and I went through each day tormented by agony. Ten years spent in pain altered my appearance and voice and rid me of all emotions except hate. In compensation, I gained the ability to recognize despair in others. It was immediately clear to me what that signified. It was for my revenge. My revenge against these murderers, the state that protects them, and a public that is ready to trample on other people's happiness."

Gray took a single deep breath, attempting to contain his anger. "I spent five years putting together my plan for vengeance. In order to carry it out I needed money and, more than anything, people who would cooperate with me. An army that was obedient, that I could trust not to betray me. I used my new talent to seek out people on the brink of suicide. It was much easier than I had expected. Japan is full of people who want to die. In three years I recruited a hundred *suitable* personnel. During that period I sold all my assets which, combined with my savings, added up to two hundred million in cash. I gradually increased my holdings through investments with the help of a recruit at a securities brokerage, and other less legal activities. Subsequently, I used the money, my new collaborators, and the support I'd cultivated to set up Tomosun Trading."

"And all of it was for revenge."

"Of course. All of it was for revenge against this country and its people and to kill these men."

Gray turned to glare at "these men." Although they were trembling with fear, apart from that they looked healthy and unharmed. At the very least there were no signs of them having been tortured.

"I would never engage in anything as savage as torture," Gray averred as though he had read Ryotaro's thoughts. "They are fed and we make sure that they are not freezing."

"But why?" Ryotaro asked, scaring himself with the question. He heard the nuance in his own voice: *These men don't deserve any basic rights.*

"Believe me, when I first locked them up, all I wanted to do was make them experience all the suffering this world has to offer. But to torture them barbarically would be to lower myself to their level. My revenge was to exterminate these three with my own hands and to take vengeance on society. For that goal I aided the weak and crushed the strong. I would thereby earn the right to exact this revenge, I convinced myself. I could not resort to doing something that would make me despise myself, like torture. I did, however, give them some homework, in the form of the looped recording you heard just now." Gray took a deep breath, collecting himself before he continued, "I have recordings from the police interrogations and their discussions with their lawyers. The recordings were obtained illegally. For the month I have had these men locked up with the tapes playing non-stop, twenty-four hours a day. Can you guess why?"

Ryotaro immediately understood what Gray was telling him. *Forcing them to confront their crimes.*

"Exactly," Gray reprised, once again as though he had read Ryotaro's mind. "It's not to deny them sleep. The tapes force these men to relive their crimes, to regret their lies, and to recon-firm the sins they committed. The volume is kept low enough, so they can sleep normally. No torture—there you have it, my morals, one of the rules I set when I swore revenge. Because I had to *transcend humanity.*"

Gray gave Ryotaro a warm, affectionate look. "That's why I was so happy when you called me 'Gray.' Something other than human. I felt I could finally be it. You qualified me, so I recruited you and gave you *the role of seeing it through.* Your recruitment was chance, but chance can sometimes be fate in disguise."

"What do you want me to do?"

"I want you to remember the truth that I have told you today. I want you to see the new world with your own eyes. And I would like you to protect Sayuri."

The last part caught Ryotaro by surprise.

Protect Sayuri? "Why me?"

"Sayuri has not had an easy life," Gray replied in a matter-of-fact tone as though to calm Ryotaro. "I took advantage of her misfortune. *I kept quiet and looked on as she was subjected to debasing behavior. All for my own purposes.* I have exploited her far more than any other recruit. From now on, she must find happiness. She is still young, and she needs a good guardian. Excuse my presump-tion, but I believe you are the most suitable."

"I'm sure there are others…"

Gray turned to Takano, paying no attention to Ryotaro's

doubts. The gesture was enough of a cue for Takano, who approached the three men, untied the ropes binding them to the chairs, and picked up the ropes attached to their collars.

"Get up," Takano ordered.

The three men staggered upright on his command. They appeared healthy but their faces were deathly pale as if they were on the edge of a mental breakdown.

"Open that door."

Takano removed the handcuffs of the man in the expensive suit, handed him a card key, and pointed to a second door. Like the one they had entered through, it looked extremely sturdy. The man in the suit did as he was told, slotting the card into the lock. There was a clink as it opened. The door swung open onto a straight corridor.

There was yet another portal at the end.

"Open that door with the same key. Walk."

Breathing heavily under their gags, the three men walked down the corridor, half-stumbling from the restraints around their feet. They walked ahead as Takano urged with their leashes in hand as if they were dogs. Gray and Ryotaro followed.

They proceeded down the long corridor through three sets of doors before finally emerging outside. They made their way along a narrow path lined with trees, the greenery forming a tunnel of foliage. The cold wind, mixed with the smell of the sea, blustered in headlong gusts that felt sharp enough to cut skin. The path was uneven and devoid of any sources of light. They moved carefully, guided only by the moonlight filtering through the canopy of trees.

The path ran out. A dead-end. Ryotaro's vision was filled by a dark expanse of water that sprawled beyond the cliff edge before them. The promontory was high and there were no railings. Ryotaro winced each time he heard the sound of waves crashing into the crags below. The three men stopped but Takano coaxed them on, pushing them from behind. He let go of their leashes when they were at the cliff's very edge.

It was 3 a.m. in the middle of winter. The sky and sea were

completely dark apart from the moonlight, and dawn had yet to make its presence felt. The three men sank to the ground, perhaps overwhelmed with fear from the height of the cliff. Takano stepped backwards.

"Good. I am giving each of you a final choice. You may repent for your sins by jumping off this cliff, or you may stay where you are. There are countless rocks at the base of the cliff so death will be instantaneous. The cross currents will ensure your bodies do not float back to the surface," Gray offered tersely, pulling a gun from his gray suit.

On seeing the gun the three men began to shake violently. The one in the suit and the overweight man eventually dragged themselves to their feet. They were crying, as though regretting their crimes. The one with animal eyes, however, stayed put and turned a hostile gaze toward Gray.

"So I see you have made your decisions. Fine. Takano and Ryotaro, you are no longer needed here. Please return to the car."

Without a moment's pause Takano began to leave, giving Ryotaro a meaningful look as he disappeared into the darkness. Ryotaro stood alone, unable to move.

"Ryotaro, what is the matter? Takano has instructions on what to do next. Hurry up and go," Gray said coldly as if to push Ryotaro away.

But Ryotaro stood firm.

He was certain that if he left Gray would kill the three men. He could not let that happen. He knew that once Gray crossed that line he would never find salvation; instead, he would perish in the endless vortex of suffering and hatred called vengeance. There was no way he could let that happen.

But... What right do I have to stop him? Would I even be able to?

Ryotaro shook his head, attempting to get rid of such feeble thoughts. Whether it was possible or not, it was his duty to save Gray from the abyss of despair, just as Gray had saved him from the darkness of death.

"Did you not hear me? There is nothing more to be said. Go, now," Gray ordered.

His voice had become harsh. But Ryotaro stayed where he was.

Gray glared at him, losing patience. Ryotaro saw the total rejection in his eyes, and it scared him. He wanted to run, but his conviction that he couldn't leave Gray to himself won out.

"Don't think you can stop me. In the ten years since the murder of my wife and child I have lived only for revenge. Revenge on the state and on these men."

"And what will you do once you've accomplished it?" Ryotaro finally managed to ask, but his voice was weak like a candle fluttering in the wind.

"Takano knows the details," Gray stated.

"Don't think of killing yourself."

Ryotaro had figured it out. Gray was planning to kill the three men then end his own life.

Gray's expression remained fixed. "With my extinction I intend to fully assume my right to avenge."

"But why?" Ryotaro had meant to shout, but his voice was so thin it was almost snuffed out by the wind.

"My life has worth only if I can take revenge. Once it is done, there is nothing to hold me to this world." Gray's speech remained polite, but his expressionless face shunned him.

Ryotaro tensed his throat, desperately trying to still his trembling voice. "You rescued us, all of us…"

"Only to reduce my sense of guilt and to turn you into obedient pawns. Still, Sayuri's value exceeded my expectations. In the end, the quickest way to exert power over those who swear fealty to lust is to use a woman's sex appeal."

Ryotaro couldn't stop his voice from shaking. "Stop it."

"Stop what? Is it difficult to hear me say that I rescued you from suicide just to use you?" Gray snorted.

Ryotaro felt no anger, no crushing sense of betrayal. He felt only sadness. He lamented his own worthlessness for not being able to cure Gray's sorrow.

Then at the very least… Ryotaro clenched his jaw. "I'm still grateful, even if you did use me. I do not want you to take your own life."

"Feel gratitude as you see fit. For you to tell me what to do, however, I find hardly desirable. No one, not even God can stop what I am about to do."

Ryotaro closed his eyes as he listened, then opened them again. They seemed to contain a new strength. "I won't stop you. I don't have the right to. But there's one thing I can do. I can take your place and accept your pain. I am not going to let you die."

Ryotaro let out a deep sigh. He could feel Gray's despair, his grief. His loved ones had been violated and murdered, abandoned by the law that was supposed to protect them, and toyed with by the public. Ryotaro's heart and mind—which had chosen death in the past—perhaps could not own Gray's sorrow, but they could at least tender thought, imagine, resonate.

To lessen his anguish, if only a little. To understand his grief, if only a little, and to share it.

He knew it was not what Gray wanted. He knew that it had no meaning. But Ryotaro needed to repay Gray in his own way for saving him. That wish steeled his resolve. He couldn't let Gray sink any deeper into the depths of despair.

Ryotaro turned to face the three murderers, looked into their frightened eyes, and pulled out the gun hidden in his inside pocket. He aimed in their direction.

"No!" Gray nearly screamed, having already understood.

Ryotaro was not sure if he was doing the right thing. He just knew he couldn't allow Gray to become a murderer. He tensed his finger on the trigger.

At that very moment—

Tap tap.

He heard a knocking sound behind him.

"Finally found you."

The voice, colored with insanity, blended into consecutive gunfire.

It took Ryotaro a few seconds to realize he was on the ground. He had blacked out as the explosion of sound ripped through his eardrums.

"Fucking bastard... Thinking you could hide from me like a damned cockroach."

Ryotaro turned to the twitchy, chortling voice and saw a man raking a hand through his hair, gun pointed downwards.

"The TV showed you barricaded up in the Bank of Japan so I raced over there. The hell was up with all those costumes? You really are fucking nuts."

The man kept his gun on Gray as he cussed him out. Gray was sprawled on the ground bleeding from his thigh and wheezing painfully.

"And the police! So freaked out by your group of cosplayers they totally let you sneak away. I was on to you from the start. It's because of you I'm in this fucking mess. I didn't even need to see you, I knew where you were from your stench." The man sucked air through his nose and spat on Gray. "I'm done for, thanks to you. The Tower's destroyed and now they're coming after me. So tell me, who the fuck are you?" the man rambled. He drooled like an overexcited doberman.

"Gray," a voice dripping with scorn answered between shallow breaths.

"Not what I'm asking, asshole! No, your real name—ah, fuck it." The man fell suddenly quiet and looked around. His eyes narrowed as he saw the three men in gags. "Who're they?"

The three men he indicated with his chin frantically shook their heads, eyes frozen with terror. *They're still alive.* Ryotaro was sure he had shot them. The moment he thought this, memories flooded back.

Gray had shouted to stop him as his finger tensed on the trigger. That was when he heard the tapping noise from behind. The bullet hit him just as the sound reached his ears. Ryotaro moved his right hand—the hand that should have been holding the gun—slowly down to his abdomen. Warm blood was leaking through torn flesh. Ryotaro's face contorted from the unbearable pain.

"I'm asking you who the fuck they are!"

Gray remained silent. The man fired a shot into Gray's left shoulder and another at his gut. Earsplitting bangs shook the air.

"Answer me!" The man looked ready to pull the trigger again.

Gray stared at him before taking a deep breath. "The ones who have kept me alive until now... My reason for living," Gray gasped, his voice disappearing like an echo.

For a while the intruder did nothing but stare at Gray. Then he twisted his neck in a snakelike motion to look directly at the three men. Still gagged, they were unable to say anything, but their eyes revealed the terror they felt.

"I see."

The man lifted the gun in their direction, his features a blank utterly devoid of emotion, and pulled the trigger three times without the slightest hesitation. Then, as though that had not been enough, he kicked their prone bodies over the edge like so many soccer balls.

He came back and planted a foot on Gray. "Now you've lost your reason for living."

"Ah, not exactly how I wanted it... But it's over now," Gray sighed, faintly smiling.

The smile seemed to irritate the man. He launched a kick into Gray. "Asshole! You think that's enough? I've lost it all. None of this shit would have happened if it wasn't for you. My organization is out for blood and Public Security is gunning for me. There's no fucking way I'm gonna get diced up like Kay. I'd be fish food by now if he hadn't tried to cover for me. Now you're gonna lose everything! I'm gonna take everything you have!" The man was out of control, as though whatever mechanism that had kept his emotions in check were disintegrating. He raved like a man possessed.

"Chu, you have already taken all."

"Don't you fucking call me that! You're telling me those three dirty bastards were all you had?" Chu sneered.

"Indeed. They took everything I had. They destroyed my dear love, my world." Gray was wheezing but spoke clearly through gritted teeth.

"The hell are you saying?" The man clicked his tongue.

"It's finished. Hurry up and kill me."

"Shut the fuck up! I'm going to destroy everything that you have. I'll kill you only then. Spit it out! What's important to you?" This time, the man drove a bullet into Gray's right shoulder.

Gray was lying in a sea of blood. "I have no such thing left. My wife and child were everything. They were my world."

"Fuck you!" The man fired into Gray's abdomen. "You ass-hole, submit to me! Scream and cry! Beg for your life!"

Blood poured from Gray's stomach. His eyes were closed, his breathing shallow. Ryotaro focused all his energy into getting up, but he had lost too much blood and his body refused to comply.

"You, the strong…"

"Huh?"

Gray's hoarse voice, a mere whisper of air through his lips, still held raw power. He looked squarely at Chu. "You who devour…" He sucked in a deep breath. *"We will come after you like your shadow."* Enunciating this clearly, Gray smiled.

"Enough. Die," the man spat as though his fun had been spoiled. Just as he spoke, Ryotaro sensed a presence behind.

At the edge of his blurred vision stood a figure. He was bleeding, and his face was pale. His complexion was now similar to Gray's.

"For my son!"

With that, Takano charged towards the crazed man who was about to take Gray's life. Chu froze for a moment, his eyes open wide at the sheer spirit of his assailant. That was all it took for Takano to close the gap, grab him with both hands, and slam him into the ground.

Chu let out a breathless grunt, but his eyes immediately focused as he brought his gun up. Yet Takano was faster. He grabbed the man's arm, hauled him to his feet, and threw him through the air towards the precipice.

Chu held his ground right at the edge. His face was a mask of insanity when he turned back to stare at Takano.

"Stay out of my way!"

Slithering upright with serpentine grace, he aimed his gun and pulled the trigger. The shot went straight through the shoulder, but Takano barely flinched. He crouched down like a fighting bull and charged again.

With a battle cry, he seized Chu with both hands. Overcoming resistance with his full strength and drawing on his momentum, Takano tossed Chu into the abyss below.

"H-Hey…" Unable to absorb what was happening to him, Chu's death throes were limited to that.

Having stood watching as the man fell, Takano collapsed to the ground with a thud and stopped moving like a puppet with its strings cut.

"Slamming into him… Not the most sophisticated tactic…"

Muttering, Gray pulled out his cell phone and pushed a button with a shaky finger before flinging it away. He dragged himself up gasping heavy spurts of breath and picked his gray hat from the ground.

"I see you're still conscious," he noted, looking at Ryotaro as he replaced his hat on his head. Gray's eyes were brimming with tears. Every ounce of love, suffering, despair, grief, and hatred in him seemed to have surfaced all at once. His face looked to be smiling and weeping at the same time.

Ryotaro desperately struggled to say something, but his voice failed him.

Gray placed one hand on his chest in a parting gesture. "All stories require an ending… My disappearing… Disappearance is the most fitting one for this tale."

Gray took step after step towards the cliff's edge then turned to face Ryotaro once more.

"You have my thanks for humoring this tale."

Ryotaro cried out voicelessly. Tears poured from his eyes and his vision blurred.

"The final curtain."

Gray bowed his head then lifted it to meet Ryotaro's gaze straight on. Never before had Ryotaro seen such a smile—it was innocence itself.

Hearing the last words he could manage but a sob.

Gray pulled down the rim of his hat and hid his eyes. Then, falling backwards, as though in slow motion, he disappeared down the cliff.

EPILOGUE

1

Having leaked to the media the info that Gray had given him, Serizawa sat at the counter of Chateau d'If, his eyes spaced out and with a cigarette in his mouth though he didn't particularly enjoy smoking. As usual, he was the only customer, but for once the TV set was on. A red-faced newscaster was furiously—hysterically—reporting on the raid on the Bank of Japan.

Serizawa thought back to when Kiyomi Takano visited his home.

Serizawa had burst out laughing when the man asked for his assistance with a crime. He'd never heard of someone approaching a detective to help break the law. He refused, of course, but what Takano said next left him in shock.

Takano revealed that brass from the very organization he worked for were accomplices in the Ikebukuro Scandal. Kiyomi Takano already knew of Serizawa's disillusionment with the force, and with that knowledge, pressed for an answer. The immense scale of the request gave Serizawa pause. Was it up to him to squeeze out the pus? Or should he turn a blind eye? He knew that his decision was the *test* Gray had spoken of. After much tormented thought he made a decision.

He would bear the burden of cleaning up the organization.

He leaked the information on Ikebukuro to the media. He had made it clear that his helping did not mean he agreed with Gray's ideology. What Gray did was, unmistakably, criminal. He'd sided with Gray only *to put a greater evil on trial*. Gray welcomed his decision and told him that Rei Yuzuki felt the same, *as though he wasn't talking about himself.*

"Rei Yuzuki's wife and kid were murdered, and he kept that hatred burning for ten whole years," Rokuzo said, making the feat sound terribly difficult.

But he was right. A negative emotion like vindictiveness was capable of laying waste to the soul. To escape ruination, an ordinary person had to counter it with other emotions and values and maintain balance. But Rei Yuzuki had kept the desire close, never letting go, and with formidable will accomplished his objective.

"He must have been an impressive man. Still, that particular case was… It gives me the creeps just thinking about it," Rokuzo muttered, blinking.

"Yeah," Serizawa nodded. He shivered, never wanting to get involved in a case that ghastly again.

That case…

By sheer chance, Serizawa had been put in charge of Rei Yuzuki's case, the kidnapping and murder of a mother and child in Miyamae. Yuzuki was thirty at the time. Mizuho, his wife, was twenty-five and their daughter, Kazumi, was about to turn six. Kazumi was not Yuzuki's daughter by blood. She was the product of Mizuho's previous marriage.

Mizuho had noticed a suspicious character lurking around from a month or so before the kidnapping. The couple had gone to the police for help. The direct trigger was that someone had attempted to kidnap their daughter, grabbing her arm as she came home from school. The police refused to take it seriously, telling the couple that there was no case until something actually happened. When Rei Yuzuki pressed harder, the police responded by assigning someone to patrol the area once a day. It was purely a token gesture, hardly effective.

Rei Yuzuki was out late on the day the kidnapping occurred and didn't return home until two in the morning. The kidnappers made their move while he was out. When he got back, Mizuho and Kazumi were missing, the living room torn apart as if there had been a break-in, traces of blood on the white carpet. Yuzuki notified the police immediately. The apartment was treated as a crime scene, the incident as a criminal case, and an investigation finally launched.

"The cops royally screwed up on that one," Rokuzo hissed.

Serizawa nodded in agreement. "Yeah, we didn't do anything. Except make things worse," Serizawa conceded derisively.

The examination of the apartment yielded no fingerprints, but the police confirmed the blood to be Mizuho's and identified three separate pairs of footprints from sneakers. The police put together an investigation headquarters and set about tracking down the criminals in an attempt to find the missing wife and child. Serizawa had been in the violent crimes section at the time and was added to the team. A quick resolution was expected since they had footprints, hair samples, and witness reports detailing the suspects and their car.

There was a new lead four days into the investigation. Copies of photos had been mailed to several houses in Tokyo's Azabu district, an area with no connection to the case. The photos contained images of Yuzuki's wife and emaciated daughter in a dimly lit room; Mizuho had a vacant look in her eyes. The police judged that the kidnappers were not looking for ransom and boosted the size of headquarters, hoping sheer numbers would help them identify the criminals. If the kidnappers were not motivated by money but rather by the desire to shock witnesses, the hostages' lives were mere playthings.

As though in mockery of the investigation, the next day saw new photos, this time mailed to houses in Shinjuku. More were posted in the public toilets of a nearby park. The photos showed Yuzuki's wife covered in cuts and clots of dried blood, her once-long hair shorn. Her clothes were torn, and fresh bruises showed that she was being beaten. There was no sign of the daughter.

The perpetrators' move to exhibit the photos to random strangers brought the horrific circumstances of the case to the public eye, effectively nullifying the media ban in place.

The police hesitated, unsure whether or not to show the photos supposedly taken by the kidnappers to Rei Yuzuki. The horrific state of his wife was eye-averting. But Yuzuki insisted, and Serizawa, who was twenty-seven at the time, took the task upon himself.

When he showed him the two photos in a lounge inside the Miyamae police station, Yuzuki took the pictures and just sat on the sofa, completely motionless, his eyes blown wide.

Two days later, more printed photos were delivered to homes in Kanagawa's Midori Ward. A glance was enough to tell that they were of daughter Kazumi. She was covered in bruises; her unseeing eyes were open.

When Serizawa handed the new photos to Yuzuki, the man expressed his emotions for the first time. He screamed and took his head in his hands, then started pounding the desk. Serizawa tried to calm him but it was of no use. Yuzuki tore at his own skin with his nails and bit his lips with enough force to rupture them. By the time officers responded to the commotion, he stood drained and still, covered in blood, with an unnatural look on his face.

After that, the investigation came to an abrupt conclusion.

The following day, in the middle of the night, another set of photos were found. In Kohoku Ward in Kanagawa, a resident arriving at his home noticed and subdued a stranger acting suspiciously outside of his house. When the lurker was handed over to the police, he was in possession of a number of photos of Mizuho, naked and lifeless as a doll.

The character's name was Makoto Goda. Age seventeen. He had dropped out of high school and held no steady job, yet drove around in foreign cars, throwing money around on all kinds of amusements every night of the week. The money was from his parents, who managed a multitude of companies.

At first he feigned ignorance in the face of the accusations, but after a mere three days of detention he burst into tears and provided a full confession, and his accomplices came under arrest.

Their names were Yuki Iwazaki and Gakuto Namiki. They were both seventeen and attended the same high school in the city. Both of Iwazaki's parents worked and were hardly ever at home. They tacitly consented to his not always coming home for the night. Namiki had been raised in a motherless household by a father who was often away on business trips abroad, sometimes for close to a month. It was in the soundproofed piano room on the second floor of Namiki's house that Rei Yuzuki's wife and daughter had been confined.

According to the youths' statements, they had set their sights on Yuzuki's wife after first seeing her on a train. For a whole month they had followed her, mapping out her routines. They decided to kidnap her while her husband was out late.

They rendered the wife and child unconscious using a modified stun gun, bundled them into the trunk of Goda's car, then confined them in Namiki's house. After two days of tireless violence where Mizuho just cried and screamed, Goda found himself getting bored and came up with the idea of using the daughter as leverage. By threatening to kill the daughter he forced the mother to succumb to his every whim. The trio reveled in the pleasure of manipulating a human being.

It was Iwazaki's idea to distribute the pictures. His motive, he stated during his interrogation, was to make his and his companions' power known to the public.

The three of them continued to indulge themselves on their captives, but eventually the daughter died, and the woman stopped reacting, like a mannequin. Namiki's father was due home at any time so they strangled the woman and took photos for evidence. They stated that they placed the daughter's body into a garbage bag and buried her in some woods in Chiba Prefecture, while the wife's body remained unattended at Namiki's house.

The detectives who found her corpse could hardly bear to

look. What had it taken to leave such injuries?

Her body was covered with innumerable lacerations, wounds made for their pleasure, wounds to make one despair, wounds to make one yield. Layers of blue plastic sheeting were thrown over the wood flooring to protect it from blood.

As Goda, the principal offender, and the accomplices Iwazaki and Namiki were all legal minors, their trial would be carried out with great circumspection behind closed doors.

Yuzuki requested the death penalty, but the culprits' status as minors made that difficult.

The day of the first hearing arrived.

Yuzuki, who wanted to attend, sat in the public gallery with Serizawa. By this time Rei Yuzuki was stick-like, tall and wiry. He was 6'4" but his weight had dwindled to less than 110 pounds. He sat there without emotion, his eyes fixed on the three kidnappers. Serizawa was alarmed by his demeanor, but more than that he felt bottomless fear.

The defense consisted of six lawyers. The principal attorney was famous for working on cases where minors had committed violent crimes. The defense he mounted was a farce.

He argued that Yuzuki's wife had attempted to seduce Goda and the other boys.

When the prosecution objected that the accusation was frivolous, he fired off a number of responses—Yuzuki's wife had been dressed to show off her curves, provocatively wearing a knee-length pleated skirt. He pointed out that the locks on the house had been intact and that this raised the possibility that Mizuho invited the boys in. He even went as far as to claim that she enjoyed "playing with fire" behind her husband's back.

Next he offered his opinion on the four photos. He insisted that the first, the second, and the final photos, namely of Yuzuki's wife covered in lacerations, betrayed an interest in S&M on her part that had spiraled out of control. He defended the third photo, of daughter Kazumi, as a memento taken after she had expired against the boys' will; one could glimpse, from this act, loving kindness even.

Rei Yuzuki literally trembled as he watched the proceedings, struggling to keep his anger in check.

The defense continued, smugly confident. The lead attorney claimed the bruises covering the mother and daughter were evidence of the young men having tried to resuscitate them, that the cuts and stabs were the mother self-lacerating for her own pleasure, that she had wanted to die. The prosecution objected against each point, but the defense always seemed to have the upper hand.

The seemingly nonsensical claims laid the groundwork for a single, clear purpose—reducing the defendants' sentences to the very minimum by reason of temporary derangement. The attorney piloted his entire argument towards that focal point, and the path was more or less in order.

The defense attempted to recast Goda, the principal offender, as a victim, arguing that his parents had only ever given him money instead of love, that they were hardly at home because they were both working, and that they were both having affairs. In the beginning Goda had shown no signs of regret, but as the case progressed he talked of nothing else, repeatedly claiming that he was the victim of an unhappy upbringing. No doubt the defense had coached him during their questioning. His testimony changed as the trial progressed. He referred to Rei Yuzuki's wife as a "classmate," to having "played with a doll" with the daughter; to having heard threatening voices in his head.

He underwent three separate psychiatric tests. In each case the examiner's report ended up sympathetic to Goda, concluding that he was suffering a mental breakdown.

The defense pleaded that Goda had not been in a state to bear responsibility. While the prosecution did their best to press for full criminal responsibility, in consideration of the testimonies of the defendant and the results of the psychiatric examinations, the court applied Penal Code 39 (Acts committed owing to insanity shall not be punished. With regards to acts committed by weak-minded persons the penalty is to be reduced.), ruling the defendant to be of diminished mental capacity.

In the end Goda, a minor and the principal offender, received a prison sentence of twelve years. Iwazaki and Namiki were ruled to have been under his coercion and were each sentenced to time in the Kanto Juvenile Correctional Facility.

Serizawa could vividly recall the moment of the sentencing, even now. The nightmarish memory was forever imprinted on his mind: the image of Goda's mouth quietly, truly quietly, twisting into a grin.

The tragic photos of the wife and child having exposed the Miyamae kidnapping to the public, many people came to regard the case as a source of amusement. They visited the scene of the crime to take "souvenir" photos. Others schemed to steal personal belongings of the victims. Still others aired opinions that amounted to bashing. The photos that had been distributed were put up for sale, and people bought them. The trend grew partly because of Mizuho's good looks.

Then something happened to accelerate the phenomenon.

The public had initially been exposed to four photos only, but the hard drives of the kidnappers' computers contained more than three thousand, of which five hundred were somehow disseminated. The leak came via P2P file-sharing software and was traced to the personal computer of a ranking police official. Why did he have the photos on his private hard drive? The force hastily put together a statement to the effect that it was only to conduct an independent investigation, but the motivation was clear from the content of the photos the offender had copied. They were all of an explicitly sexual nature.

The photos spread across the internet like wildfire as inconsiderate people collected them out of curiosity and even went as far as to upload digital photo books. Visitors flocked in droves to Iwazaki's house and the victims' residence like pilgrims to a holy site, driving Rei Yuzuki further and further into a dark place.

The police official responsible for the secondary wave of damage had to and did face disciplinary action, but the penalty, a ten-percent reduction in pay over ten months, was woefully lukewarm.

Yuzuki tormented himself for having failed to save his wife and daughter. He became distrustful, and his bottomless rage grew to target not just the perpetrators, but also the government that failed to punish them, the public that made a mockery of his suffering, and the police force that allowed the photos to spread.

Two years after the kidnapping he left the country and vanished. His whereabouts a mystery, the public soon forgot about him.

Serizawa came back to the present and returned his gaze to the documents in his hands. They were the sum total of all the data he had compiled on Rei Yuzuki since Gray and Kiyomi Takano had approached him.

Rei Yuzuki had graduated from the National Defense Academy of Japan and joined the Self-Defense Forces, with which he served in Afghanistan in 2000 as part of the peacekeeping operation. He spent half a year there before returning briefly to Japan, then left the SDF and moved to Abu Dhabi. Serizawa had no information on Gray's movements since the kidnapping, but in light of Tomosun Trading winning the rare earths project, it seemed probable that he used that period to make a number of connections.

It was impossible to find any more data on the man.

Be that as it may...

Serizawa flopped the documents onto the counter, one side of his mouth curled upwards as he took a swig from the whisky in front of him.

What would I do if someone damaged me to the point that all I wanted to do was blind and deafen myself? What would this individual called Takeshi Serizawa do in the face of such enemies? What could he do? How far would he go?

"Are you okay?" Rokuzo, suspicious of Serizawa's brooding, was watching him instead of the TV.

Serizawa shook his head and gave up thinking about it. "I'd be toast," he muttered.

Rokuzo appeared to have misheard him. Taking hold of his

own glass of whisky, he tipped it upwards.

2

Everything passes. A wind rages, strong enough to steal away all. Yet no matter how much pain it causes it moves on, beyond one's grasp, and is gone.

Ryotaro breathed in and out quietly. He felt a nebulous, subtle sadness as he looked out the window at the cloudless sky.

That time…

Ryotaro, who'd lost consciousness after Gray had gone off the cliff, woke up in a room at a mid-size hospital, where he had been unconscious for a whole day. The attending physician announced himself as a friend of Gray's.

Before his death, Gray had called Sayuri. Sasaki and Kozue had traced the call and the three of them had raced to Ubara Utopia in Chiba where they found Ryotaro and Takano lying unconscious.

Sayuri was with Ryotaro when he woke up in the hospital room. Her eyes cast down at the white tiles, she took her time telling him about Kiyomi Takano.

Takano's son had been part of Chu's gang. Unable to bear working at the Tower, however, he'd attempted to leak to the police. Chu kept him under ball and chain, dealt with the evidence, then murdered him, but he'd already confessed to his father about the place. Takano told the police what he knew, but the police refused to take him seriously. Moreover, they made no attempts to uncover the reason behind his son's death, insisting they couldn't open an investigation. Takano came to suspect that some part of the police bureaucracy was trying to cover up evidence of the Tower's existence. In order to *do right* by his son and to take revenge on the government and the police, he fell in with Gray and his overwhelming resources.

While Ryotaro was still in the hospital, Shindo showed up, her attitude the same as ever, and handed him a deposit book for an account full of freshly laundered funds. She told him that

Gray had set aside money for everyone who assisted him in his final plan. Each of the accounts held four hundred million yen— more than enough for any typical lifetime. Shindo complained about how setting up the books had been the most boring thing she'd ever done. She left saying she was going to forget about Gray, buy some uninhabited island, and live the high life.

Once alone, Ryotaro turned on the TV and watched the news. The screen regularly showed footage of the Bank of Japan swarmed by a sea of gray. The reports detailed that the people in gray suits arrested were either unemployed or poor, that they had all been recruited by a man in gray, but that each described the contact as being a different age or height, leading to speculation that the Gray Man was in fact a number of different people— none of whom had been arrested.

The theft of bills from the Bank of Japan plus the destruction of the National Printing Bureau presses had plunged the country into chaos. This, together with Gray's exposure of *the scandal* involving the elite, brought Japan under heavy international censure. The loss of face was severe enough to threaten the nation's very status as an advanced one.

Ryotaro had no idea what lay in store for Japan after such a shattering drop in the value of the yen. Still, he was sure the country was not about to come apart. It was one that knew how to crawl out of bottomless pits. Replacing all its leadership, preparing for reconstruction like it's been there and done that, it would return to develop.

"Daydreaming about something?"

The voice brought Ryotaro back from his thoughts. Takano stood there, arms folded. His wounds had been potentially fatal, but his formidable, yakuza-grade presence was no hollow prop. His doctor had lavished praise upon his powers of recuperation as being many times that of a normal person, and indeed he'd recovered faster than Ryotaro.

It was two months since the raid on the Bank of Japan.

Ryotaro, discharged from the hospital, was completing his recuperation at his new home.

"Amazing, huh?" Takano gestured towards the TV with his chin. It was showing footage of protests in a foreign country. "They're a dictatorship, aren't they?"

Ryotaro couldn't tell just from the footage which country was being shown. Similar protests were currently erupting all over the world.

The footage of the Bank of Japan awash with gray had spread like wildfire with the caption "Rebellion of the Weak." It had given rise to a new phenomenon.

The masses were staging "rebellions" across the world. Tackling the full spectrum of sources of their suffering, the oppressed all over the globe were putting on gray garbs and making their voices heard. A new wave of Grays encircled the planet.

"I'm back," Sayuri's bright voice echoed from the doorway. "It started to rain. Can you believe it? The weather report didn't say a word about rain. Dammit!" Sayuri grumbled and rubbed a towel over her wet hair.

Ryotaro got up carefully and looked to the sky sprawling outside the window. He thought of the role Gray had given him, "seeing it through." The original meaning had been to bear witness to Gray's final moments and to deal with necessary arrangements. According to Takano, Gray wished to be buried at the Dairakuin temple, the resting place of Rei Yuzuki's wife and daughter not far from Tamagawa Station.

But the role meant something different now.

Seeing through what happened to Japan. Not only observing, but taking an active role. And—as Gray had requested—protecting Sayuri. Ryotaro had sworn to the memory of the vanished man to do this.

No one talked of Gray's death. Everyone felt the same sense of loss and sadness, like a hole had been knocked through their chests, but no one wanted to believe that he was gone.

Ryotaro had yet to decide what to do next. If possible, he wanted to bring down a hammer on wrongdoers and aid the weak. But he knew quite well that he possessed neither the power nor the talent for such mighty deeds. Instead, he could protect those close to him. That was a good enough place to begin.

He sighed.

The weather's bad when it rains. That's obvious enough. But even when it's pouring, the sun is just hiding behind the clouds, never truly gone.

Besides...

Ryotaro strained his eyes as he looked into the blue of the sky.

"I mean, come on. It's supposed to be just a shower, the sun's out. What's with the downpour? I got drenched!"

Sayuri's gripe brought a faint smile to Ryotaro's face.

Sometimes it's sunny even when it's raining.

About the Author

Born in 1985 in Kanagawa Prefecture, by day Tomotake Ishikawa is a gainfully employed salaryman. In his spare time, including on his commute, he writes. When *Gray Men* won the Grand Prize of the second annual Golden Elephant Award—bestowed on new genre fiction with the potential to reach a global audience—he became a published author. He cites among his influences the master storytellers of yore such as Alexandre Dumas.